BLINDSIDE

When a passenger jet crashes in Denver, Colorado, nobody survives. In Glasgow, Alex Cahill gets a call from the wife of a former US Secret Service colleague — a man supposedly travelling on the doomed plane. However, there's no record of his name on the passenger list. And Cahill's connections in the US intelligence agencies are unforthcoming. Desperate to uncover the truth behind the disappearance of his old friend, Cahill and Logan Finch head to Denver to confront the FBI. Meanwhile, a perfect storm of events gathers across the globe, from Colorado, to war-torn Afghanistan and to the mean streets of Glasgow — where DC Rebecca Irvine is investigating a new drug that is killing users. It is a deadly storm that will engulf them all.

Books by G. J. Moffat
Published by The House of Ulverscroft:

DAISYCHAIN

G. J. MOFFAT

◆

BLINDSIDE

Complete and Unabridged

CHARNWOOD
Leicester

First published in Great Britain in 2011 by
Hachette Scotland
an imprint of Hachette UK
London

First Charnwood Edition
published 2012
by arrangement with
Hachette UK
London

British Library CIP Data

Moffat, G. J. (Gary J.)
    Blindside.
    1. Finch, Logan (Fictitious character)- -Fiction.
    2. Irvine, Rebecca (Fictitious character)- -Fiction.
    3. Lawyers- -Scotland- -Glasgow- -Fiction.
    4. Women detectives- -Scotland- -Glasgow- -Fiction.
    5. Suspense fiction. 6. Large type books.
    I. Title
    823.9′2–dc23

    ISBN 978–1–4448–1195–7

For my grandparents, who all served one
way or another — Jimmy, Hannah,
John and Isobel.

Acknowledgements

For my family as always — KayCee, Bee and LuLu.

All the crowd at Hachette/Headline. Particular thanks to my publisher Bob McDevitt and my editor on this book Ali Hope.

I am amazed and humbled again by the generosity of those who spent their time talking to me and sharing their experiences. This book would not be what it is without them. They are Graeme 'The Enforcer' Pearson former Director General of the Scottish Crime and Drug Enforcement Agency, Sergeant Larry Subia of the Denver Police Department, Fiona Taylor for the introduction to Iraq veteran Joe Stewart and Joe for his memories. And finally my brother-in-law (and chemistry doctor) Paul Clingan for starting the ball rolling.

Chris Hannah for the new brand.

Prologue

FBI Field Office, Denver, Colorado
Midnight, Sunday

The top floor of the Federal Building at 1961 Stout Street at the edge of Downtown Denver was dark except for two rooms at the end of a long corridor. Peter Ames, a twenty-five-year-old Special Agent not long out of the Academy at Quantico, Virginia, moved along the corridor quickly. He was carrying a rolled sheet of paper which he twisted in his hands as he walked.

Ames passed by the first of the lighted rooms, seeing the faint silhouettes of three men sitting around the conference table inside. He stopped at the next door, glancing at the name plate on the wall beside it that told him it was occupied by the Special Agent in Charge of the Denver field office — SAC Randall Webb. Ames cleared his throat, flattened out the sheet of paper and opened the door.

Webb did not look up at Ames as he entered the room. His chair was facing the window and Ames could see from his reflection in the glass that Webb had the phone to his ear. Ames stared out the window but could see nothing in the dark. He wondered what Webb saw out there.

'I'm still waiting to hear,' Webb said into the phone. 'I don't have that information yet.'

Ames stepped around Webb's desk until he

3

was in his boss's line of sight and held out the sheet of paper. Webb looked up at Ames and nodded, reaching out to take the paper from him.

'Wait,' Webb said into the phone. 'I'm getting it now. I'll call you back.'

He swivelled his chair round and hung up the phone, placing the paper on the desk in front of him.

'It's there, sir,' Ames said, putting his finger on the paper next to a name on the flight passenger list: John Reece. Webb stared at the sheet for a long moment then leaned back in his chair. He was a trim black man in his early fifties. A native of Baltimore, his reputation in the Bureau was impeccable. He looked at Ames.

'Do we have any confirmation from the scene yet? I mean about survivors.'

'No, sir. It's still too early for them to make a formal assessment on that.'

Webb sighed. 'I know the official line, son. What I'm asking for is their best guess right now.'

Ames swallowed, his throat feeling dry in the air-conditioned environment.

'No survivors is what they're saying, sir.'

Webb glanced at the flat-screen television mounted on the wall to the side of his desk. The sound was on mute and the picture showed the crash scene from above as a news helicopter circled the flaming wreckage of the jet.

'Where's Coop?' Webb asked, turning back to Ames.

'He's next door with the others.'

'Go get him for me.'

4

Ames left and Webb picked up the phone to call the man he had been talking to before: an assistant director at Bureau headquarters in Washington. The AD answered on the first ring.

'What's the news?'

'I got the list.'

'And?'

'The name John Reece is on it.'

The AD was quiet.

'They're saying no survivors,' Webb added.

'I need to wake the Director and give him the bad news. We'll talk later.'

The door to Webb's office opened again and Special Agent Cooper Grange walked in, followed by Ames. Grange was taller than the six-foot Ames by a good couple of inches and had twenty years on him. His trademark black suit looked tailored to fit his athletic frame and was offset by a greying crew cut.

'Did he tell you?' Webb asked Grange.

'Yes.'

Grange was never one to waste words.

'This thing just moved to a whole new level.'

'I know. You want me to get the rest of the task force in here now?'

Webb put his hand on the passenger list still sitting on his desk. There was a 'Joint Terrorism Task Force' stamp in the top right-hand corner in red ink.

'Yes.'

'We need to take this guy down. Hard.'

'I know, Coop. I know.'

Grange and Ames left. Webb went back to staring out into the night.

Part One: Missing

1

Monday

Alex Cahill fumbled on the table by his bed for the phone that was vibrating, the light from it seeming incredibly bright in the dark of his room. His wife Sam stirred and huffed out a sigh.

Cahill grabbed the phone, looked at the screen and saw two things: that it was five a.m. on a Monday morning in April and that he did not recognise the number displayed on the screen — except that it had a US dialling prefix.

He pressed the button to answer and swung his legs out of bed, rubbing sleep from his eyes.

'Is this Alex Cahill?' a woman asked.

He didn't recognise the voice.

'Take it downstairs,' Sam said.

Cahill stood and went out of the bedroom, past his daughters' rooms and downstairs towards his study at the back of the house.

'This is Cahill,' he told the woman on the phone.

'I'm calling about Tim,' she said.

The woman's voice was thick, like she had been crying. Cahill rubbed at his hair, his mind not functioning yet at full capacity.

'Tim who?' he asked as he padded barefoot into his study, closing the door behind him.

'Tim Stark. This is his wife, Melanie.'

Cahill sat in the leather seat behind his large desk and swivelled to look out the window into his garden.

'Sorry, Melanie,' Cahill said. 'It's early here. What about Tim?'

'I didn't know who else to call,' Melanie Stark said. 'I mean, I've tried the police and the people at the airport but they won't tell me anything.'

Cahill closed his eyes, forcing himself to think despite the fuzz clouding his brain.

'Melanie, I haven't seen Tim in a while. Not since I was in the US last summer. In Washington. And it's five in the morning here. What's this about?'

'Sorry, I forgot about the time difference. It's just . . .'

Cahill switched on the desk lamp and reached for a pen, writing 'Tim Stark' at the top of a blank page in his notebook. He could hear Melanie sniffing back tears and felt a knot of anxiety form in his stomach. Tim was a good friend and something was clearly wrong.

'Okay, listen, Melanie. I need you to slow down. I mean, let's start with the basics. You said something about an airport. Which airport?'

'Denver International.'

Cahill jotted that down underneath Tim's name in the notebook.

'Are you there right now?'

'No. I'm at home in Kansas City.'

'I'm not following you, Melanie.'

'It's the crash,' she said. 'It's all over the TV. Haven't you seen it?' The knot in his stomach twisted inside.

10

'Give me a minute.'

Cahill got up, still holding the phone to his ear, and went to the couch where he lifted a remote and pointed it at the TV. The screen came to life and he switched to a news channel.

Fractured images showed onscreen in a loop: firefighters tackling a huge blaze and ambulance crews rushing in and out of frame while the blue lights of their vehicles filled the night.

Cahill muted the volume and looked at the info bar scrolling along the bottom of the screen, describing a plane crash outside Denver, Colorado. His home town.

He sat on the couch watching the screen.

'I see it now,' Cahill said into the phone, his voice sounding hollow.

'Tim said he was going to be on that flight,' she said. 'He was in Denver and called me to say that he had business in Washington and that he'd got a late cancellation on the flight. He took it and — '

She was speaking in a rush.

'I'm not sure I understand why you're calling me,' he said. 'Or what you think I can do to help you. I'm based in the UK now. In Scotland.'

'I know that,' she said. 'I found your contact details in Tim's desk. You were in the Service together, weren't you? The Secret Service.'

'We were.'

'He talked about you and the other guys a lot. About what it was like back then. Said you were the best.'

She stopped talking and sobbed. Cahill didn't know what to say. The info bar on the TV screen

11

continued to scroll, telling Cahill that there were no survivors expected from the crash.

'Melanie, I'm real sorry about this. Tim was a good man. A friend.'

Cahill ran a hand over his face and up through his hair, feeling like all he wanted to do was sleep. But he knew that he would not get to sleep with images of the plane wreckage seared into his mind.

'Tim got fired from the Service in the Fall of last year,' Melanie said. 'Didn't even get his pension.'

'I didn't know. He seemed fine when I saw him.'

'He wouldn't tell me why he got fired. Then he got another job. Said it was something he couldn't tell me about but that it paid well.'

Cahill's antennae started to twitch.

'But it didn't pay well,' Melanie went on. 'I mean, not so far as I could see. It didn't pay at all. Not officially. But there were always cash deposits in our account. Nothing huge, just enough for what we needed. Like he was being careful not to put any more in the account. I was worried and I looked for something, anything, to show me what he was doing. I mean, a payslip or a contract. Anything.'

'And you couldn't find anything, right?'

'Yes. There was nothing. And he was away for days on end. Sometimes more than a week.'

'You do know what that sounds like, Melanie.'

She said nothing.

'It sounds like he was involved in something bad,' Cahill said. 'Something criminal.'

12

'I know,' she said.

She sniffed loudly and when she spoke her voice wavered.

'But I can't believe that about him. Not Tim. It's not like him, you know?'

Cahill did know. Stark had been such a Boy Scout — joining the Secret Service from the FBI after receiving a bunch of commendations for his work there. Mr All-American, a smart, tough operator. And he hadn't changed in all the years Cahill had known him.

'It doesn't sound like the man I know,' Cahill told her.

'Thank you,' she said, sounding genuinely pleased.

'What's the problem there? Why are the police not talking to you?'

'Oh, it's not that they haven't been talking.'

A man appeared on the TV. The onscreen caption identified him as a Colorado official of the NTSB — the US National Transportation Safety Board. The NTSB would normally be responsible for investigating the cause of the disaster.

'I don't understand, Melanie,' Cahill told her. 'I thought you said that they wouldn't tell you anything.'

'They won't.'

Cahill sighed.

'I know he was on that flight, Alex. I mean, he called me from the airport before he boarded and told me the flight number, when he'd get to Washington, the name of his hotel there. But he sounded weird. Not like himself.'

Cahill wasn't following her at all now and said so.

'They say they don't have any record of him on the flight,' Melanie said. 'His name isn't on the passenger manifest.'

2

Now Cahill was wide awake.

'Have you called Tim's cell phone?' he asked.

'Yes, of course,' Melanie replied. 'It defaults to voicemail.'

'What about his car?'

'What do you mean?'

'Is it at the airport somewhere, maybe in a long-stay car park or something?'

'I don't know. I hadn't thought of that.'

'Look, get back in touch with the police and tell them that he said he would be on the flight and that he's ex-Secret Service. That should get their attention. Ask them to check for his car and call the airline as well.'

She took a few deep breaths.

'I'll do that.'

'They'll have access to security cameras covering every inch of the airport so if his car is there they'll find it. But you realise that will just confirm he was at the airport. Not that he got on that flight. Or any flight.'

'It would be better if he wasn't on it, you know. They're saying that there are no survivors.'

'Take small steps right now. Find out what you can.'

Cahill was about to end the call when something jagged into his mind, a shard of mental glass.

'Melanie, you said he got fired from the

15

Service. Have you tried calling there?'

'I did. I couldn't get past the front desk. It was almost like they fed me a script. I don't know what's going on.' She started crying. 'I trusted him,' she said. 'And he never let me down before.'

'He was always someone I could trust,' Cahill told her.

'He said the same about you. He looked up to you so much.'

Cahill didn't know how to respond.

'Look,' she said. 'I'm going to go talk to the police again and I'll call you after. But let me give you my numbers so you know how to get me.'

Cahill jotted down her home and mobile numbers.

'Is there anyone there with you? Any family?'

'My son's coming with his wife. He'll be here soon.'

'Good. Take care, Melanie.'

* * *

Cahill sat at his desk staring at the TV screen and the devastation wrought by the crash. It would be just past midnight in Washington. He scrolled through his contacts until he found the name he was looking for — Scott Boston, his old boss in the Secret Service.

Cahill called Boston's office number. Had a hunch that if he was still the same man he might be at his desk even at midnight on a Sunday. He liked to work when it was quiet.

16

Boston picked up on the second ring.

'Scott, it's Alex Cahill.'

Boston said nothing for a moment.

'Alex, Jesus. It's been a while. How are you?'

'I'm good, Scott. How's life in the Service?'

Standard platitudes.

'You know, same old same old. What can I do for you at this time on a Sunday?'

'Actually it's early Monday for me.'

'I forgot. How's it working out for you over there?'

Cahill's hand went involuntarily to his side. He felt the ribs he had broken in an explosion last September during what was supposed to have been an easy gig protecting an actress at a film premiere. He was sure Boston would have heard about it through government channels — would have heard that Cahill had lost one of his men, Chris Washington, in the same incident.

'It's been an interesting couple of years, you know. Listen, I'm calling about one of the guys. Tim Stark.'

'Uh-huh.'

Cahill heard the caution in Boston's voice.

'We stayed in touch after I left and I just heard he got fired from the Service.'

'Alex, you know I can't talk to you about that stuff. Who told you that anyway?'

'His wife.'

'Melanie? When did you speak to her?'

'Just now. She called me from Kansas. Said she thinks he was on that plane that went down over there.'

Cahill heard a noise on the other end of the

17

phone, like Boston had stood up quickly and his chair had shot back and hit something.

'What plane?'

'You didn't hear? The one that went down outside Denver. It was headed your way.'

'He was coming to Washington? Tim Stark was coming here?'

'Looks that way.'

Boston was quiet.

'Scott, what's going on with this?'

'Alex, I've got to go. Sorry.'

Cahill held the phone away from his ear as Boston slammed the receiver down to end the call. He was left in the quiet of his study listening to nothing but the dial tone.

3

Cahill called Tom Hardy: a six-foot-four Texan hard-ass and his second in command at CPO — the company he ran to provide close protection for anyone who needed it and could afford the best. They had set up CPO together after a career in the army and the US Secret Service.

'You up yet, Tom?' Cahill asked when Hardy answered.

'Fixin' breakfast,' Hardy said in his Texas drawl. 'Been for a run already.'

Cahill believed him.

'You in contact with any of the guys from back in the Service?' Cahill asked.

'A couple,' Hardy answered. 'Why?'

'You remember Tim Stark?'

'FBI guy?'

'That's the one.'

'What's going on, Alex?'

'I got a call from Tim's wife this morning. She thinks he was on the plane that went down over in Denver.'

'I saw that on the news. Looks bad.'

'They're saying no survivors.'

'Why'd she call you?'

'Me and Tim stayed in touch. Anyway, she said Tim got fired last year and might be caught up in something illicit now.'

'Tim? No way.'

19

'That's what I said. He told her he was going to be on that flight but his name's not on the passenger list and apparently the cops are being tight-lipped about it.'

'What's this got to do with you?'

'A good friend might be in trouble, Tom. Or worse.'

'She didn't call the cops?'

'Yeah, but they won't talk to her. Plus, I called Scott Boston and it sounded like he almost had a heart attack when I told him that Tim was supposed to be on a plane heading for Washington. Wouldn't tell me why Tim got fired — or much of anything, for that matter.'

'Let me call the guys I know. See what I can find out.'

Sam came into the study as Cahill finished the call with Hardy, walked over to him and sat beside him on the couch, laying her head on his shoulder.

'Can't sleep?' Cahill asked.

Sam shook her head.

'What's up?' she asked. 'Anything important?'

'I don't know. Could be something, could be nothing. One of the guys I knew back in the Secret Service might have been on that plane and his wife called me looking for help.'

Cahill nodded at the TV screen and Sam sat up to watch the news, Cahill turning the sound back on.

'Want some breakfast?' Sam asked.

'Sure.'

Cahill watched the news feed some more while Sam made scrambled eggs with toast and coffee.

20

He began to feel a little more human with food in his belly. Sam ate her breakfast with him and went back upstairs when she heard their two daughters — Anna and Jodie — starting to stir noisily.

It was close to seven when Cahill called Logan Finch, his best friend and in-house lawyer at CPO. They shared a history of more than just business dealings.

Logan sounded alert when he answered the phone; Cahill heard lots of voices in the background.

'Hey, Logan,' Cahill said. 'Sounds like you had a sleepover last night?'

Logan was heavily involved with Rebecca Irvine — a detective constable in Strathclyde Police. She was divorced with a young son and they socialised with Logan and his daughter, Ellie, at weekends. Sometimes the socialising for Logan and Rebecca went on into the night. Cahill was glad. It was a good relationship for both of them.

'What can I say?' Logan answered. 'It was fun.'

'I'll bet.'

'I take it this is more than a friendly call, given we're due to be in the same office in less than two hours.'

'Yeah, it is. Did I remember right that when you were in private practice you had a couple of cases with the US Government? Or at least some kind of organisation connected to it?'

'It was at DHS. Homeland Security. I defended them against a couple of claims in the courts over here by Scottish tourists who did not

21

appreciate their very thorough customs examinations.'

'Criminals, eh?' Cahill said. 'Never happy getting arrested.'

'Something like that,' Logan said, laughing.

'Can you make contact?'

'I don't know. I can try. Why?'

'I'll fill you in later.'

'Okay. We've got to get the kids ready for nursery and school. Can we catch up about it in the office?'

'Okay. But get there as soon as you can, okay? I get the feeling the longer we wait on this the more likely that the lines of communication will close up.'

'Sounds mysterious.'

'You ain't heard nothing yet.'

4

CNN was showing a helpline number for families to call at the airline in the US if they wanted information about the crash. Cahill thought he'd give it a go while he waited to hear back from Hardy.

It took a while for the call to be connected and a man's voice came on, sounding harassed.

'Uh . . . it's about the crash.' Cahill did his best to sound upset and distracted.

'How can I help, sir?'

'My brother. He's — ' *Cough.*

'I know this is difficult, sir,' sounding sympathetic now, 'but before I can do anything for you I need a name.'

'Sorry, of course.' *Sniff.* 'His name is Tim,' Cahill said. 'Tim Stark. I just know he was on it. He told me he would be.'

'I'm checking for you now, sir.'

Silence.

Cahill heard fingers tapping on a computer keyboard. Then some more tapping.

The guy started talking to someone beside him, but was covering the mouthpiece of his phone.

The talking stopped.

'I'm going to put you on hold for a minute, sir,' the man said. 'Please stay on the line.'

Cahill held.

Held some more.

Looked at his watch and saw five minutes tick by. No way to treat a grieving brother, he thought.

'Good evening, sir.' A different male voice came on the line. 'You're asking about your brother. About Tim Stark.'

'Yes.'

Cahill had given up the pretence of trying to sound upset. This man sounded like he was not in the mood for anyone's bullshit.

'What's your name, sir?' the man asked.

'Alexander Cahill.'

Pause.

'Sir, I don't understand.'

'We're half-brothers.'

The line went dead again — back on hold. Cahill had given his own name because he knew that they would check him out and find out that he had been a serious player, and had a connection with Stark in the Service.

He held again for a while. It was approaching ten minutes this time when the same man came back on to the line.

'Mr Cahill,' he said, 'what's your interest in this matter?'

'Are you with the airline?' Cahill asked.

'I think you know that I'm no more with the airline than you are Mr Stark's half-brother.'

'We're being honest with each other, are we?'

'Let's see how we get on.'

'Tim and I go back a ways.'

'We know. We looked into it.'

'So you know that he's on our side, right?'

'I know that he *was*.'

'His wife called me today in a state. Tim told her he was going to be on that flight but his name is not on the passenger list. And no one will tell her anything. So I offered to help. I'm good that way. Helpful, I mean. Especially where my friends are concerned.'

'The information she was given is correct. His name did not appear on the passenger manifest for the flight.'

'That's a very carefully worded answer.'

No response.

'Which agency are you with?' Cahill asked. 'FBI?'

'I'm sorry I can't be of any more help.'

'Are you there because you think that plane was brought down deliberately?'

'This is a very serious incident and a lot of families are suffering tonight. A lot of people lost their lives.'

'I understand that. All I want to know is whether Tim Stark boarded that plane and if he was still on it when it took off.'

'You have no official role in this and I am not able to release any further information to you as a result. No matter what your relationship with Mrs Stark.'

Cahill didn't like the innuendo.

'That was a cheap shot. Are you trying to piss me off? Because most people who do usually end up regretting it. Not a wise move.'

'Are you threatening me? It's a federal offence to interfere with a law enforcement official — '

He stopped himself.

'Look,' Cahill said. 'You know who I am. What

25

I did for our country. What's going on?'

'I'm ending the call now, Mr Cahill. Goodnight.'

Click

Cahill called Tom Hardy again.

'Any luck yet?' he asked.

'No. I didn't reach anyone.'

'I spoke to a Fed at the airport. Don't know which agency exactly. Probably FBI. They're all over this.'

'What's the story? What do you think Tim was into?'

'I don't know. But I'm starting to believe that he was on that flight. Or at least that he boarded it. Whether he was still on it when it took off, I don't know.'

'So what now? I mean, I know you, Alex. Don't make this a crusade. We just got confirmation that the UK Government is renewing our contract for another three years. I don't need to remind you that it's our most profitable gig. Your head needs to be in the right place.'

'I'm going into the office. Logan might have someone he knows who can help, from back when he was a scumbag lawyer.'

Hardy laughed in spite of himself — Cahill having completely ignored what he had just said.

'He's still a lawyer, Alex.'

'You know what I mean.'

26

5

Logan Finch watched from the couch as Rebecca Irvine tied his daughter's hair in a French plait. He liked watching Ellie and Irvine together, was happy that they were getting on better now.

Irvine saw him watching and made a face. He smiled at her, stood and went to the kitchen.

Irvine's three-year-old son, Connor, was sitting on the floor tracing shapes in the orange juice he had spilled. He saw Logan and lifted his arms up, laughing.

'Let's get you ready for nursery, buddy,' Logan said, lifting him off the floor and skidding in the juice puddle.

Domesticity.

'Time to make a move, everybody,' Logan shouted as he went from the kitchen into the hall of his flat.

Irvine came out of the living room and grabbed Connor from him.

'You in a hurry?' she asked.

'Kind of. Alex called and he needs me to look into something this morning. Sounded urgent.'

'Want me to drop the kids off?'

'Would you? That would be great.'

Irvine smiled. He was transparent.

'All you had to do was ask.'

'But it's more fun when you think that it's all your own idea, right?'

'Oh, sure.'

Logan leaned in past the flailing arms of her son and kissed her. Irvine's hand slid up his back and on to his neck as their lips opened on one another.

'I had fun this weekend,' he told her.

'Me too. Let's do it again sometime.'

He kissed her again before going to his bedroom to grab a jacket, stopping by the bed and putting a hand on the mattress. Feeling the last heat from their bodies lingering there and remembering . . .

'Logan . . .'

Ellie stood in the door with a knowing smile. He didn't mind that she sometimes still called him by his name instead of Dad. She had only come into his life three years ago — after the murder of her mother. But at fourteen, she seemed far more mature than he remembered being at that age.

'I gotta go, Ellie,' he said, brushing past her and kissing the top of her head.

'Piano practice tonight,' she said. 'Did you remember?'

'Sure,' he said, not meaning it. 'Pick you up at seven from Valerie's?'

'You forgot again.'

'Did not.'

★ ★ ★

Logan walked through the CPO reception, nodding at the woman behind the desk. The company name — the 'O' a stylised target of concentric rings — was on the wall above her. Cahill and Hardy were waiting for him in the War Room — the biggest of the meeting rooms in the CPO office suite. The two men were sitting at a small conference table in the centre of the windowless room, spotlights shining on the glossy table top. A large TV was mounted in the centre of the wall to the right of the door.

Cahill looked up and put a finger to his mouth when Logan came into the room, pointing at the conference phone that was sitting on the table. Logan pulled a chair out from the table and sat quietly.

'Guys,' an American voice sounded from the phone, 'I can't help you on this. Not right now anyway. Place is locked down tight and no one is telling me anything.'

'Thanks, anyway,' Hardy said before pressing a button to end the call.

Logan looked at Cahill.

'We're getting exactly nowhere,' Cahill said. 'Nobody wants to talk to us.'

'You need to fill me in on this before I make the call to the woman I know at Homeland Security,' Logan told them.

Cahill picked a remote device from the table top and aimed it at the TV. The screen ran a feed from an American news network — still focusing on the crash outside Denver.

Cahill let Logan watch for a while before telling him what was going on.

Logan stared at the screen some more.

'They think it was brought down deliberately?' he asked. 'The plane, I mean.'

'Who knows. The news people aren't suggesting anything like that.'

'Would explain the secrecy, though, right?'

'Maybe. But the only reason that Tim's name would raise a flag in those circumstances is if he was a suspect.'

Logan nodded like he agreed.

'But he can't be. Not the Tim I know.'

'So it's something else?'

'Can you make the call?'

'Sure. But she's based in New York so it'll be the middle of the night over there. We'll have to wait, you know. Plus, if this thing is sensitive, she might not be able to tell me anything.'

Cahill stood and went to the TV, watching the images from less than six feet away. He turned to face Logan.

'If I remember correctly,' he said, 'it was more than just professional between the two of you.'

Logan felt heat rise in his cheeks.

'Am I right?'

Logan nodded.

'Okay, then.'

'Not okay,' Logan told him. 'It was a brief thing. We only saw each other like that a few times when I was over in New York. I don't feel comfortable using the relationship this way.'

'I'm not asking you to.'

'What are you asking?'

'Make the call. Ask the question. If she says no, then that's the end of it. Don't put any pressure on her.'

Logan looked at Hardy. He was non-committal, shrugging his shoulders.

30

'Fine,' Logan said, turning back to Cahill. 'But I'll do it like you said. Ask her the question in a businesslike way. Nothing else.'

'That's all I'm asking.'

'So, what do you want to do now?' Logan asked.

'Let's call Tim's wife.'

6

Melanie Stark answered Cahill's call on the first ring.

'I've got some people with me,' he told her before introducing Logan and Hardy.

They both said hello quickly.

'You get anywhere with the cops?' Cahill asked.

'Not really. I mean, they weren't interested in talking to me. Couldn't get me off the phone quick enough.'

'What about the airline?'

'Same story as before. His name's not on the list and there's nothing more they can tell me.'

'That's not surprising.'

'I don't know what else to do.'

She sounded on the verge of tears.

'We've called some people too,' Cahill said.

'What did you find out?' She sounded more hopeful.

'Nothing concrete.'

'Oh . . . '

'But, I mean, it's what they didn't say that's interesting.'

'I don't understand.'

'Well, I called the airline helpline. You know, the one they're showing on the TV? I pretended to be Tim's brother and said that I thought he was on the plane. Then the airline guy put me on hold for five minutes and someone else came back on the line in his place.'

'Who was it?'

'He didn't say, except that he was with a law enforcement agency. And it wasn't the police.'

'Then who?'

'I figure it's probably the FBI.'

'What is Tim mixed up in?'

'I don't know. And I also called our old boss at the Service, Scott Boston. Do you know him?'

She was quiet for a moment.

'Yes,' she said finally. 'He's the one who fired Tim.'

'Well, I don't know what's going on over there, but he sounded shocked that Tim was supposed to be on a flight heading for Washington. Hung up on me real fast.'

Melanie sighed.

'What the hell is going on?' She was angry now. 'Why won't anyone tell me what happened to my husband?'

Her voice broke into a choked sob. Cahill's mouth went tight, his lips forming a narrow line.

'We haven't exhausted our lines of inquiry yet,' he told her. 'Logan's a lawyer and he knows someone in Homeland Security.'

'Are you going to call?'

'Yes,' Logan said. 'As soon as the office in New York opens.'

'I want to go to Denver,' Melanie said.

'Best if you don't,' Hardy said. 'You'll end up stuck in a room for hours and they still won't tell you anything.'

'Stay by the phone,' Logan said. 'We'll let you know as soon as we've spoken to my contact.'

A doorbell sounded behind Melanie.

'I think that's my son. Call me as soon as you can.'

'We will,' Cahill said, ending the call.

He turned to Hardy and Logan, telling them to reconvene in the War Room this afternoon to call Homeland Security.

'Someone better start talking,' he said. 'Or I'll be going over there myself to raise hell.'

7

Rebecca Irvine's phone sounded as she got in the car outside Ellie's school, waving to Ellie as she disappeared into a crowd of her friends. Her son was in his car seat in the back.

'DC Irvine,' she said when she answered the call — recognising the number as the Strathclyde Police HQ.

'Becky, it's me.'

Detective Superintendent Liam Moore — her boss.

'Morning, sir.'

'Where are you?'

He sounded cranky. Not an encouraging start to the day.

'I'm going to drop my son off at the childminder. Why, do you need me?'

'Yes. What are you working on right now?'

'The Johnson case. You know, the body in the Range Rover? Ewen Cameron's the DS on it.'

'It's stalled, right?'

He was right. They had identified the victim as Andrew Johnson: soldier, turned private security mercenary, turned . . . something else. Shot twice in the head. 'Execution style' was how the newspapers described it. Beyond that, they had nothing to go on.

'No need to be defensive about it,' Moore said when she didn't answer. 'I know you guys are working it. Maybe you need something new.

Freshen things up, you know.'

Irvine said maybe.

'No one else is free right now anyway,' he said. 'We're getting slammed.'

So what's new?

'What have you got?' she asked.

'It's a floater. Fished out the Clyde this morning down on the Broomielaw.'

Irvine closed her eyes. Those were never good.

'There's a twist with this one,' Moore said.

'Okay. What is it?'

'It's a drug squad investigation. Those guys are at the locus already. They've asked for CID assistance.'

'Am I volunteering?'

'You already did.'

Irvine cradled the phone with her shoulder while Moore talked, reached inside her jacket and took out a notebook. She wrote the location of the body. Was about to write the name of the drug squad contact on site when she paused.

'Did you say the Director General is there?' she asked Moore.

'Yes.'

'Why is the head of the SCDEA at a crime scene?'

'I didn't ask. Must be big time, eh?'

'I guess. Are we going to be in charge of the scene?'

'Yes. I briefed Jim Murphy already.'

Murphy was a veteran detective sergeant who had turned the latter half of his time on the force into a career as a crime scene manager. It was a desk job that he was entirely happy with as he

36

headed rapidly downhill towards retirement. That wasn't to say that he was a bad detective. He just preferred a life behind a desk to a life stepping over bodies.

Who could blame him?

'Leave it with me,' Irvine told Moore. 'I'll head over there as soon as I can.'

'Brief me when you get in.'

'Yes, sir.'

Irvine had very little experience of dealing with the SCDEA — the Scottish Crime and Drug Enforcement Agency. But she knew enough about police hierarchies to realise that if the head man — the DG — was at a crime scene, then it was a very big deal.

8

Irvine felt cold in spite of the sun overhead as she walked along the riverside towards the small crowd gathered behind the yellow crime scene tape. She saw uniformed officers standing around looking bored and Scenes of Crime staff in the full regalia: white overalls, hoods, masks and booties.

The sun was clear in the sky, only wisps of cloud spoiling the blue canvas. Irvine knew that it was her core temperature that had dropped, not the heat of the sun.

When she reached the crowd, Irvine eased her way through, showing her warrant card to a uniformed officer who stepped up to block her. She saw two thirty-something men in dark suits with SCDEA gold shields fixed to their jackets. She could almost feel the sense of entitlement radiating from them.

She approached the two men and introduced herself. They did the same: Detective Chief Superintendent Eric Thomson, head of operations at the SCDEA; and syndicate leader, Detective Inspector Bryan Fraser. Irvine didn't know the jargon.

'What's a syndicate?' she asked.

'What we call our investigation teams,' Thomson told her.

Irvine wasn't really sure what was wrong with the word 'team', but said nothing. She was here to make friends.

Thomson was a short man with a neat beard and square-rimmed glasses. It looked to Irvine like he took some care over his appearance. Fraser was much taller — over six feet — with hair gone prematurely grey.

'What's the story here?' Irvine asked.

She looked past the two men at a white-suited technician on hands and knees going over the ground inch by inch for evidence.

Fraser turned in the direction she was looking.

'Young girl found this morning,' he said. 'Face down in the water.'

'How old?' she asked.

'Eighteen or nineteen, we think.'

Irvine winced.

'Where's the body?'

'The pathologist was here with the shell a half-hour ago.'

Irvine knew the jargon this time: 'the shell' was the name given to the unmarked van that ferried bodies to the mortuary.

'What do you want me to do?'

Fraser didn't answer this time, looked at Thomson instead.

'You should speak to the DG,' he said. 'And Kenny Armstrong. They're around somewhere.'

He swivelled his head, scanning the crowd.

Irvine had seen photographs of the Director General — Paul Warren. He liked being high profile and was often front and centre when a big arrest was made.

'Here they are,' Thomson said, waving at two men making their way through the crowd.

Warren was in his early fifties and wore a

charcoal-coloured suit. He had short, greying hair and a narrow face. The man with him was about Irvine's height with heavy stubble and close-cropped hair. His clothes looked like they had seen better days: stained jeans, a V-neck jumper and a black leather jacket.

Thomson made the introductions. The man in the leather jacket was Detective Sergeant Kenny Armstrong.

'Sorry about this,' Armstrong said, looking down at himself as he shook Irvine's hand. 'I've been out all night on this and didn't get the chance to change.'

Irvine noticed that he had a bit of a Highland accent.

'No worries,' she said. 'I know what that can be like.'

'Kenny's been working hard on this the last couple of weeks,' Warren said. 'Since it started.'

'Not that it's got us anywhere,' Armstrong said, rubbing his hands over his face.

'Since what started?' she asked.

'Sorry,' Warren said. 'We need to get you up to speed, don't we?'

He turned to Armstrong.

'Kenny, can you get some steer from DC Irvine on working the scene and we can meet back at Pitt Street later today with the full team for a briefing. I'll call you and let you know what time.'

He told Irvine it had been nice to meet her then moved away with Thomson and Fraser in tow.

'Not sure how I can steer you until I know

40

what this is about,' Irvine told Armstrong. 'I mean, I'm a little in the dark.'

'Welcome to Operation Red Square,' Armstrong said flatly.

9

'CID are the experts,' Armstrong said to Irvine as he walked with her to the top of the concrete embankment leading down to the river's edge. 'I mean, on murder investigations. It's why we asked for your input.'

They stopped at the top of the embankment. Irvine saw another of the forensic technicians being helped down the embankment wall to the muddy river's edge. She turned to face Armstrong.

'You've had more than one body?' she asked.

'Yes.'

'And the reason CID haven't been called in before is that you didn't think they were murders. Am I still on track?'

Armstrong nodded. 'You're good,' he said, smiling for the first time. 'How many?' Irvine asked.

'How many what?'

'Deaths.'

'This is the fourth.'

A line creased between Irvine's eyes. 'You're saying you have four murders?'

'Well, we're not sure if they're all murders.' He opened his hands.

'Okay,' Irvine said, feeling more confused now than when she had arrived. 'Let's deal with what we have here then we can talk about the rest. What was it about this girl's body that made you

42

think someone killed her?'

Irvine looked down at the technicians working in the shallow edge of the river, water halfway up their boots.

'We're not certain that she was killed,' Armstrong said. 'Not in the way you mean. By someone doing violence to her.'

'But this one is different to the first three?'

'Yes. The girl was naked.'

'And who goes out at night in Glasgow like that before taking a swim, right?'

'That's what we thought.'

'So at the very least someone was with her when she died. Stripped her and dumped her here.' A further thought occurred to Irvine. 'Why do you think this is linked to your operation? I mean, what's the connection to the other bodies?'

'We don't know for sure that she is connected,' Armstrong said. 'I mean, the other deaths were overdoses so far as we can tell. But there are needle tracks on this girl's body and no immediate signs of any other cause of death.'

'Seems a bit of a stretch.'

'You're right. But it makes sense to treat it as potentially connected for now so that we can get a head start on working the case. If we're wrong, we've lost nothing. You've got to understand that with three bodies already and now this one, it's at the top of the list of priorities.'

'Okay, I can see some sense in that. Anything else to go on? I mean, do we have an ID on the girl?'

'One of the uniforms that responded to the

call recognised her. She's a working girl with a record for possession. Don't have a name yet.'

'We'll need to speak to the uniforms.'

Armstrong nodded.

'Why strip her?' Irvine asked. 'I mean, if none of the other victims was stripped?'

'I don't know.'

Irvine thought about that. It was a significant departure if this was connected to the earlier deaths.

'Maybe because whoever she was with didn't want to be connected to her,' Irvine said. 'It's a way of trying to obliterate evidence.'

One of the Scenes of Crime team working down on the bank picked something off the top of the mud and slipped it into an evidence bag.

'Okay,' Armstrong said. 'I can see that could be it.'

'Which might mean different things,' Irvine went on. 'I mean, a celebrity or a politician would want to avoid a scandal.'

'Or someone in the supply chain who might not want to be connected to the drugs that have killed these people.'

Irvine looked at Armstrong again.

'That's the link?' she asked. 'The same bad drugs?'

He nodded.

'We can fill you in on all of that at the briefing later today.'

Irvine peered across the river, squinting at sunlight reflected on the surface of the water. The crowd behind them started to thin as it became clear that there was nothing much to see

44

any more except a bunch of cops going about their painstaking business.

'This is your investigation now,' Armstrong said to Irvine. 'So, what's the plan?'

'Work the evidence. We want to get the ID on the girl and information on other girls who know her. Interview them and her family too, if she has any here. Check CCTV as well: see if we can track her movements yesterday.'

Armstrong took out a notepad, flipped it open and made some notes as Irvine spoke.

'If we know who she is, then we can check where she lives. Speak to anyone who lives with her.'

'Anything else?'

'Find her clothes. Or maybe what's left of them. If I know criminals, the first thought is usually to dump them or dump *and* burn them. Probably won't be too far away either. Something like this, they like to get it over with fast. We might get some residual evidence from that — hair, fibres or fluid samples. And we need to ask the pathologist to look out for that kind of thing during the post-mortem. She might have had sex before she was killed.'

'Should we find out who she bought her regular supply of drugs from as well? And who her regular customers were.'

'If we can. The other girls might know.'

Armstrong wrote in his pad some more.

'It's always personal,' Irvine said.

'What?' Armstrong asked.

She looked at him and shook her head, she had been talking to herself more than anything.

45

'I mean, that's pretty much the rule in CID on murder investigations. It's usually someone that the victim knows.'

'Uh-huh.'

'So I'd bet whoever dumped her here had met her before today. And that's how we break this case.'

10

Logan had gone back to his office to work on a backlog of contracts for new CPO jobs before the call to his contact at Homeland Security. He was putting the finishing touches to the last document when Cahill came in. It was a small room next to Cahill's and Logan kept it simple: a walnut desk, swivel chair and a unit with a low-level cupboard and shelves above it. He glanced at the photograph of Ellie on the middle shelf as Cahill walked to his desk.

'You ready?' Cahill asked, holding up his watch and tapping on the face of it. 'Just gone two.'

Logan looked at his own watch, surprised to see that Cahill was right. He had worked through lunch without noticing.

'I guess I got caught up in this stuff,' Logan said, standing to follow Cahill as he left the room.

Hardy was waiting for them back in the War Room, sipping from a bottle of water and watching more news coverage of the crash.

'Anything new?' Cahill asked.

'Nope. Usual talk about recovering the black box and waiting till they know more before reaching any conclusions.'

'Still no mention of terrorists?'

'Nothing. Looks like it was an accident from what they're saying, but who knows what they might be holding back?'

Logan sat beside Hardy and pulled the conference phone towards him.

'If it's not terrorists, then why all the secrecy about your friend?' Logan asked.

Cahill shrugged and sat beside Logan.

'Let's call your contact and see what she can tell us.'

Logan picked up the phone handset and punched in the number he had for Susan Jones at the Department of Homeland Security in New York.

'I'm looking for Susan Jones,' he said when a man answered.

He was put on hold and pressed a button to activate the conference setting on the phone. A Tom Petty song started playing.

'Nice hold music,' Hardy said, tapping a pen on the table in time with the music.

The music stopped and the same man came back on to the line.

'Sir, who may I say is calling?'

'Logan Finch.'

Tom Petty was back on. Hardy started humming along.

'Logan, hi,' Susan Jones said after a minute. 'It's been a while. How are you?'

She sounded incredibly bright and upbeat, which was what Logan remembered about her. That and the killer cheekbones.

'I'm good. How's things with you?'

'Oh, you know. Still trying to keep the world safe from harm.'

She laughed — a high, flutey sound. Logan

always thought that it was totally at odds with such a tall, athletic woman.

'I've got you on speakerphone, Susan. Is that okay?'

Letting her know not to talk about anything other than business. Logan glanced at Cahill who winked at him.

'Sure. Who have you got there? Clients getting roughed up at one of our airports?'

'Uh, no. I'm not with Kennedy Boyd any more. I mean, I left private practice altogether.'

'Good for you. I never did like lawyers.'

The laugh again.

'I'm with a security company. Close protection. I've got two of the team here. Alex Cahill and Tom Hardy.'

They both said hello.

'Fine, upstanding Americans, by the sound of it.'

'Yes, ma'am,' Hardy said.

'Southern manners,' she laughed. 'What's up?'

'Have you heard about the crash over in Denver?' Logan asked.

'Of course. Awful, isn't it?'

There was no tell-tale change in her tone.

'We had a call from someone who thinks that her husband was on the flight . . . '

'Uh-huh.'

' . . . but the airline has no record of his name on the passenger manifest.'

'Okay. I'm not sure what this has to do with DHS.'

'Well, Alex called the airline and they put him on hold and when they came back on it was

49

someone from law enforcement.'

'FBI, I think,' Cahill said.

Jones was silent, though they could hear the sound of her fingers tapping on a keyboard.

Cahill hit the mute button.

'She's going to cut us off,' he said to Logan. 'More cover-up bullshit.'

Logan held up a hand and re-activated the phone.

'Susan, is there anything you can tell us about that flight?' Logan asked.

'I'm checking our systems. Hold on.'

Tap-tap-tap

'No alerts at our end that I can see. What's your friend's name?'

'Tim Stark,' Cahill said. 'Used to be FBI and then Secret Service.'

'Oh my. Let me check the name and see what I can find. Call you back in five.'

Five stretched to ten, stretched to twenty.

The phone rang. Logan pressed the button to answer and activate the speaker.

'Logan, it's Susan.'

'That was a long five minutes.' He tried to keep his voice light.

'I know. There's a flag on your man Stark.'

Cahill frowned. 'Why?' he asked.

'I can't tell you that. In fact, I shouldn't really tell you anything else.'

'He's just about the most patriotic guy I know,' Cahill said. 'Bleeds red, white and blue. And he has a wife at home who's tearing her hair out in a panic because nobody will tell her anything about what's going on.'

50

'I'm sorry. I can't say any more.'

'Can you tell us if he was on the flight?' Logan asked.

'At least that,' Cahill said. 'Please.'

She was quiet.

'Susan . . . ' Logan said.

'Tim Stark wasn't listed on the flight,' she said. 'But the manifest shows that John Reece was on it.'

Cahill leaned back in his chair, looked at Hardy and shook his head.

'Thanks, Susan,' Cahill said. 'I appreciate it.'

'No problem. And I'm sorry.'

She ended the call.

Logan looked from Cahill to Hardy and back again. 'What's going on?' he asked.

'She just told us that Tim was on the flight.'

'That's not what she said.'

'What she said was, he was on the flight using an assumed name.'

'Which means what?'

Cahill didn't reply.

'It means that he's dead,' Hardy said.

11

Cahill stood and stretched.

'Is that it?' Logan asked.

'It's as much as she can tell us, and she shouldn't even have said that. We can't push it with her any further.'

'So what are you going to do now?'

'I'm going to make a very difficult phone call to Melanie Stark to tell her that her husband is dead. I need to do it alone.'

Cahill left Logan and Hardy in the War Room and walked to his office at the south-west corner of the building. It was bigger than Logan's office, but not ostentatious. He had a couch as well as a similar desk and shelving unit. His desk was covered with photographs of his wife and two girls.

He sat at the desk and lifted his phone. After a moment, he dialled Melanie Stark's number. A man answered.

'I'm looking for Melanie Stark,' Cahill said.

'This is her son. Can I help?'

Cahill thought: your mother will need your help shortly.

'No, thanks. I need to speak to Melanie.'

'What's this about?' He started to sound tense.

Cahill heard a woman's voice in the background asking who was on the phone.

'My name is Alex Cahill and I'm a friend of

your dad. Your mom will want to speak to me, son.'

'Hold on.'

The phone clattered down on a hard surface. Cahill pulled his own phone away from his ear at the noise. He couldn't blame the boy for being upset — angry even. Cahill felt some of that himself.

'Alex,' Melanie Stark said, picking up the phone. 'What have you heard?'

'Does the name John Reece mean anything to you?'

Pause. 'No. I mean, I don't think so. I never heard it before.'

'Never seen that name written down anywhere in the house?'

'Alex, what's this about? Does this man Reece have anything to do with what Tim's caught up in?'

'Sort of.'

'Alex . . . ' She knew that he was stalling.

'Melanie . . . '

Always the bad news is preceded by the name, spoken softly. Like it helps.

'No . . . '

'I can't be totally certain, but the information I have makes me believe that Tim was on that flight out of Denver.'

No sound this time.

'I'm so sorry, Melanie. I really am.'

He could hear the scream starting way down inside her, rising up from a place so deep inside that no person should ever have to know the pain it brought as it burst up and out. Cahill had heard it before. Too many times.

'If it helps,' Cahill said, 'I can't believe that Tim was involved in something illegal. That's not the Tim I knew.'

He knew he'd said it already today, but what else was there to say?

'Are . . . you . . . sure?' She was barely able to get the word out between sobs.

'As sure as I can be. He was on that plane when it went down.'

'I can't . . . '

The line disconnected.

Cahill stood and went to the window, looking down at the people passing by outside.

What were you doing on that plane, Tim?

12

Irvine found DS Ewen Cameron when she got back to Pitt Street from the riverside. She explained that she had to go to a briefing on a new case and that she didn't know how long it would be. He didn't seem too bothered, his head buried in a mountain of paperwork that was expanding on a daily basis.

Kenny Armstrong headed off to find the senior SCDEA guys. They had called to say the briefing was already set up somewhere in the building.

Irvine didn't want to hold things up, but she was keen to get a head start on the inquiry: knew that the first couple of days were crucial in solving any murder. She called the mortuary to find out about the post-mortem and was told that it was scheduled for tomorrow.

After that she called the CCTV ops room down at the Fruitmarket and spoke to someone about getting the recordings for the last few days sent over to see if they could track the girl's movements in the city centre. They said they'd do what they could, but they were short-staffed this week.

Armstrong came into the room and waved at her to come over.

'They're all set upstairs,' he said.

'Okay. Can we hold for another couple of minutes? I want to check in with DS Murphy, our crime scene guy.'

'You go see him and I'll tell my guys to wait. We're on the second floor, last door on the left.'

'I'll walk up with you. Murphy's on the same floor.'

★　★　★

Jim Murphy stared at Irvine over rectangular glasses that had slipped down his nose, a heavy fringe flopping down on to his forehead. He reminded Irvine of her old history teacher, sitting there in his black V-neck with a white shirt and paisley-patterned tie.

'The floater?' he asked as she reached his desk.

She nodded.

'I got nothing for you yet. Still waiting for the lab geeks upstairs to let me know what they collected at the locus.'

'Okay. Let me know when you do get anything.'

Irvine knew that Murphy could be ponderous and sometimes needed a kick. Murphy preferred to think of it as being methodical and diligent.

'I called the Fruitmarket,' Irvine said as she turned to leave. 'You know, for the CCTV.'

He knew: nodded slowly.

'And the pathologist. Post-mortem is tomorrow. Can you keep on top of all that for me?'

His head retracted like a tortoise.

Irvine took it as a 'yes'.

★　★　★

56

The briefing room at the end of the hall was already busy with other officers and was set up conference-style with rows of chairs facing a long table that had three more chairs behind it. Everyone was in plain clothes except Eric Thomson and Bryan Fraser — the senior SCDEA officers Irvine had met at the scene that morning. They sat at the long table.

She was glad to see that there was a coffee pot on a table at the side of the room. She filled two cardboard cups and sat next to Armstrong, handing him one of the cups. He gulped at it. The woman on the other side of Armstrong fidgeted with a thin blue folder which was open on her lap. Irvine had seen her around the building and guessed she was one of the force's drug officers and not with the SCDEA.

Paul Warren — the SCDEA Director General — came into the room and pushed the door closed before taking up position behind the empty third chair at the long table. There were seven people sitting in the chairs facing the table.

'Everyone say hello to DC Irvine from the CID,' Warren said.

Irvine held her hand up. The others looked at her and nodded.

'There should be packs under your seat with the briefing material,' Warren said. 'So grab one if you don't have it already.'

Irvine now saw that everyone except her and Armstrong had one of the blue folders with a sheaf of papers inside. She put her coffee down on the floor and reached under her seat to grab the folder there. Armstrong followed her lead and did the same.

Irvine flicked through the papers quickly, seeing extracts from three post-mortem reports for the previous deaths and some jargon-heavy stuff about drug types. The drug references went over her head.

'Eric is going to take you through this.'

Warren sat down and his Director of Operations stood.

'I'll give you the basics,' Eric Thomson said. 'We had, as most of you know, a fourth death this morning. It's a different ball game now. Young girl. Teenager.'

He paused to let this sink in.

'The main substance found in the three previous victims was fentanyl. And there were also the same lower levels of heroin.'

Someone spoke from the front row of seats.

'Same levels in all the victims?'

'No,' Thomson replied. 'Slight variations in each of the three. And we'll have to wait for the post-mortem results from the victim today.'

'Somebody experimenting?'

'Too early to say definitively. But we've brought more people in to this task force because that's how it looks. As of today we're treating all the deaths as suspicious. I mean, beyond the fact that illegal drugs were involved. That's why CID is here.'

Thomson looked quickly at Irvine before scanning the room.

'We're treating them all as murders now,'

Warren said. 'Someone knowingly sells bad gear, they deserve all they get.'

'What we seem to be dealing with here,' Thomson went on, 'is a new product in the market. From what we've been able to find out so far it's being distributed in the usual channels. There are no new dealers we know of and the deaths can be traced back to buys from different dealers.'

'That's why we think it's probably a new wholesaler,' Warren interrupted. 'If all of a sudden it was a new retail crew on the scene there would be the usual territorial flare-ups. We'd have seen, and heard, something from our informants. A wholesale business can keep it under the radar more easily.'

'Yeah,' someone shouted from the other side of the room. 'Four bodies. Way to keep it under the radar.'

There was a ripple of laughter.

'This is a relatively high level of organised crime,' Thomson said. 'It may be a foreign outfit because our usual sources don't seem to know much about it.'

'Any sign of increased smuggling into the country anywhere?' someone asked.

'Not that we've seen. But then, that doesn't mean much. Could be the supply network is using entry points we don't know about yet and, of course, that's something we need to look into. Or they may just be smart. Or lucky.'

'We are looking at increasing our resources on the smuggling front,' Warren said. 'We need to look at the budget first, though.'

Irvine felt a little lost, decided to ask some basic questions.

'For my benefit, can you say a little more about the drugs?'

Warren looked at DI Fraser.

'Of course,' Fraser said as he stood, stretching above Thomson. 'Fentanyl is not something that you hear much about but, in fact, it's actually more potent than heroin. It's similar in that it's an opiate . . . '

'What does that mean exactly?' Irvine asked.

'Okay, an opiate is a drug that affects the central nervous system and also breathing. Slows everything down. It's used to manage pain, like in cancer patients.'

'I thought they used morphine for that?'

'Also an opiate. The effects of fentanyl are a little different from heroin. The high is not as pronounced and it also doesn't last as long. So, because of the shortened period of the high, it can be even more addictive.'

'Combine the two to get the best of both, so to speak?'

Fraser smiled and nodded.

'Exactly.'

Irvine took a pen from her jacket pocket and scribbled notes on the back of one of the post-mortem extracts.

'But why the deaths?' someone else asked.

'We think that whoever is supplying this hasn't quite got the mix right yet. Which explains the different levels found in the first three victims. You see, the negative effect fentanyl has on the respiratory system is much more pronounced than with heroin and so if it's sold as heroin to a user, he can OD on it without knowing. Basically, it stops him breathing.'

Irvine wrote some more. At the top of the page she wrote the operation name, looked up at Fraser.

'Why Operation Red Square?' she asked.

'There are stories out there that the Russians used a fentanyl-heroin derivative against some terrorists, kidnappers, in Moscow a while back.'

'You think these guys are Russian?'

'We don't know. Haven't ruled anything out as yet.'

Warren stood, taking control of the meeting.

'This fourth death is the one we want to focus on for now. Young girl found like that will get lots of ink in the press. Let's see if we can get any better leads on it than we have from the others. I've asked for CID input not just because the deaths are unlawful, but also to give us a different perspective on the investigation.'

He looked at Irvine.

'If you and DS Armstrong could wait behind after we break up, DC Irvine, we'll take you through how we want to do this.'

Irvine nodded, feeling a little surge of excitement now — the buzz of the job.

13

When the meeting finished, Irvine and Armstrong waited while the room cleared, then went to the front of the room.

Warren came around the table and stood in front of them, leaning back against the table edge.

'Now you know what we're dealing with,' Warren said to Irvine. 'Kenny's been immersed in this for a while and doesn't think that we're going to get anywhere by focusing on our usual sources.'

'We won't,' Armstrong said.

Warren smiled, like a parent dealing with an irascible child. Irvine wondered if there was tension in the relationship between the two men.

'My view', Warren said, 'is that we need to look at this from all angles. Leave no stone unturned, if you know what I mean.'

Irvine didn't want to get stuck on the wrong side of a fight.

'What do you want me to do?' she asked.

'I want Kenny to brief you on the local drugs scene, the supply chain and the like. Give you a feel for what we're dealing with. Then he'll take you on a tour of the earlier crime scenes. How does that sound?'

'Fine by me.'

'Good,' Warren said, straightening up.

Warren left the room and Irvine followed

Armstrong to the table where the coffee was, picking up a shortbread biscuit and taking a bite.

'You don't like the DG?' Irvine asked.

Armstrong looked sideways at her.

'He's all right for a boss. I mean he's a purist, you know. A bad bastard, if you're a criminal. And he didn't take the DG job for political reasons.'

Irvine had always assumed a job like DG of the SCDEA was a way to make a career splash. A politician's job, not a real cop.

'Why, then?'

'Because he wants to do something about the shit that flows through this country. The drugs, I mean. He's about as straight a cop as you'll find anywhere.'

'How did this thing start?'

'I flagged it up to my syndicate leader, DI Fraser, and from there it went up the chain fast. The DG likes to keep his hand in on operational matters. Doesn't like sitting behind a desk all day.'

'He came up with the name of the op?'

Armstrong nodded. 'He wants people to think he has all the big ideas. Fine with me.'

Irvine took another bite from her biscuit and put the remains back on the plate. She liked shortbread but this stuff was cheap and not particularly good.

'What about your DI?' she asked. 'What's he like?'

Armstrong picked up her half-biscuit and put it all in his mouth. Irvine didn't know what to make of that.

'Now, *he* is a politician. More concerned about his next promotion than anything else.'

Armstrong scrunched his cup before throwing it into the bin.

'Look, never mind me. I'm crabby today because I haven't had a good night's sleep in about a week and we're getting exactly nowhere with this investigation. And then the girl this morning . . .'

He didn't finish that thought.

'I'm not normally like this,' he told her.

He tried to smile, but it wasn't convincing.

Irvine didn't mind crabby, so long as there was good reason. She kind of liked him, in spite of his poorly developed social skills.

'Where to now?' she asked.

'Want a tour of my nightmare?'

Part Two:
Soldiers

1

Denver, Colorado
Monday morning

Seth Raines went to the kitchen in his apartment on Capitol Hill, poured himself a glass of orange juice and drank it in one go. He switched on the coffee machine and sat at the table rubbing sleep from his eyes. The images from a dream ran through his head: a dream of war and death. The details precise and the sounds and smells resonating like it was only yesterday.

Back in another life, Raines had served in the Helmand Province of Afghanistan as Staff Sergeant for Third Platoon, Charlie Company, First Reconnaissance Division of the US Marines. That was before a simple mission two years ago to monitor the eradication of an opium poppy field. Before his convoy was ambushed on the trip back from the field to the British camp outside the city of Lashkar Gah — brigade headquarters for Four-Two Commando, the Royal Marines.

In his dream, he saw only brief, fractured images of that day: the ragged stump of a severed leg and blood soaking into desert sand. But now that he was awake, the memory of it all rushed back, hitting him like a physical blow.

★ ★ ★

Raines was sitting next to one of his men — Private First Class Matthew Horn. They were sweating heavily under body armour listening to a briefing by the commanding officer of the British Marine brigade. He was a very British soldier, immaculately uniformed with a neatly clipped moustache and a deeply tanned face.

The door of the room was open and Raines saw a Union flag fluttering outside in the low wind. Two marines were standing at the base of the flagpole taking custody of the now deposed Stars and Stripes from their British counterparts. Raines nudged Horn and nodded for him to look at the exchange taking place outside.

'Most of you already know the lieutenant,' the British officer said, pointing at a young-looking woman in the front row of the briefing room. 'She is our Civil Military Ops Cell representative today and will communicate with the ANP contingent through our interpreter.'

If there was one thing that both armies had in common, Raines thought, it was their love of TLAs: Three Letter Acronyms.

ANP — Afghan National Police.

'This is a hearts-and-minds job for the local population,' the officer went on. 'The ANP will burn a designated opium poppy field in a very public manner and our job is to ensure that nothing untoward happens while this is taking place.'

The Brits were good at that sort of thing, Raines knew — hearts-and-minds jobs. They'd had plenty of practice during the troubles in Northern Ireland.

'We also have two colleagues from the US Marine force today. Sergeant Raines and PFC Horn.'

There were a total of twelve soldiers in the room for the operation and Raines and Horn were the only Americans. The Brits turned to look at them. Raines nodded his head in greeting.

Raines knew what kind of first impression he made on people. He had identical, Maori-style tattoos on his shoulder blades — all loops and curls with pointed ends — and they extended up on to his neck. The very topmost points curled around on to the sides of his neck and were visible even above his body armour. His hair was shaved down to a fine bristle and his eyes were so dark in colour that even from a modest distance they looked almost black.

Next to him, Horn was like a choirboy with his razored blond hair and fresh face.

'They will travel in the lead Snatch,' the British commander continued. 'With the lieutenant and Corporal Johnson of the Royal Military Police. Everyone clear on what they have to do? Good, let's get going. It's going to be bloody hot today so the quicker we get this done the better.'

Raines stood with Horn, both men lifting their helmets and rifles and moving with the other soldiers out of the room and towards the heat that they could feel as they neared the open door.

Outside, Raines saw the three Land Rovers that were going to be used for the op: two 'Snatches' — lightly armoured versions of the

vehicle — and a WMIK — an armed Land
Rover. The latter had a .50 calibre machine gun
mounted on top.

'You boys up for this, today?'

Raines and Horn turned as the female
lieutenant approached behind them. She was
wearing regulation desert camo fatigues, body
armour and helmet. She had a sidearm in a
holster on her hip but no rifle. Loose strands of
dark hair fell from under her helmet.

'Yes, ma'am,' Raines said. 'Happy to help.'

'Good. How long have you got left?'

'We're done end of this month. Twelve
months in.'

'Lucky you, eh? I just got here.'

'It'll go quick,' Raines told her.

'Let's hope so.'

She walked ahead of them heading for the lead
Snatch. Raines looked at Horn, seeing his young
private watching the lieutenant. Horn looked
sheepish when he saw that Raines had caught
him.

'She seems nice,' Raines said.

'Yes, Sergeant. She does.'

★ ★ ★

It always ended the same way for Matt Horn: in
dream or memory.

Raines forced himself to think of something
else, ran his hand over the rough scar of the
bullet wound on his shin and watched the coffee
start to drip into the pot fixed under the
machine.

70

The apartment was sparsely furnished: a simple table and two chairs in the kitchen, a couch and TV in the living room and a bed with a table beside it in the bedroom. Raines didn't think of it as home. It was a place to live. That was all. The furniture was second-hand, bought mainly from ads he found in local shops and newspapers. He could leave it all behind and never give it a second thought.

The place was perfect for what he wanted: a one-bed, one-bath apartment in a big, Victorian redstone building. He was the quiet, dangerous-looking guy with the tats who lived alone and didn't have anything to do with anyone else. He said hello to all his neighbours and smiled but didn't know any of them by name. It was how he liked it. No one invited him to parties and no one stopped him to talk about work or football or anything else.

Raines didn't think of himself as having a home anywhere any more. Not the apartment and certainly not the place in the mountains outside of the city.

The phone rang and Raines went to the counter to pick it up.

'It's me,' a man's voice said.

'Yeah.'

'Did you hear?'

'No.'

'Stark got on the plane last night.'

Raines said nothing, scraping his nails at the stubble on his face.

'The plane that went down,' the man said.

'You saw him get on? You're sure of it?'

71

'He was on it. But he wasn't using the name Stark. The ticket was under the name John Reece.'

Raines listened to the hiss and burble of the coffee machine.

'There's nothing more to be done about it, then,' he said.

He hung up and went to the window, opening the blinds. Sunlight slanted in through the narrow slats.

He felt numb. It was all he had ever felt since coming back from the war.

2

Raines drove into Lower Downtown Denver, glancing at a sign welcoming him to 'LoDo'. He passed by converted Victorian warehouses housing bars and shops and parked his pick-up truck on the street outside a diner at the corner of Seventeenth and Market.

Inside, he told the waitress that he was meeting someone and needed a table for two. She grabbed a couple of menus and led him to a table set against a bare brick wall. The place was nice, but nothing out of the ordinary — anonymous.

Raines liked anonymous.

He rubbed at his jeans where the scar was on his leg, feeling an ache starting to throb.

He stared out of the window fronting the street, light from the sun reflecting in the glass of the shop fronts across the road. Remembered the baking heat of the sun that day at Lashkar Gah. Remembered the oven-like interior of the Land Rover they travelled in to get to the poppy field.

★   ★   ★

Raines and Horn got to the Land Rover and waited at the rear door with the British lieutenant and the RMP corporal. Two privates came over from the body of British soldiers,

73

unlocked the rear doors and went round to the front.

The corporal looked no older than Horn, who was twenty-three. Raines still found it hard to believe that Horn had left college, where he was studying chemistry and physics, to join the army and come to this god-awful place. Plus, he'd had his shaggy, student hair shaved off in a regulation military cut. Raines had turned forty on this tour and for the first time in his military career was starting to feel old.

The lieutenant motioned for Raines and Horn to get in the back of the Land Rover. They climbed in and sat facing each other on parallel benches immediately behind the front seats. They shifted, trying to get comfortable in the heat, swatting at flies that buzzed in from outside. Horn wiped his sleeve across his face, smearing sweat on his uniform.

'Christ it's hot,' the British RMP corporal said, climbing in and sitting next to Horn.

The lieutenant sat next to Raines and pulled the rear door shut.

'Yeah,' Horn said. 'Wait till next month, then complain.'

The corporal stared at Horn as though he had insulted his mother. He caught himself and tried to smile. It was less than convincing.

Raines knew the type: way too much testosterone and always on the verge of a fight. Even the most innocuous of comments or a look out of place was likely to set him off. He knew, because it was how he used to be.

'What's your name, son?' Raines asked him.

'Andy Johnson, Sarge.'

The lieutenant leaned towards the soldiers in the front of the vehicle.

'Let's get this moving, please, gentlemen,' she shouted over the sound of the diesel engine starting up.

'Yes, ma'am,' the driver replied.

'Hold on to your hats,' Raines said. 'We're heading for bandit country.'

* * *

A man sat opposite Raines in the diner and put his newspaper down on the table; waved at the waitress to bring him some coffee. He was a stocky man with dark hair cut military short.

'Penny for them?' the man asked.

Raines said nothing and waited for the waitress to finish and leave. He thought about Matt Horn. About how it all went so wrong.

'How did it go last night?' the man asked.

Raines put his hand on the newspaper and turned it to read the headline on the front page about the crash. The man waited.

'He was on that.' Raines tapped the photo under the headline. 'Stark, I mean.'

'That won't be the end of it. You know that, right?'

'Of course I know.'

'So what do we do now?'

'Nothing. I mean, it's business as usual. I've got my meeting with the . . . investor tomorrow.'

The man looked at Raines for a long beat, leaning back in his seat.

'You know if that's the way you want to do it I'll go along with it. So will everyone else. But it's risky.'

Raines snorted.

'Like it was all fun and games up to this point.'

The man held his hands up.

'I'm just saying, is all.'

Raines remembered another man doing the same thing in very different circumstances. A British field medic in an operating theatre at the camp in Afghanistan. The man's hands covered in Matt Horn's blood. His hands up like he was giving in, letting Horn go. Raines didn't care much for surrender. Made that plain to those medics.

Raines looked at the man across the table.

'We can't stop now,' he told the man. 'And I don't want to anyway. I'm owed. We all are.'

The waitress came over and they ordered breakfast, Raines staring at the photograph of the downed plane on the front page of the newspaper.

Now they'll really come after me hard, he thought.

Bring it on.

Part Three:
Secrets

1

Nobody was talking.

Cahill tried Scott Boston again at the Secret Service in Washington. Couldn't get his call taken. Boston dodged him every time.

It was the same for Tom Hardy's contacts. They had all clammed up. Not that they had been talkative that morning. But it was worse in the afternoon. As though a communications smart bomb had been detonated. Don't talk about Tim Stark. It was working.

Hardy even tried to see if he could get anything via their contacts in the British Government. Same story.

'I'm going for a walk,' Cahill told Hardy at four-thirty. 'Clear my head.'

Hardy watched him go. Didn't say anything. Knew that there was nothing that would calm Cahill.

★   ★   ★

Cahill sat on a stool by the window of a café on Buchanan Street. A teenager walked by nodding his head in time to music on his iPod, oblivious to all around him. He had long hair and wore a vintage AC/DC T-shirt advertising a tour from 1984. The kid wasn't old enough. Probably bought it on eBay. He reminded Cahill of Bruce, CPO's resident ethical hacker and IT director.

Bruce had a quite astonishing collection of rock band tour T-shirts. All of them purchased at a gig on the tour. Cahill couldn't remember the last time he saw Bruce wearing anything to work other than jeans and a tour T-shirt.

'Yo,' Bruce answered when Cahill called him.

'It's me.'

'Boss. What's on your mind?'

'Can you run a check on the names Tim Stark and John Reece for me?'

'Sure. Are there likely to be flags on the names already? I mean, if I run a search will it come back at us?'

'They'll be flagged.'

'Uh . . . '

'I kind of want it to get back to us.'

'I get it.'

Bruce paused.

'You want me to check it out on any, eh, official sites?'

'No.'

'Good. When do you need it?'

'I'll be back in the office in ten minutes.'

'I'm on it.'

What Bruce meant by 'official' sites was law enforcement sites. And not the publicly available ones. The ones that required hacking, Cahill was wary of that. The firewalls and security systems on those things were good. Bruce was better, but the risk of accidentally tripping up was too great. Even being on such a site was a serious criminal offence.

Sometimes such an approach was necessary. This time, Cahill thought that staying on the right side of the law would be enough.

Cahill walked back to the office and straight to Bruce's room.

Today's T-shirt — ZZ Top.

'Old school,' Cahill said, pointing at the T-shirt.

Bruce puffed out his chest.

'Best live band I ever saw,' he said.

Bruce started playing an air guitar and making a noise with his mouth roughly approximating a ZZ Top riff. Cahill thought he recognised it, though he was no fan.

''La Grange'?' he asked.

Bruce stopped his elaborate air guitar histrionics.

'You the man, boss.'

Cahill nodded.

'Results?' he asked.

Bruce turned to one of five computer monitors in his room and tapped it meaningfully with a finger. There was an archived news story from the States about an FBI investigation several years ago. Stark was mentioned as one of the agents.

'Okay,' Cahill said. 'Why are you showing me this?'

'That's all I can find on the guy,' Bruce said, sweeping hair behind his ears.

'What do you mean?'

'Archives. Old stuff. Nothing recent at all. I'd normally expect something to show up even if it's a simple Google search, you know. But this is it. I mean, unless your man is a schoolteacher from Manchester with a Facebook page extolling the virtues of bondage?'

Cahill said nothing.

'Coz that's all I got,' Bruce went on. 'Strictly weirdos and normals.'

'What does that tell you?'

'That there may have been some kind of recent effort to hide your boy's activity. Law enforcement types usually show up somewhere.'

Cahill looked around the room. It was exceptionally clean and organised. Most people assumed from Bruce's external appearance that he was a slob, expecting his workspace to be littered with McDonald's wrappers and empty Coke cans.

Nope.

'You want anything official looked at now?' Bruce asked.

'No. Thanks, Bruce.'

Cahill went back to his office and slumped in his seat. He stared at the paperwork in front of him but found it hard to concentrate. He knew that his singular nature was both his biggest strength and weakness — his inability to change his focus once he had zeroed in on something.

And he had zeroed in on Tim Stark now.

2

It was after six that night when Irvine and Kenny Armstrong got back to Pitt Street. The sun was falling, painting the sky orange. A streetlight above them buzzed on and off.

They had been to the three previous crime scenes and taken a tour of the areas where drug dealing was now most prevalent, stopping only for a quick sandwich over lunch. Irvine realised how much things had changed since her days in uniform. It seemed that the territories changed every few years as new dealers and gangs took over.

There was a note on Irvine's desk telling her that a uniformed officer had called to identify the girl in the river as Joanna Lewski — pronounced *Leff-ski*. A Polish immigrant and known prostitute. She showed Armstrong the note.

'That's one of the uniforms who found the girl today,' he said, looking at the name on the note. 'I'll set up a meeting with them tomorrow. Get the full story.'

Irvine nodded.

'Have you made a connection between any of the victims?' she asked.

Armstrong was sitting across the desk from her. Most of the staff had gone home for the night and the place was nearly empty. Irvine saw a light on in Liam Moore's room, but the boss

83

was nowhere to be seen. Never was after six.

Armstrong stretched in his chair.

'Other than the fact that they all died of overdoses and that the drugs were the same, no. Why?'

Irvine opened the file for the third victim and took out a set of photographs. The first one showed a young man lying curled on a mattress on a floor. His skin was pale, his lips blue. The room he had died in was bare other than a mattress on the floor. It was stained and dimpled where the springs had gone.

'This is probably just my CID brain working overtime, but did you explore the angle that these deaths might not have been random?'

Armstrong leaned forward, resting his forearms on the desk. 'You mean, like, could these people actually have been targets rather than having the bad luck to buy some bad gear?'

'It's just a thought.'

He scratched his face.

'I appreciate you guys are going to come at this from the perspective of the drugs,' Irvine said. 'Looking for dealers or suppliers or whatever. But maybe there's another angle, you know. Maybe it's about who the victims are.'

'That would make it a serial killer?'

Irvine raised her eyebrows. 'Yes it would.'

'You start throwing those two words around and it's going to take this thing on to a whole 'nother level. I mean, Warren wouldn't like it.'

'Why?'

'Well, for starters, the case would be pulled from him. CID would take over. He likes nothing more than breaking a big case. Helps him when he goes to get budget increases for us. And he'd look like an idiot for not making the connection before. Four deaths is a lot to explain away.'

'I suppose . . . '

Irvine flipped through the files, checking the locations of the deaths and anything else that might link them. They were all within a five-mile radius, but that didn't mean much. Glasgow wasn't a big city, really. And drugs were prevalent in the deprived council estates, many of them bounding one another. So there was nothing unusual about them being that close.

Armstrong watched her in silence, content to let her work through it on her own.

So far as Irvine could tell, there didn't seem to be a family connection between any of the victims and none of them were reputed to have any gang affiliations.

Two men: thirty-one and twenty-three.

One woman: twenty-four.

And the girl this morning — Joanna. Irvine couldn't think of her as a woman.

So young.

Irvine closed the files and stifled a yawn.

'You should head home,' Armstrong told her. 'You've done well to get up to speed on all of this in one day. There's plenty more to do tomorrow.'

'I want to be ready for it.'

'You are. What else is there for you to do today?'

'Just feels like we should do something, you know?'

'Listen, we're both exhausted. Can't work at your best like that. And I thought that maybe you'd like to go home.'

'I do. It's just . . . '

'What?'

How much to tell this guy?

'I got divorced not long ago,' she said. 'Last year. And I went through . . . some other stuff. A friend of mine got killed.'

Armstrong frowned.

'It was a difficult time and I didn't work much. The boss was good about it, you know.'

'And now you want to make up for lost time. Is that it?'

'Maybe. I just know that since I came back I've been dealing with the usual crap this city throws up on a daily basis. Robberies and fights and everything else. And the one murder on my desk is at a dead end.'

'Hey, I get it,' Armstrong said. 'We all feel like that sometimes. But you're tired. Go get some rest and we can start again tomorrow.'

Irvine sighed.

'You're right,' she said, not looking at him.

'Plus, a good sleep, a shower and a shave and I'll be brand new.'

He jutted his chin out.

'I need to make a call first,' Irvine said.

She stacked the case files on top of one another and Armstrong walked out into the hall to give her some privacy.

Irvine called Logan. She told him that she'd be late and could he pick Connor up from the childminder. He said sure.

'That your husband?' Armstrong asked, coming back in from the hall.

'No.'

'But you have a kid?'

Irvine didn't feel like having a getting-to-know-you conversation right now. Not after what she'd seen today.

'No offence, Kenny. But can we save this till later?'

He tilted his head as he looked at her and nodded. 'Sure.'

'It's not you.'

'Don't sweat it.'

Armstrong pulled his jacket on. 'Come on, I'll give you a lift,' he said.

Irvine looked at the new files on her desk.

Four more deaths. It seemed never ending.

3

Logan was waiting for Irvine at his flat, leaning on the door frame. Irvine smiled and gratefully walked into his embrace, breathing deeply of his scent. She heard Ellie playing the piano somewhere inside.

They went into the hall together, Logan asking how her day had been.

'Depressing and exhilarating in about equal measures.'

She followed Logan into the living room.

'Ellie,' he shouted, turning back to the hall. 'Finish up for tonight, okay?'

The piano tinkled for another few seconds and stopped.

Irvine went into the room and saw Connor asleep on the couch, his hair mussed and his top pulled halfway up his back. The TV was on with the sound turned down low.

'How was he?' she asked.

'Good as always. He followed Ellie around like a pet dog. I think she secretly enjoys the attention.'

She leaned down and smoothed Connor's hair back off his forehead, kissed him gently there. One of his hands came up, fluttering where she had kissed him. Irvine felt a wave of emotion hit her and swallowed it down.

Logan was watching her from the window, leaning back against the sill.

'You want to get home?' he asked.

Irvine felt tired, but wanted to get to her place after spending the whole weekend here. As much as she loved being with Logan, she wasn't ready to live with a man again. Not yet.

She nodded at him and sat beside Connor, resting a hand on his leg.

'Tough day?' he asked.

'Yeah. Not only do I have an unsolved murder on my desk, but I got co-opted into a drug operation. Pulled a teenager out of the river today.'

He reached out and pushed a strand of hair behind her ear.

'How was *your* day?' she asked.

He told her about the plane crash and that Cahill was making noises about going over to America to kick up a fuss.

'Sounds like Alex.' She smiled.

Cahill was growing on her. Slowly.

Ellie came into the room and stood by the door. Irvine smiled at her and got a smile in return. Their relationship was still a little tentative so Irvine tried to give her space, let her breathe.

'You're getting good,' she said to Ellie. 'I mean, with the piano.'

'My teacher says I should think about drama school or something. I don't know.'

'Well, sounds good to me.'

Logan glanced at the guitar on a stand under the window. He didn't get so much time to play it any more.

★   ★   ★

They drove to Irvine's house and Logan carried Connor inside while Ellie waited in the car. When Connor was in bed, Logan hugged Irvine and said see you soon. Kissed goodnight.

After soaking in a hot bath, Irvine poured herself a glass of red wine and lay on the couch in her living room flipping through her notes from today. She couldn't see any connection between the four victims and felt a little foolish for having mentioned it even as a possibility to Armstrong.

Her eyes got heavy and so she turned off the lights and went to bed. As she lay there, she turned on her side and rested a hand on the space beside her, hoping to feel the warmth that Logan left there when they were together. There was nothing but cold.

4

Cahill sat in his study at midnight going through e-mails on a laptop but not seeing them. He gave up and closed the machine, leaning back in his chair and lacing his fingers behind his head.

His wife Sam came in and sat on the couch.

'You're not doing anyone any good right now, Alex. I mean, you look like you need a good sleep.'

He smiled and nodded.

'Thanks, hon. You look great too.'

'You know what I mean.'

Sam got up and walked round behind Cahill, kissed the top of his head and started massaging his neck. He leaned forward.

'You're not getting any younger. Maybe it's time you left the action man stuff to the newer guys?'

'People don't hire the company, Sam. They hire me. And Tom.'

'You've got to let the younger ones take up the slack. Otherwise, who's going to look after the business when you're done?'

He reached up and grabbed her hands, squeezing them lightly.

The phone rang. Cahill picked it up and said his name.

'Alex, it's Scott Boston.'

Cahill sat forward.

'Scott. At last.'

'I was just checking . . . I mean, how did you get on with Tim Stark? The plane thing, you know?'

Boston didn't sound like his usual confident self. His language was hesitant, staccato.

'I'm still working on it.'

Cahill didn't want to say too much. Susan Jones had stuck her neck out to give them even the little information she had. It wouldn't be right to drop her in it.

'Anything I can do?'

Sam backed away from Cahill and pointed up, telling him she was going to bed. He nodded at her.

'I don't know, Scott. The last time we spoke I didn't get much chance to say anything. And you've been dodging my calls ever since.'

Boston laughed. It sounded strained, like he was trying too hard.

'Sorry about that,' he said. 'I mean, it kind of took me by surprise. Tim and the crash and all.'

'Sure,' Cahill said, waiting for Boston to say what it was he had called to say.

'I needed to clear some things up before I could say anything.'

'What's on your mind?'

'It would be a big favour to me if you could lay off with the crash. I mean, you asking around is making life difficult for a lot of people.'

'Difficult how?'

Boston sighed.

'You haven't changed, Alex. You never could leave well enough alone.'

'It's not in my nature, Scott. I mean, I don't like getting fed bullshit. Especially by people who I thought were friends.'

'Maybe I deserved that.'

'There's no maybe about it. Why don't we start again and you tell me what's really going on.'

'Don't push it.'

Cahill was pissed at that.

'So, what you're telling me,' he said, trying to keep his voice level, 'is that it's okay for everyone to lie to Melanie Stark about how her husband wasn't on that plane and let her think he was into something illegal.'

Boston said nothing. Cahill heard him breathing.

'And you and I both know that Tim Stark was as clean as they come.'

'He was,' Boston agreed.

'So, tell me, Scott. What's this all about? Why did you fire Tim? Why was he on that plane using a different name?'

'Who told you — ' Boston stopped himself from saying any more.

'You forget I know how all of you guys operate. I've been around the block more than most.'

'I can't tell you anything.'

'But you can tell me to back off, right?'

'Yes.'

'Scott . . . '

'Alex, you know me. I've always been straight with you, haven't I?'

'So far as I know, yes. But there's always a first time.'

'Well, this isn't that time. Believe me.'

It was Cahill's turn to sigh. 'Is that all you've got?' he asked. 'Riddles?'

'People's lives are at stake, Alex. You have to leave it alone.'

Cahill heard the strength of feeling in Boston's voice. 'This is nothing to do with the Service, is it?' he asked.

'No.'

'So why are *you* calling me?'

'I'm the messenger, that's all.'

'What, they thought it would sound better coming from you?'

'I suppose.'

'And what exactly is the message? I mean, let's not be coy about it.'

'Fine. You push any harder and life will get difficult.'

Cahill closed his eyes. 'What about Melanie?' he asked.

'You told her he was on the plane? That he's dead?'

'Yes.'

'Then she knows what she needs to know. For now.'

'Christ, Scott. What's fair about that?'

Boston laughed, a harsh sound. 'When has this kind of thing ever been fair, Alex?'

Cahill knew that he was right. But it didn't stop him feeling anger bubble inside.

'Can we rely on you, Alex?'

Cahill stared out into the night through the windows of his study.

'Alex?'

'I won't tell Melanie anything else.'

'That's not exactly what I asked.'

'That's all I've got for you.'

5

Cahill went to bed but couldn't sleep after the call with Boston. He pulled back the covers and swung his feet out of the bed, listening to the steady rise and fall of Sam's breathing beside him. He turned and put a hand on her shoulder, feeling her skin warm under his fingers. Her breath hitched and went back to its steady rhythm.

He went down to his study and called Melanie Stark. It was early evening in Kansas. He had no idea what he was going to say to her.

'Alex,' she said, her voice a flat monotone.

'How are you holding up?'

'You know . . . ' She faded into silence.

Cahill did know.

'It takes time,' was what he said.

A cliché. Still, it was true.

'Why are you calling? It must be late there.'

Cahill looked at the clock on his desk. 'It's after one. But that doesn't matter, I was working anyway. Have you spoken any more to the police or anyone else?'

'No. There's no reason to, is there? Tim's dead. That's what you told me.'

'But don't you want to know why, or what he was doing on that plane?'

'I thought I did. But I'm not so sure any more. What good would it do? I mean, what if I find out he was mixed up in something . . . bad? Then what?'

'That won't happen. I know Tim.'

'Maybe nobody really knew him.'

'Melanie . . . '

'Bye, Alex.'

He sat at his desk, clenching and unclenching his fists, wanting to hit something. He'd known too many people who had died. And he couldn't shake the anger he felt about this. About what they were doing to the memory of a good man. And his family.

He didn't like not knowing. Hated being lied to and bullied, which was how he felt now after the call from Boston. It wasn't just Melanie Stark's problem now. It was his.

And maybe he would make it someone else's problem.

6

Irvine went to Liam Moore's room and knocked on his open door. He beckoned her in with a wave of his hand, not looking away from his computer screen. She sat and waited while he typed something on his keyboard. Irvine had not yet worked out if Moore was always in the middle of something when she wanted to speak to him or if he pretended to be so that he could make her wait. Maybe he was checking his Twitter account.

'How did it go yesterday with the SCDEA thing?' he asked eventually, pushing the keyboard forward and resting his arms on the desk.

'It was a long day.'

'Anything you need from me?'

'No. It's too early to really know where the investigation is going.'

He watched her silently.

'They're retaining overall control of the investigation, right? I mean, the SCDEA.'

'Yes. They're happy for me to lead on the latest victim. The girl.'

'Territorial boundaries and all that. Plus, they think they're better than regular cops. Hand-picked, you know?'

'Yeah.'

'I appreciate that boundaries are not your

97

strong point, Becky.'

She smiled. He did not.

'Try to play nice, okay? Stay out of trouble.'

'Sure.' She frowned. 'Of course I will.'

★   ★   ★

Armstrong had changed and washed his hair but the stubble was still in place, grown heavier overnight. It looked like he didn't need much time for a full growth to develop.

'You going for a beard?' she asked.

He rubbed at his chin.

'If it was good enough for Serpico . . . '

'So what's the plan for this morning?' she asked.

'Chase up the lab results,' he said. 'Talk to the uniforms. See what shakes loose.'

'*See what shakes loose?*' She squinted at him. 'Kenny Armstrong, LAPD.'

'You're a little weird. And potentially very annoying.'

'Thanks.' She beamed at him.

Armstrong took a large bite out of a chocolate muffin. Crumbs stuck in his beard and he wiped them away with his hand.

'Uniforms are here,' he told her. 'They're downstairs.'

'When were you going to tell me this?'

'I just did.'

Irvine called down to the main reception and asked them to direct the officers to her desk. When two men came on to the floor she raised a hand in greeting and they started over.

'DC Irvine?' the taller of the two male officers asked.

'That's me. And this is DS Armstrong.'

Nods all round. The uniforms took their hats off and set them on the empty desk next to Irvine's then pulled up two spare chairs to sit down. It looked to Irvine like the taller man was probably in his mid-thirties and the shorter one not yet out of his twenties. They were both lean, with short brown hair.

'You responded to the call-out yesterday morning, right?' Armstrong said. 'The body in the river. Joanna Lewski.'

'Yes,' the taller one answered again. 'She called herself Tanya. For the punters, you know. I guess she thought it was exotic.'

'And you arrested her before. When was that?'

The taller man lifted a plain file and placed it on the desk in front of Irvine. She hadn't even noticed he had been carrying it. She opened the file and skimmed the arrest report.

'Picked her up for soliciting down on Waterloo Street about nine months ago,' the tall cop went on. 'She was high as well and had some gear on her. Heroin.'

'Says here that she got community service.'

'Six weeks. And she did it, to be fair to her.'

Irvine looked up at the man.

'How is it that you remember her?'

The man held Irvine's gaze.

'She was new. I could tell. And, well, she was just a wee thing, you know. I felt for her.'

'You've been on the job how long?'

'Does it never get to *you*?'

99

Irvine had felt the same resentment of detectives herself when she had been on patrol. She looked back down at the file, finding an address for the girl south of the river in Bridgeton.

'Who does she live with?' Irvine asked.

'Another girl. An older one. Real hard case name of Suzie Murray.'

'Someone put her up in the flat to keep an eye on her while they got her started?'

'That's the way it works.'

'Do you know who?'

'No. Sorry.'

Irvine slid the file to Armstrong who picked it up and sat it on his lap to look through it.

'Any family here that we need to know about?'

'No. Far as we know she came over here on her own.'

'Seems awful young.'

He shrugged.

Irvine tapped a finger on the desk and bit at her lower lip.

'I saw her later,' the shorter man said.

The tall one twisted in his seat to look at his partner. The short one stared at him.

'When?' Irvine asked.

'Couple of weeks after she got sentenced. Her community service was helping clean graffiti, you know. I saw her and said hello. Asked how she was doing.'

'Was she high?'

'No. But she didn't look too healthy.'

Irvine glanced at the photograph of the girl in the file that Armstrong was holding. She was an attractive girl.

Armstrong closed the file.

'Anything else that might help us?'

The two men looked at each other and shook their heads.

After they were gone, Irvine asked Armstrong what he thought of the girl — and the reaction of the two uniformed officers. Armstrong flicked the file open nonchalantly and looked at the girl's picture.

'She looks young in this picture. Vulnerable. I can see why men would react to her.'

'What, you're not a man?'

'I try to keep the job separate.'

'Good luck with that.'

The corner of Armstrong's mouth twitched.

'You heard of her room-mate, this Suzie Murray?'

'Can't say that it rings any bells. But I know the type.'

'What does that mean?'

'She'll not be well disposed towards us.'

7

Cahill was late getting into the office. He walked past Logan's room and raised a hand in greeting before going into his own room and closing the door. He took his jacket off and draped it over his seat, stood looking out of the window thinking that he should have stayed at home today.

Cahill glanced at a photograph on the shelf by his desk — him and Tom Hardy in uniform in the desert with their arms around one another.

He heard the door open and turned to see Logan come in wearing a pair of faded jeans and a navy blue shirt, open at the neck. Lately Logan had decided that he didn't want to wear the CPO combats and polo shirt. It felt too much like a uniform. Cahill still wore his.

'What's up?' Logan asked, seeing the fatigue in his friend's face.

'This thing in Denver . . . '

Logan sat on the couch.

'Is it that soldier thing?' Logan asked. 'You and Tim Stark.'

'We didn't serve together.'

'No, but you know what I mean. Army, Secret Service. Same thing, right?'

Cahill looked at the photograph again.

'I know you, Alex. You're pissed off at the attitude of the Feds and everyone else. You don't like it when they give you the silent treatment.

Just stirs you up even more.'

Logan smiled, knew that he was right about it.

'You're saying I'm a stubborn bastard who likes to pick a fight?'

'I am.'

'Tim's got a family. You know what that's like — making sure that they don't come to any harm?'

Logan nodded. Knew all too well.

'You think they're in danger?'

'Christ knows,' Cahill said, standing. 'But I'd hate to find out that anything had happened and I could have done something about it.'

'You thinking of going over there?'

'Yes.'

'For how long? I mean, we've got contracts lined up here for the next six months.'

'Tom can handle it. All the clients know him.'

'This is for free?'

'Of course. It's for a friend.'

'Well, if you feel that you need to do it, you should go.'

Cahill nodded, staring at Logan.

'What?' Logan asked.

'Come with me.'

'What do you need me for?'

'Look, I know what I'm like. I fuck with people just to get a reaction. I only know one way of doing things and that's to move forward. Pushing all the way.'

'So?'

'So, you're different. You know the . . . softer stuff. How to talk. Negotiate. This isn't the kind of operation I usually handle so I might be a little bit out of my depth.'

'And I won't be?'

'Sometimes when you say that you're a lawyer I can see people change. The way they react to you. They get careful with their words.'

'Not the cops. Not usually.'

'It's a different world now. It's run by the lawyers, not soldiers. That's where the power lies.'

'You're saying people don't fear violence or action so much as a sharpened pencil?'

'Exactly.'

'Me? I'd rather have a gun.'

'What's this about a gun?' Tom Hardy asked as he came into the room.

'They threatened me, Tom,' Cahill said. 'Scott Boston called last night and made it plain that it would not be good for me to keep asking questions about Tim.'

'Scott doesn't know you too well, does he?'

Cahill turned to Logan.

'I'm going over there with or without you. Let me know your decision by the end of the day.'

He left the room without saying anything else. Logan looked at Hardy.

'I think it would be a good idea if you went with him,' Hardy told Logan. 'He's not good when he's in this kind of mood. And it's been a while since I've seen him like that.'

He walked to the door, pulling it open.

'I don't know,' Logan said. 'I mean, I've got Ellie and everything . . . '

Hardy looked down and closed the door again.

'This is where you repay some of that debt

you've accumulated,' he said. 'This is how it works with us, you know?'

Logan knew. And both Hardy and Cahill had done more for him than he could ever do for them. More than he could ever possibly repay in kind.

'I understand, Tom.'

'I'm asking as a personal favour. Go with him and make sure he doesn't kill anybody. Or, at least, anybody he doesn't have to.'

8

Logan went to find Cahill to tell him that he would go to Denver with him. He wasn't anywhere in the office. Logan walked to the reception desk.

'Did Alex leave?' he asked the woman there.

'A couple of minutes ago,' she told him.

'Did he say where he was going?'

'Said something about blowing off steam at the range.'

Logan said thanks and went to the elevator to go down to the underground car park. He was hoping to catch Cahill before he left for the CPO gun range at their building on the south side of the river — an old warehouse on Scotland Street.

Cahill's car wasn't in its usual spot so Logan got in his car and drove up the ramp to follow him.

★   ★   ★

Logan used a remote control device to activate the electronic gate at the warehouse. He waited in the road as the metal gate slid smoothly open and saw Cahill's car parked inside. He drove in and parked beside it, the gate closing behind him.

The warehouse was not just a shooting range — it was also where CPO stored its armoury.

The security at the site was tight. Logan punched a five-digit code into a keypad beside the metal entrance door. The light on the keypad turned green and Logan used his key to open the door.

The building exterior was deliberately shabby. A Hollywood set decorator would have recognised the skill that had gone into making it look like that. Inside was a different story.

Logan walked along a corridor with a polished concrete floor and clean, grey walls, turning right at the end. Spotlights embedded in the floor and recessed in the ceiling lit the way to another door with a keypad. Logan heard faint gunshot reports behind the door. The sound did not carry beyond the building's walls.

After entering a different code, Logan went into what looked like a large cupboard. He pushed at the rear wall and it opened into the range. The room was long and narrow with various weapons arranged neatly on mounts on the walls at either side of the door. Beyond that were two separate ranges, about twenty-five metres long with target boards on rails suspended from the ceiling. The targets could be moved along the rails via a control panel in the enclosed booths for each range.

Logan had been here many times, but was still surprised at how loud the gunshots sounded in such an enclosed space. Cahill was in a classic shooting stance in the right-hand booth, firing at a target around fifteen feet from his position.

Logan grabbed a pair of ear defenders and put them on. He waited behind Cahill until he had emptied his magazine at the target. It was never a good idea to surprise a man with a loaded weapon. Especially one in a mood like Cahill.

Logan noticed from the number of bullet holes that Cahill had already fired a full clip at the same target.

Cahill's gun clicked on an empty chamber and he stood straight, ejecting the magazine from the handle of the weapon.

'You mad at someone?' Logan shouted, taking his ear defenders off.

Smoke hung in the air around Cahill, the smell of cordite sharp in Logan's nostrils.

Cahill turned quickly, taking his own defenders off and putting them on the counter in front of him beside the gun.

'I'm plenty mad,' Cahill replied.

'So what's new?' Logan smiled, trying to lighten the mood. He walked to the booth and pressed a button to bring the target closer.

'Hasn't affected your accuracy,' Logan said, looking at the target with its close grouping of bullet holes.

'The old man hasn't lost it yet.'

Cahill was the most accurate shooter in the team. He never lost a challenge. Logan was getting better all the time, and was now giving some of the others a close run in their challenges. Cahill encouraged competition — thought that it was a good way to maintain their edge outside of a real engagement. His plan was always to get into as few fights as possible. He knew from experience that no matter how good you were, bad luck had a way of catching up with you eventually.

'You're dead set on this mission of yours?' Logan asked. 'I mean, going over to Denver.'

'I booked our flights last night.'

Logan stared at him.

'We leave at seven tomorrow morning. Sam's getting the spare room ready for Ellie to come over tonight. It's all set.'

Logan looked at his watch — saw that it was not far off noon. Ellie would be at school for a few more hours yet and so there was nothing Logan could do about speaking to her just yet.

'I'm that predictable?' he asked, shaking his head.

'Not predictable. Reliable.'

'How long will we be away?'

'I don't know.'

'But you've booked a hotel, right? I mean, we'll have to stay somewhere.'

'Sure. I booked somewhere in Downtown. It's corporate and anonymous.'

Cahill frustrated Logan sometimes.

'How long did you book the hotel for?'

'Three nights.'

'You think that'll be enough?'

'If it's not, we'll extend the stay there or somewhere else.'

Cahill spread his arms out.

'If you don't want to go . . . ' he said.

'I'm going. Okay. I just . . . '

Cahill waited. Logan sat down again.

'I mean, I feel a little lost when I go into the field with any of you guys. It's not me. I don't know what to do. I'm a lawyer not a soldier.'

'Bullshit. You've done more than okay when you've had to. I mean, for someone chucked into the fire with no warning and little or no training.'

'But — '

'And it's not like I'm asking you to shoot anyone this time, you know. It'll be a different kind of thing.'

'Just talking?'

'Interacting with the law enforcement agencies.'

Logan puffed out his cheeks and shook his head.

'What?' Cahill asked.

'Alex, you can't interact with *anyone* without starting a fight.'

'Not true.'

'Almost true.'

Cahill picked up his gun and ear defenders and went to the wall beside the entrance. He put the magazine back in the gun and placed it on a mount. He hung the ear defenders up beside the others on the wall.

'Have you told Tim's wife yet?' Logan asked as he joined Cahill to put his ear defenders on the wall.

'No.'

'You should. She'd want to know.'

'You're right. Why don't you go home to get packed. Pick up Ellie and tell her what's going on. I'll call Melanie.'

'The dream team,' Logan said, following Cahill out of the room.

He glanced back at the shredded target. Hoped it wouldn't come to that.

9

After Logan left the warehouse, Cahill went to call Melanie Stark from another room in the building — a functional meeting space with a round table and six chairs.

It was still early in Kansas, but Cahill figured that she wouldn't be sleeping much.

Turned out he was right.

'How are you holding up?' he asked, when she answered the call.

'Ask me again in six months.'

He thought that she sounded a little brighter than she had last night. Which wasn't saying much.

'I wanted to let you know that I'm not going to let this go. That I want to help you.'

'Alex, I appreciate the sentiment, you know. But Tim's dead. What's left after that? Whatever we do, he won't be walking back through the front door, will he?'

'No. You're right about that. But that doesn't mean that we can't honour his memory.'

'I don't mean to be rude, Alex. But that stuff sounds so hollow right now.'

'I know. Doesn't mean it's not the right thing to do.'

She sighed. 'Okay,' she said. 'Suppose that I agree to let you help me. What are you going to do? And how much will it cost me?'

'First, it won't cost anything. I don't charge

friends for helping them out.'

'Sorry. I didn't mean anything by it.'

'No need to apologise. It was a perfectly sensible question.'

'So, what is it that you can do from over there?'

'Not much. That's why I'm flying out to Denver tomorrow.'

'What?'

'I need to be where it happened.'

'You organised this before speaking to me.'

She sounded a little angry. Maybe that was good — showing something other than grief or hurt.

'Yes. I was going to do it anyway. For Tim.'

'Are you going alone?'

'No. I'll have someone with me. Logan — the lawyer you spoke to before.'

'I don't expect that the cops or FBI like lawyers much, do they?'

'They don't. That's kind of the point.'

She made a noise. Cahill wasn't sure if it was a sniff or the best attempt at a laugh that she could manage right now.

'I'll speak to the cops and the FBI and anyone else who I think will help. Or might be trying to hide something. In my experience, if you stir up enough people it usually gets results in the end.'

'Will this come back at me? I mean, will they — '

'I'll make sure it doesn't.'

'Thanks. I guess. Though I'm not sure what it is that you're going to find. Maybe I don't want to hear it. Have you considered that?'

'I won't tell you if you don't want me to.'

'No. I mean, I want to hear it. Good or bad.'

'It won't be bad.'

'I appreciate your confidence.'

'Listen, there's something that you can do to help me.'

'What's that?'

'Can you go through all of Tim's stuff: clothes, bags, papers, computer. Everything. Look for anything that's unfamiliar to you. It might be something that you wouldn't ordinarily notice. Just a scribble on a piece of paper or a phone number you don't recognise. If it's there, you'll know it when you see it.'

'I'll do that today.'

'I'll call you when I get in to Denver.'

She paused.

'Is this how you all are?'

'What do you mean?'

'You know. Soldiers and cops and people in the Service.'

'I suppose. The bond you have with someone you've stood beside and risked your life with is different from any other.'

'Even that with your own family? Your children?'

'Yes. I'm not saying it's stronger, because it's not. Just different.'

'Well . . . thanks. I think Tim would have done the same for you.'

'I have no doubt.'

'Take care, Alex. I don't want you to . . . you know. To get hurt for this.'

'Don't worry about me.'

Cahill drove back to the city centre, parked under the office building and went up to find Tom Hardy in his own room. Hardy was on a call with a client so Cahill waited until he finished before speaking.

'Tom, I'm going to Denver tomorrow with Logan. I'll be gone for three days at least. Maybe more.'

'As long as it takes?'

'Yeah.'

'I can't talk you out of this?'

'You know me better than that.'

Hardy nodded. 'You need anything else from me?' he asked.

'I'll need a contact over there.'

Meaning: someone who can supply a weapon.

'Of course. Can't go walking around naked.'

'Do you know anyone?' Cahill asked.

'No. But I can find someone. Don't sweat it.'

'Nothing fancy, Tom, you know?'

Translation: a handgun.

'I hear you. Watch your back.'

Part Four:
Exit Strategy

1

Seth Raines drove his pick-up truck west towards the Rocky Mountains with a man in the passenger seat beside him. They cleared the city limits and moved on to 1-70 quickly in light traffic, the sun rising into a clear, blue sky. Raines reached into the door pocket and pulled out a pair of sunglasses, unfolding the arms with one hand while watching the road as it rose into the mountains. There had been a light snowfall in the mountains the night before and the sun sparkled in the fresh, crystalline snow.

The road continued to climb up, snow-capped peaks high above them. It twisted through a pass before rising again into the town of Grant. As they passed through the town, Raines turned west again and, after about a mile and a half, pulled on to a track that wound up through dense woodland to a high clearing. This high up, snow covered the track and crunched under the wheels of his truck. A short distance along the track they came to a tall, metal gate. Raines stopped his truck next to a pole with a speaker on top and said his name, his breath visible in the sharp morning air.

'Come on up,' a voice answered as a buzzing sounded and the gates swung slowly open.

They reached a clearing after another mile of the snow-covered track. There were three wooden structures built just behind the tree line

117

at the northern edge of the clearing. Two men in green camo jackets and jeans stepped down off the porch of the middle building, the largest of the three, and walked towards the truck as Raines stopped. The men were carrying assault rifles and wore ballistic vests over their jackets.

Raines and his passenger got out.

'Heard about Stark,' one of the men said to Raines. 'Bad business.'

'We stick to what we're doing,' Raines said. 'What happens is what happens.'

'Sure thing, boss.'

Raines's passenger sensed something more than respect emanate from the man to whom Raines had spoken. Something like fear.

Raines nodded at the man and walked on, his passenger following behind and staring at the dark tips of the tattoos on Raines's neck. They mounted the steps of the middle building where Raines stopped, turning to his passenger.

'Those are sealed,' he said, indicating the other two buildings.

The passenger looked left and right, noticing now that the other buildings had no external windows. Only heavy steel access doors broke up the otherwise featureless wooden exteriors.

'The wood is just cladding,' Raines went on. 'An external shell to cover the actual building construction.'

'I like it,' the passenger said. 'So it looks like any other private cabin if anyone gets interested?'

'Correct. That's the way we planned it.'

Raines opened the door from the porch into the main building. Inside, the space stretched up to a double-height ceiling with a large, central area that was split into an office space at the back and a modest living area at the front — with couches facing an open fire.

There were two more men inside, both sitting in the office area working at computer monitors. They were dressed in jeans and heavy cotton shirts. Only the handguns in holsters fitted round their waists gave away their military background.

Raines went to the men and leaned over, looking at the spreadsheets open on both screens.

'Looks good,' he said, no emotion apparent in his voice.

Raines moved to the living area and motioned for the passenger to follow. They took their coats off and sat on separate couches, the passenger looking around the room and shifting in his seat. Raines looked at the man, trying hard to keep his hatred for him hidden. In this business, he didn't have the luxury of choosing whom he worked with. The man wore what looked like an expensive suit and a white shirt open at the neck. His black leather town shoes were flecked with melting snow.

'Perimeter security?' the man asked.

'Motion sensors. We have them linked to the computers back there.'

The man frowned.

'No fences?'

'Other than at the front, no.'

'Doesn't sound very safe.'

The man picked an imaginary piece of dust

from his immaculately pressed trousers. Raines noticed his accent now for the first time. He did a good job of hiding it.

Raines resisted an urge to pull his handgun and shoot the man in the face.

'It's completely safe,' Raines said instead, leaning forward and resting his elbows on his knees.

'How?'

'Well, I mean, you saw the fence at the gate we came in through, right?'

The man nodded.

'That stretches both ways to sheer drops down the mountainside. So we're covered on both flanks by the natural terrain. No one's getting in that way unless they're prepared for a long climb.'

'And even if they do get up, you have the motion sensors?'

'Now you're getting it.'

'And at the back?'

'The only way in to the back is over the top of the mountain from the other side. Ain't gonna happen.'

'And, again, the motion sensors.'

'Those are located a minimum of one mile from here. And we have ordnance planted in the ground and on trees a half-mile in. Either remote triggered or via tripwires.'

'Impressive.'

Raines leaned back in the couch.

'Anyone comes here up to no good and they end up dead.'

'You consider the federal authorities carrying

out their lawful duties to be up to no good?'

'Especially the Feds.'

Raines stared at him but did not reply. The man turned away from Raines's hard gaze, pretended to look around again at the interior of the building to demonstrate that he had not been intimidated.

'Let's talk business,' Raines said.

2

After their brief discussion, Raines waited in the main building while one of the men from the office showed his passenger around the rest of the compound.

He walked to a door at the back of the living area and went through it into his own private office space. He sat at the sparse desk and breathed deeply, feeling more tired than he ever had.

The drive up the track to the compound brought back the memories again: him and the other soldiers inside the Land Rover as it pitched and rolled over the rutted dirt tracks that passed for roads in Afghanistan.

★ ★ ★

They had waited at the site of the opium field for less than an hour, the splash of pink flowers almost surreal in the washed-out haze of the desert.

The soldiers kept mobile, not resting in one location and aware of their surroundings. Never straying too far from the track around the field for fear of wandering into an active minefield. Raines had seen two men from his platoon with traumatic amputations from mine blasts. They had survived, thanks to the swift treatment they received from the medevac team, but their lives

122

would never be the same again.

After the local ANP contingent had set fire to the field and the blaze had well and truly taken hold, they went back to the Land Rovers. The temperature was now close to forty degrees and was taking its toll on them.

They took up the same positions on the rear bench seats as before. No one said anything as the Land Rover moved off, all of them watching the dark smoke rising from the poppy fields into the clear, blue sky.

They drove back through Lashkar Gah and Raines was again struck by how primitive the place was, although he had been there many times before. The buildings were almost invariably made from mud and bricks and the roads were no better than the track they had followed from the camp.

There were no women to be seen anywhere and men with lines etched in their faces watched the convoy pass by. Occasionally a group of children would run alongside, shouting and waving at the soldiers.

Horn turned in his seat and waved back at one particularly enthusiastic boy who kept pace with them for a good fifty metres. Johnson shook his head.

'What?' Horn asked, annoyed.

'Nothing,' Johnson said.

Horn stared at him.

'Even after being here this long you can still relate to these people?' Johnson said after a moment.

'What else is it that we're supposed to do?'

Raines sensed the animosity between the two men, but did not interfere. Soldiers have to learn by getting their hands dirty. Or bloody. And aggression was part of the job description. But he admired Horn's resilience — wasn't such a bad kid for a soft, middle-class boy who volunteered to go to war. Raines thought, not for the first time, that if his own son had lived past his sixth birthday he would have been proud if he had turned out like Matt Horn.

They passed through a more modern-looking part of town and the lieutenant asked why the rest of it was so primitive.

'This is Little America,' Raines told her. 'We were over here in the sixties. Built some stuff and headed home again.'

'No one ever stays in places like this for long,' she said.

'Is that what your job is about?'

'What do you mean?'

'Trying to make it right with the locals. I mean, build their trust. Tell them we'll be here till everything is all right. That it will be different this time.'

'Yes. Don't you have something similar?'

'We do,' Raines said, smiling.

A look of annoyance passed over her face.

'And there's something wrong with that in your mind, Sergeant?'

'No. I mean, I recognise that the intention is pure.'

'But . . . '

Raines shifted in his seat and turned to face

124

her. He noticed up close how young she was — like a lot of the officers over here in both armies. Probably straight out of officer school and posted here with no in-theatre experience.

'But it doesn't help us much,' Raines went on. 'When we call in fast air support to drop a couple of five-hundred pounders on a suspected Taliban compound and go in to clean up the mess only to find children's body parts and screaming women.'

The lieutenant's eyes narrowed.

'That's what happens in a war,' Raines went on. 'We can't avoid civilian casualties. How do you explain that to their mothers and fathers?'

'We can only do what we can. But we still have to try. Or don't you believe that?'

Raines turned from her and saw that Johnson was watching their exchange intensely.

'I wanted to know what you thought of it,' Raines said.

He looked back at the lieutenant, saw that she was staring at him, trying to figure out if he was testing her.

'It's a pity your tour is up so soon, Sergeant,' she said.

'Why is that?'

'I think maybe I'd enjoy debating the finer points of our strategy with the local population some more.'

Raines saw a smile twitch at her lips.

'She got you there, Sarge,' Horn said, laughing.

He turned to speak to Horn and the front of the Land Rover disappeared, metal screeching

125

as the IED in the road detonated under the vehicle.

Raines had a split second to see Horn's right leg torn from him just above the knee and then everything went dark.

3

Raines picked up the phone from his desk and dialled a number for a house back in Denver. It rang for a while and he waited, aware that it could take some time for the owner of the house to answer.

'Yeah,' the answer came eventually.

'I met the guy today. You know the one?'

'How did it go?'

'He's getting the full tour.'

'You're still up there, then?'

'Yes.'

'I don't like the idea of working with this guy.'

'So you said. We're not in this to make friends. I told you that already.'

'But it's not necessary. I mean, for what we want to achieve. You haven't lost sight of that, have you?'

Raines hated the pleading quality he heard in the man's voice.

'I haven't lost sight of anything. I can see for miles. And this is the way we're going, so quit whining about it already. You think there's some other way, something more noble?'

The man on the other end of the line was quiet. Raines pinched the bridge of his nose between his fingers.

'I don't want to have this conversation again,' Raines said, angry now. 'We've done it more than once.'

'Sorry. It's just that — '

'Just nothing,' Raines snapped. 'This is the way it is. We get this guy on board and we do what's necessary. After that, we're outta here. And I'm never coming back to this goddamned country.'

There was a pause on the other end of the line.

'Is this what they've done to us?' the man asked. 'To you.'

'You can get out any time you like. Just say the word.'

'What happens to me then, Seth? Tell me that. The same thing that happened to Johnson?'

Raines didn't need to tell him.

'That's what I thought.'

Raines wasn't sure that he could trust the man any more. Wondered if he would have to do something about that.

'Come see me when you get back, okay?' the man said.

Raines said that he would and ended the call. He sat quietly for a moment, looking at the framed photograph on his desk. It was a shot of Charlie Company the day after they had arrived in Afghanistan.

He picked the photograph up and looked at the faces of the young men who had been in his charge. He counted, for what seemed like the thousandth time, the faces of those who had not come back.

He stopped when he got to Matt Horn's face — closed his eyes and remembered.

He's back in that British Land Rover, opening his eyes and choking on the smoke billowing from the ruined front section of the vehicle. The two British soldiers who had been there were gone.

Something sticky clogged up his eyes. He wiped at them, looking down at his hands and seeing his own blood there.

He felt panic start to rise in him, patted himself down and felt that everything was intact. His head throbbed from the concussive blast of the explosion. Didn't know how long he'd been unconscious.

He figured the device must have been a mine triggered by the front tyre of the vehicle on Matt Horn's side. It was the only explanation why Raines had survived intact.

He looked at Horn. Not so lucky.

Tonk-tonk-tonk

Bullets impacted the armour of the Land Rover.

Raines looked back, saw that the soldiers in the vehicles behind them were out and returning fire, using their own vehicles for cover. Dirt kicked up around them where bullets hit the ground.

Horn had lost most of his right leg and was bleeding heavily from the wound. His right arm hung limp by his side, the sleeve of his uniform in tatters and blood staining what little cloth was left.

His left foot was a mangled mess.

Horn watched Raines, his eyes blinking and breaths coming in short gasps.

Andy Johnson was in shock beside Horn, his eyes wide: staring at the female lieutenant opposite him.

Raines turned to look at her and saw that her helmet had been split in two by a piece of shrapnel. Maybe a part of the vehicle shorn loose by the explosion. The shrapnel had done the same to her head. Raines looked away.

Tonk-tonk-tonk-tonk

Have to get out of here.

Raines got up and went to the rear door. Couldn't get it open. The armour had warped in the blast preventing the doors from opening. He kicked at them, made a little daylight. Kicked again.

He heard the whoosh of a rocket-propelled grenade, flinched instinctively. The explosion was loud and he saw that it had landed twenty metres in front of the Snatch immediately behind them.

He grabbed his rifle, forced the butt into the gap between the door and the frame of the vehicle and used his weight to lever it. The door resisted and then burst open. Raines staggered forward, almost falling out. Dirt kicked up in the ground and he heard the crackle and fizz of bullets in the air.

Johnson was still staring at the lieutenant so Raines stepped in front of him and grabbed his face with both hands.

'We need to move, soldier,' he shouted. 'Now.'

Johnson looked at Raines. Looked out the open rear door at the soldiers behind them.

He turned back to Raines, nodded and grabbed his rifle.

'Give me cover fire while I get Horn out of here, okay?'

Raines realised that he was shouting everything at the top of his voice to be heard over the din.

Johnson stepped down out of the Land Rover, turned to go around it to get cover, and started firing.

Raines shuffled back to Horn, grabbed him by his body armour under both arms and heaved him to the back door. When he got there, one of the soldiers from the other vehicles ran up and helped take the weight as Raines pulled Horn free. Raines knew that they were exposed to the enemy now but there was no choice. He couldn't leave Horn in there.

They managed to get Horn around behind the vehicle and sat him on the road, his blood leaking out rapidly and staining the ground.

Raines pulled his belt free and wrapped it around what was left of Horn's right thigh in a makeshift tourniquet. Horn's eyes fluttered and he shouted out in pain. Raines pulled the belt as tight as he could and was pleased to see the flow of blood ease. Still, he knew that they needed a medevac as soon as possible if the boy was to have any chance of surviving.

'Where's the support?' Raines shouted at Johnson as another RPG whooshed above them and exploded in the desert.

'There's an Apache on its way,' Johnson replied, still firing. 'It'll torch those fuckers.'

Raines reached into one of the pockets in his trousers, pulled out his morphine needle and stuck it into Horn. He motioned for Johnson to give him his morphine too and gave Horn the second dose. Horn's face muscles slackened as the drug took effect.

Raines stood, went to where Johnson was standing and joined him in firing at the enemy position.

An Apache gunship swooped overhead and its thirty-millimetre cannon roared. The pilot of the helicopter fired two missiles at the enemy position and sprayed them again with his cannon. Raines stopped firing his weapon and watched in awe at the devastation the Apache wreaked.

A bullet ripped into his combat trousers and went straight through the flesh and muscle of his leg, clipping his shin bone on the way.

Raines fell, more bullets thudding into the dirt around him.

Above, the Apache's cannon continued to roar.

4

Raines was quiet on the drive back from the compound and his passenger seemed content to watch the scenery pass by.

'When do you leave?' Raines asked finally as they passed the first sign for Denver.

The passenger smiled.

'I know that you don't like me,' he said.

'Is it that obvious?'

'It doesn't matter. We don't have to be friends.'

'We won't be.'

'I like it that we are able to define our relationship now. So there are no misunderstandings later.'

Raines glanced sideways at him but said nothing.

'So you'll do it?' Raines asked. 'I mean, we're in business.'

'Yes. We are most definitely in business.'

Part Five: Excursions

1

Logan called Irvine while he waited outside Ellie's school.

'I'm leaving tomorrow,' he told her when she answered.

She didn't say anything for a moment. He realised that it was probably a confusing opening gambit.

'I mean, I'm flying to Denver with Alex. The plane crash I told you about. Sam is going to take Ellie.'

'How long will you be away?'

'I don't know. Three or four days maybe.'

'The timing isn't such a bad thing. I think this new case of mine is going to keep me busy nights anyway.'

'I'll come over tonight for a while. After dinner. Say goodbye properly.'

'I'd like that. I'll call you when I get in.'

★ ★ ★

Logan could tell from the look on Ellie's face when she saw his car and the brief but excitable discussion with her friends that followed that she wasn't happy to see him there.

Ah, fatherhood.

Ellie opened the rear door, threw her bags in heavily and got into the front passenger seat. She made a show of huffing and sighing while she put the seatbelt on and shifted around in her seat in an overt display of petulance.

Logan tried to ignore her and drove off. She waved at her friends from the car.

After a couple of minutes, she rummaged in the door pocket and took out a CD to put in the stereo.

'You had plans?' he asked her eventually.

She turned her head slowly to look at him and said yes.

'Sorry. There's some stuff we need to talk about.'

'Sounds serious.'

'Depends on your perspective.'

Logan used the controls on the steering wheel to lower the volume of the stereo.

'I have to go away on business for a few days. Maybe even a week.'

'When?'

'Tomorrow.'

She turned back to look out of the windscreen. Logan glanced at her, couldn't read her expression.

'I've got school.'

'I know, Ellie. You can't come with me.'

'I had kind of worked that out.'

She was trying to be sassy. That was her way. But he could tell from the uncertain edge in her voice that the confidence was just for show.

'I'm going with Alex, and Sam said you can stay at their house.'

Ellie chewed on her bottom lip and squinted as sunlight fell across her face.

'What do you think?' Logan asked.

'Might be kind of cool,' she said.

'Right. No dads.'

'Hmmm.'

'We're going over for dinner tonight and you'll stay there so we need to get you packed this afternoon.'

'Fine.'

Logan was relieved. Her continuing maturity still surprised him. He reached over and ruffled her hair with his hand to annoy her. She pushed him away and tried to look perturbed, not really succeeding.

★ ★ ★

When they got home, Ellie went straight to her room and started laying out most of her wardrobe on the bed while Logan got a suitcase from the cupboard in the hall. He put it on the floor in her room, stared at all the clothes and shook his head.

'It won't be that long,' he told her.

'Just being prepared.'

'Right. I mean, you are planning on coming back here when I get home? You're not leaving me.'

She stopped and looked at him — serious now.

'Don't say that.'

His heart contracted.

She returned to packing. They didn't dwell on difficult emotions, preferring to confront them and deal with them in a straightforward way.

He realised she had grown a lot even over the

139

last few months. Maybe in some weird way the death of his cat, Stella, a while back had helped. It was from natural causes. She was an old cat. And Chris Washington's death too. It had shown Ellie that death is a way of life and that it touches everyone. She wasn't special, at least not in that way. She hadn't been singled out for any unique suffering.

'What about Becky?' Ellie asked, surveying the clothes on her bed and nodding her head as though she was satisfied with her work.

'What do you mean?'

She turned to him.

'You'll miss her.'

'Yes. But she's got an important job and so she needs to be here to do that.'

'Uh-huh.'

That seemed to be the end of it.

Logan went to his room and double checked his own carry-on bag. It didn't look like he was taking much, not compared to Ellie, anyway, but it was all he needed. And he could always pick up extras over there.

Ellie shouted that she was going for a quick shower and he heard the bathroom door close then the sound of the shower going on. He went back to her room to check her packing and was surprised to see that she had put a lot of stuff back in her wardrobe and the suitcase was ordered and ready to go.

He bent down to shut it and saw a mobile phone he didn't recognise. It was wedged down the side of the suitcase, only the top of it showing above the clothes. He pulled it out and turned it over in his hands. It was an old Nokia, which would have looked new maybe three years ago.

He sat on Ellie's bed and switched the phone on. It took a moment to warm up and then the logo for the phone company came on the screen. Logan paid the bills for Ellie's phone and this one was on a different network. He frowned, not sure what he was looking at.

★   ★   ★

Ellie came out of the bathroom twenty minutes later in her robe with her hair piled up in a towel. Logan was on her bed, leaning back against the wall. She stopped when she saw him.

He held the phone up.

'What's this?'

Her eyes flicked to the phone.

'It's a phone.'

He raised his eyebrows at her.

'I can see that, Ellie. I mean, why do you have it when I already pay for one? I've never seen this one.'

'Becky got it for me.'

Logan sat forward, frowning.

'What?'

Ellie came over and sat beside him, took the phone from him and started pressing buttons. He waited to see what it was she was going to show him, but when she was done she put it against his ear.

He heard her mother's voice. Heard Penny.

'Hi, baby. This is your mum calling to say

congratulations on your very first phone. Hope you like it. Love you.'

Ellie took the phone and switched it off.

Logan blinked away blurred vision.

'Becky said they were getting rid of the evidence in my mum's case after Christmas. At the police station. And was there anything I wanted. She showed me a list.'

'She never said.'

'Told me it was our secret. Anyway, I knew that message was on my old phone. I never deleted it.'

'And Becky knows about the message?'

'No. I didn't tell her why I wanted it. It was just for me.'

Logan put his arm around her shoulders and pulled her against him. She didn't resist, leaning her head on his shoulder and toying with the phone in her hands.

'Why didn't you tell me?'

She shrugged in his embrace.

'You've got Becky now,' she said.

Logan gently eased her away from him and faced her.

'Your mum was special to both of us,' he said. 'Becky knows that. You could have told me.'

She looked down at the phone and back at him. She surprised him by saying okay, leaning in and kissing his cheek before getting up to plug in her hairdryer.

She was stronger than him, that was for sure. And he loved her all the more for it.

2

Armstrong had left Pitt Street after the interview with the two uniforms — telling Irvine that he wanted to catch up on his other work. He promised to be back before five to go and see Suzie Murray with her.

Irvine typed up statements for the officers and filled out internal reports. She hated the paperwork and it took her more than three hours to finish all of it. Sometimes she thought that modern policing was more about documenting what was done — rather than actually doing it.

She called Jim Murphy at four in the afternoon to chase up the post-mortem results and to see if anything of note had turned up from the lab analysis of whatever was found at the locus.

'I think the drug squad instincts are right,' Murphy told her.

'How so?'

'Well, blood analysis isn't back yet but I'm betting that she died from an overdose. I spoke to the pathologist and his preliminary view is that she wasn't killed by someone. There are no signs of violence and no water in her lungs.'

'She was dead when she went in the water?'

'Yes.'

'CCTV show up yet?'

'No.'

'Call over there and see if they can put a rush on it, will you.'

'I'll do it now. Talk later.'

Five o'clock came and went with no sign of Armstrong. The clock crept towards six, then past it. She called her mother to ask her to pick Connor up from the childminder and endured a lecture about parental responsibility. After that, she called Armstrong's mobile and left a message on his voicemail to call her when he could.

Then it was six-thirty.

Her phone rang and she picked it up without looking to see who it was.

'It's about time,' she said.

'What?'

It was Logan.

'I thought it was someone else.'

'You waiting for a call? We can speak later if you like.'

'No. No, it's fine. I'm a bit frustrated. Are you still planning on coming over later?'

'I am. It's just that, well, I wanted to ask you about something. About the phone you got for Ellie.'

She'd forgotten about that.

'Why didn't you tell me?'

'Ellie asked me not to.'

'She's a kid, Becky. Did you not think I should have known about it? I could have helped her. I mean, who knew how she was going to react to hearing Penny's voice. She could have regressed.'

'What about Penny's voice? You're not making any sense, Logan.'

He told her about the message on the phone.

144

'I didn't know. How did she react?'

'She's fine.'

He sounded terse, angry.

'I said I didn't know,' she told him, aware that he was reacting this way because he was upset — probably unsure how he felt himself about hearing Penny's voice again.

He didn't respond. She closed her eyes and rubbed at them with her free hand.

'Listen, I'm sorry,' she said. 'If I'd known about the message of course I would have talked to you about it first.'

He sighed.

'We can talk about it later,' she said. 'I'll call when I get home, like I said.'

'Fine.'

Click

Was there any other word in the English language so often used to mean something entirely opposite to its meaning as *fine*? She didn't think so.

She called Armstrong again, still pissed off at him. Got his voicemail and left a short message that she would go and see Suzie Murray on her own and he could meet her there if he liked.

She put on her jacket, grabbed her bag and headed out of the building.

Way to stay out of trouble.

3

Irvine stood outside Joanna Lewski's building in Bridgeton. It was on the corner, three storeys built in red sandstone with a charity shop at street level and flats above. The sun was sinking in the sky and it glowed red-orange.

She looked at the address she had scribbled on a piece of loose paper. Lewski's flat was on the top floor, back right. She went to the entrance door and was looking for the buzzer for the flat when she noticed that the door wasn't locked. She pushed at it and it swung into the common hallway. She wasn't much of a fan of the red and yellow paint job in Logan's building, but this one had bare plaster walls in charcoal grey. She could barely see the stairs at the far end in the murky light cast down from the grimy window on the landing.

For a moment, Irvine thought about going home. This was something she could do tomorrow when Armstrong was with her. If he was happy to leave it tonight, maybe she should be as well.

Nothing to do with the less-than-inviting interior, of course.

She pushed the piece of paper into her bag and stepped into the hall.

'Get on with it,' she whispered.

Halfway along the hall she was startled by the sound of her mobile ringing.

'Hey,' Armstrong said. 'Where are you? I thought we were going to see this Suzie Murray together.'

Irvine closed her eyes.

'Before five you said. It's now ... ' she checked her watch — 'nearly seven.'

'Yeah, sorry about that. Had a bit of a domestic.'

'You're married?'

'Why so surprised? But, no. It's my girlfriend. Where are you?'

'I'm at Murray's building now. I was going to see her on my own.'

'You want me to come too? I can be there in ten minutes.'

'Do what you want. But I'm going up to her flat to get started. It's late enough already.'

'Go ahead. I'll be there.'

Irvine put her phone away and walked to the stairs at the end of the hall. The dirty grey walls continued up to the next floor and, if anything, it looked even darker.

She started up the stairs and heard a noise above — like shouting. A male voice. She strained to hear but it had stopped and she wasn't sure where exactly it had come from. It could have been at the end of the first floor hall or higher up. Sound echoed off the walls and down the stairs, distorted from its origin.

She waited for a moment and started up again when there was no further sound. The stairs were old stone, polished by the foot traffic that had passed over them since the place was built over a hundred years ago. The centre of each stair was dimpled where the heaviest traffic had worn it away. Irvine was careful to look where she was walking, one hand on the rail screwed to the wall for support.

As she neared the top of the stairs leading to the second floor she heard more noise. This time it was like a thump, followed by someone choking back a sob. It sounded like it was coming from the far end of the hall. Where Suzie Murray lived. Where Joanna Lewski had lived.

Irvine stepped up into the hall and looked along to the door of the flat. There was a narrow window seeping dirty yellow light from the streetlights outside.

She waited, straining to listen for any more sounds from down the hall. She thought she could hear whispers, but couldn't be sure. There was another thump, this time definitely emanating from the flat she was going to visit. Irvine stepped back, wondering if maybe it would be a good idea to wait for Armstrong after all.

She turned to look back down the stairs, didn't see the door to Suzie Murray's flat slowly open, revealing the black interior of the flat.

She heard a slow creaking sound behind her as the door to the flat opened all the way, turned and saw the silhouette of a man against the light from the window. His face was indistinct in the gloom of the hall.

She heard what sounded like a woman crying.

The man didn't move.

Irvine reached into her bag and took out her warrant card, holding it up.

'I'm a police officer. DC Irvine, Strathclyde Police CID.'

Her voice sounded stronger than she felt. That's how they taught you — got to *sound* like a cop, even if you don't feel it.

The man turned his head and looked inside the flat. She saw him in profile — long hair with a prominent brow and a boxer's flat nose. Realised now that he was tall and wide.

Wished to Christ she'd waited for Armstrong.

The man turned back to look at her.

'Bad timing,' he said, and walked towards her.

4

Irvine held her ID out in front of her, as though it would act as a shield. The man continued to advance on her. She stepped back, felt her foot slip on the edge of the top stair — nowhere to go but down.

He was close now, ten feet from her. She pushed her other hand into her bag and grabbed the canister of pepper spray, pulled it out and pointed it at him.

'Stay where you are or I'll use this.'

She said it loud and it was enough to stop him. Still couldn't make out his face. She smelled alcohol and aftershave.

His head cocked to one side.

He ran at her.

Irvine saw his face clearly for a moment and pressed the button on the spray.

He ducked his head and held a big hand up to protect his face from the spray. Irvine tried to angle the liquid into his eyes.

Then he was on her.

He shoved his leading hand into Irvine's face, cracking her face back on to the wall. She felt the impact on her eye socket and cheek, the whole side of her face going numb from the blow.

She kept her finger on the spray and moved the canister rapidly from side to side hoping to catch him in the face. It worked.

He shouted out and pulled his hand off her face.

Irvine kicked out at his legs and felt the side of her shoe connect with his shin. She stepped up into the hall and swung her fist at his head, the canister of pepper spray still grasped in it. She caught him with a glancing blow and he staggered on to the stairs, grabbing at the railing with one hand and swinging the other one round at her.

She saw the blow coming too late. His hand closed into a fist and hit her high on the head, just below her hairline. The force of it made her stagger and she fell back against the wall.

The man rubbed at his eyes. Turned and ran, half falling down the stairs.

Irvine leaned against the wall and listened to the sound of him running on the stairs and the main door crashing back against the wall as he went out on to the street.

She slid down the wall and dropped the pepper spray, her whole body shaking. She felt on the verge of tears but forced herself not to cry, taking in deep lungfuls of air to slow her pulse.

The side of her face felt hot and tight. She put her hand to it and felt swelling around her eye, pulled it away and saw blood. She wiped the blood on the wall, smearing it red.

Irvine searched in her bag for a packet of tissues, pulling out a handful of them and pressing them to her face. She felt blood soak them almost immediately.

'Are you okay?'

Irvine looked up at the sound of the woman's voice. She was leaning against the doorframe of her flat staring at Irvine.

'Did he hit you?'

Irvine nodded and pushed herself up. She bent down to lift her bag and felt her head swim, light flashing in her vision. When it passed, she grabbed her bag and walked towards the woman, the wad of tissues still pressed against her face.

'Are you Suzie Murray?'

She nodded.

'I'm a police officer. Can I use your bathroom?'

Murray straightened and looked inside her flat. Her eyes darted furtively back to Irvine.

'I don't care what you've got in there,' Irvine told her. 'I came to ask you about Joanna Lewski.'

As she drew level with the door of the flat, Irvine saw that Murray's lip was cut and there was swelling to her jaw. She had been crying.

'Did he do that to you?'

Murray nodded but said nothing. Irvine thought that she looked to be in her mid-thirties, with a bad blonde dye job showing dark roots, but was probably five to ten years younger than that. Being in her line of work tended to age women rapidly.

'Can I come in?' Irvine asked, taking the tissues from her face and looking at the crimson stain on white.

'What is it about Joanna?' Murray asked, unable to look Irvine in the eye.

It hadn't occurred to Irvine that Murray

152

would not know that her flatmate was dead. *Had nobody told her?*

'Let's go inside, okay?'

Irvine went past Murray into the flat. She followed Murray's directions to the bathroom, a narrow room at the far end of the hall. The bath was stained where the tap dripped constantly and clothes were strewn across the floor.

She went to the sink and looked in the mirror, turning her face to see the damage that had been done. There was a half-inch cut running down past her right eye and the side of her face was already swollen and discoloured.

Irvine took some more tissues from her bag and dabbed at the cut. Murray came into the room and took a box of Elastoplast from a drawer under the sink.

'It's all I've got,' she said, handing it to Irvine.

Irvine took them from her and said thanks. Murray left her alone as she tore the backing off two plasters and crossed them over the cut, pressing down and seeing a bloodstain rise where she had applied pressure.

She was going to have some heavy bruising but there was nothing she could do about that for now.

Murray was in the living room when Irvine came out of the bathroom. The place was a mess — dirty clothes and dishes all over the place and a single, stained sofa against the wall opposite a window which looked down on to the street outside. Irvine decided she would stand.

Murray pulled her hair back from her face and looked at Irvine.

'Place is a mess.'

Irvine wasn't sure what the correct response to that was. She said nothing.

'You said this was about Joanna?'

'Yes. I'm sorry but she died yesterday.'

Murray looked away but otherwise did not react.

'We found her body in the river. She was naked. Somebody stripped her and dumped her.'

Again, no reaction.

'You don't seem surprised or upset, Suzie.'

Murray shrugged.

'Stuff like that happens to us, you know. Comes with the territory.'

'How well did you know Joanna?'

'Not that well. She moved in a month ago.'

Irvine knew the score: getting any worthwhile information from Murray was going to be difficult. Her inherent distrust of the police.

'Sounds like maybe you didn't have a choice in the matter? Her moving in, I mean.'

'I don't own this place. Someone else does.'

Her handler. Pimp. Irvine made a note to check the Land Register to see who the owner was.

'Who was that man? The one who was just here.'

Murray rocked back and stood, walking over to the window and wrapping her arms around herself. Irvine couldn't tell if it was because she was scared or trying to avoid talking about him.

'Suzie?'

'I don't know his name.'

'That's not really an answer.'

Irvine heard her sigh.

'He sold us some stuff.'

'Drugs?'

She nodded, still looking out the window.

'Have you used any of it?'

'No. He came here with Joanna the other night. Said they were going to party.'

Irvine looked around. Not much of a place for celebrations.

'Did they?'

'What, you want the details?'

Irvine said nothing.

'They didn't stay here long. They went out.'

'And they took the stuff with them?'

Murray nodded.

'Had he sold you drugs before?'

She shook her head.

'He showed up a couple of weeks ago with Joanna. She was the one who knew him. Said he had better stuff than anyone else.'

'And he didn't take cash from Joanna for it?'

'You want a prize for figuring that out?'

There was a knock at the door. Murray looked at Irvine, her eyes wide with fear.

Another knock, louder this time.

5

Irvine held her hand up, telling Murray to stay where she was. It didn't sound like whoever was out there had gone away.

Irvine's mobile rang. It was Armstrong.

'Where are you?' he said.

'I'm in Suzie Murray's flat. Someone was here. I think it might have been the guy who dumped Joanna Lewski's body. And I think maybe he's come back.'

'I don't think so.'

'What?'

'Well, I mean, I'm standing outside her door waiting for someone to answer and I'm the only one here.'

'That was you?'

'Yeah.'

Irvine ended the call and went to open the door. Armstrong looked at her face and winced.

'Jesus *Christ*,' Irvine almost shouted. 'Why didn't you say anything when you knocked?'

'It's not something I'm in the habit of doing.'

'Wait here.'

Irvine went back to the living room and gave Murray one of her cards. Told her to call if she could remember anything else that might help. Asked if she had anywhere else to stay in case he came back.

'What do you care?' Murray said. 'And, anyway, there's nowhere else.'

156

'I'll have someone call in on you. Take a full statement.'

'Look, lady. No offence, right, but I'm not telling you any more.'

Irvine stared at her.

'Want to know how I keep out of trouble? I don't get involved. You'll have to sort it out without me.'

Irvine wanted to say more, couldn't work out what might help.

'Let's go,' Armstrong said, from the hall outside the flat.

Irvine turned to look at him.

'She's said all that she's going to say,' Armstrong told her. 'That's the end of the story.'

Murray shrugged at Irvine.

'Unbelievable,' Irvine said, stepping out into the hall and closing the door to the flat.

'Where to now?' Armstrong asked.

'You're taking me to the hospital to get this looked at,' she said, pointing at her face.

'It wasn't my fault.'

Irvine stopped at the top of the stairs, looked around and kneeled to lift the canister of pepper spray from the floor.

'Was lucky I had this.'

Armstrong looked at her and shrugged.

'Sorry.'

Irvine turned and went down the stairs without waiting for him.

6

Logan was sitting at the Cahills' dining table when he heard the phone ring through in the study. He looked at his watch and saw that it was after nine. Wondered why Becky hadn't called yet.

Cahill got up and went out to answer the phone. Noises sounded from upstairs where Ellie had gone to play with the Cahill children. Sam looked up at the ceiling and then at Logan, smiling.

'How's she doing? Ellie, I mean.'

'Pretty good. We haven't been to the counsellor for a while and she's not quite as raw now when we go to Penny's grave.'

'She's awful grown-up now.'

Logan nodded.

'You're doing a good job. I mean, of bringing her up.'

'I hope so. But how can you tell, really?'

'Ask me that again in twenty years' time.'

It was Logan's turn to smile.

Cahill came into the room holding the phone to his ear and motioned for Logan to follow him. They walked briskly to the study where Cahill activated the speaker on the phone base station.

Logan heard a woman's voice before Cahill cut across her.

'Melanie, I've got you on the speaker now with

Logan. He's the lawyer who's coming over with me.'

They exchanged brief greetings before Cahill spoke again.

'What did you find?'

'I don't know if it's anything. But you said it didn't matter how small it was.'

'Go ahead.'

'It's just this one thing. I went through Tim's stuff and couldn't find anything. Then I remembered that I hadn't checked our e-mail account since, you know . . . '

No one said anything.

'Anyway, I logged on and found this e-mail which Tim sent from his phone. It's timed just before the flight. He must have sent it here in a hurry.'

'What does it say?'

'It says 'D. Hunter, Denver'. That's all.'

Cahill looked at Logan and shook his head.

'Does it mean anything to you?' Melanie asked.

'No. What about you?'

'Nothing. I never heard the name before. You think it might be connected?'

'I don't know,' Cahill said. 'The timing is certainly interesting. Like he was sending himself something that he thought was important. And also maybe that he wanted someone else to see if anything happened to him. Can you forward that e-mail to me?'

'Okay. What's your e-mail address?'

Cahill told her and said he would check it out and call her back if he found anything.

'What do you think?' Cahill asked Logan after ending the call.

Logan shrugged.

'Sounds like it might be something. The timing, you know.'

Cahill nodded and dialled another number on the phone. A man with a strong Glasgow accent answered.

'Bruce, it's Alex. Can you look at something for me?'

'Sure. What is it?'

'I need you to check any connection between Tim Stark and a D. Hunter from Denver.'

'Not much to go on.'

'It's all we have.'

'That's it? No documents or anything?'

'That's it.'

'When do you need it?'

'Tomorrow is fine. Or the day after. I'll be in the States so call my mobile.'

Cahill ended the call, opened his laptop and waited for it to boot, drumming his fingers on his desk. He accessed his e-mail and waited for the message from Melanie Stark to download. He clicked on it and printed off a copy.

Logan got up and went to the printer, lifting the page from the tray and handing it to Cahill.

'Doesn't look like much of a lead,' Logan said.

Cahill looked over the printed copy of the e-mail and when he was done he forwarded the e-mail to Bruce and shut down his laptop.

'What's the plan tomorrow?' Logan asked.

'I'll come pick you up. We can leave my car at the airport.'

'And after we get there?'

'We play it by ear.'

'You realise that it's likely our names will raise a flag now with Homeland Security when we get over there and hit the US customs' desk?'

'I'm kind of counting on it. I mean, where else do we start?'

'That's your idea? You make enough of a nuisance of yourself that they lock us in a small room at the airport for several hours and threaten to send us straight back here.'

'Something like that, yeah. I find it works most of the time.'

Logan stared at him.

'Look, they're not going to send us to Guantanamo Bay or anything.'

Logan's eyes widened.

'And we need to get in touch with whichever law enforcement agency is really in charge of this thing. They *will* come to speak to us.'

'If they don't?'

'We make our presence felt over there. Go see the Feds and the cops and anyone else that we can think of.'

'What if they ignore us? I mean, have you thought about that? Then you go to the press, is that it?'

Cahill smiled. 'Not bad. I hadn't thought of that.'

'I was kind of kidding.'

'No,' he was excited now, 'it's a good idea. There's nothing they hate more when they're trying to keep something under the radar.'

'Let's see if we can get into the country

161

without getting arrested first,' Logan said, regretting even mentioning it now. 'Take it from there.'

Sam Cahill came into the room and held up Logan's mobile.

'This was ringing. I think it was Becky.'

Logan stood and took the phone from her, walking past her to go out of the study. Sam looked at her husband.

'You look after him over there,' she told him.

7

'Is everything okay?' Logan asked Irvine. 'I mean, it's getting late now.'

'I'm fine. It's nothing.'

'What's nothing?'

Irvine sighed.

'I had a bit of a confrontation tonight. This case I'm working on.'

Logan wanted to ask more but let it go for now.

'Are you at home?'

'Yes. But you don't need to come over tonight if you don't want to. I know you've got a long trip tomorrow.'

'I'm coming over.'

'Good.'

★ ★ ★

Logan parked a little way along the street from Irvine's house and walked back. When she opened the door he stared at the discoloration on her face, her eye half closed from the swelling.

'Jesus, what happened?'

She lifted a hand self-consciously, trying to cover it.

'I thought you said it was nothing.'

She stepped back and told him to come inside. He followed her down the hall, through the

163

dining room and into the kitchen where she sat at the table.

She poured herself a cup of tea while Logan went to the fridge and poured himself a glass of orange juice. He sat next to Irvine and pushed her hair back to look closely at the damaged side of her face. He saw now that she had three stitches in a cut beside her eye, which was heavily bloodshot.

'Some confrontation,' he said. 'Did you get in a fight?'

'Sort of. Somebody I wanted to talk to on my case wasn't quite so keen to speak to me.'

'Don't you work these things with a partner?'

She looked sideways at him. 'Yeah, usually. This time I went on my own. Turned out not to be such a good idea after all.'

Irvine put her mug down and turned in her seat to face him. Her lip trembled.

'Logan . . . '

She moved forward and wrapped her arms around him, crying quietly. Then not so quietly.

'I was so scared. He was much bigger and stronger. If I didn't have the pepper spray — '

She didn't finish the thought.

He held her and stroked her hair. After a moment she pulled away and took a tissue from her pocket, dabbing at her eyes.

Her phone rang, shrill in the quiet of the room. Irvine grabbed it and answered.

'DC Irvine?' a male voice asked.

'Yes.'

'It's DS Jim Murphy. Listen, sorry to disturb you at night, but I thought you might like to

164

know what we found.'

'You got something new, Jim?'

'Well, we think it's the clothes from your victim. Lewski.'

'What do you mean, *think*?'

'There's not much left of them. They were found in a skip outside a building site about a half-mile from the locus. Someone set fire to them.'

'Is there enough left to do us any good?'

'Don't know till the forensics people go over it. It'll be tomorrow now before they make a start.'

'Thanks, Jim.'

She finished the call and held Logan's hand.

'How do I look?' She straightened her back and sniffed, lifting her chin.

Logan tilted his head to one side.

'You really want me to answer that?'

'Yes, actually.'

He leaned towards her and kissed her gently on the lips, moving up the injured side of her face and kissing her eyes as she closed them.

'How's that for an answer?'

'Pretty good. You practise that?'

'Only on you.'

They moved through to the living room and sat together on an oversized couch. Logan put his arm around her and pulled her to him.

'What is this case anyway that causes you to get beaten up?'

'It's a drug squad thing that I got pulled into because there've been some deaths.'

'What, like gang hits or something?'

'No. Not like that. Overdoses.'

'Why is CID interested in overdoses?'

'They think there's a new strain of drug going around. A heroin derivative. If the suppliers know that it's potentially lethal we might be able to charge them in relation to the deaths, not just the supply.'

'I hadn't thought about it that way.'

'Can we not talk about it any more? When do you leave tomorrow?'

'Alex is picking me up at seven.'

'How's Ellie taking it?'

'Better than I thought. Sam said you can go over there any time. If you want.'

'I will, if I get the time. This case feels like it'll keep me busy.'

They sat for a while without talking, watching the fire crackle in the hearth and enjoying the quiet.

Irvine turned her face and kissed his neck, small and soft. Her hand slid across his chest and inside his shirt. Logan kissed her.

'You have to get up early,' she said, bringing her hand up to his face.

'Not that early.'

Part Six: Patriots

1

The place looked smaller than Seth Raines remembered. He got out of his pick-up truck and walked up the steps to the front door of the single-storey house. He rapped his knuckles on the door and waited. He looked back at his truck sitting in the dirt driveway behind the crumbling front wall.

'That you, Seth?' a voice sounded from inside.

'Yeah.'

'Come on in. It's open.'

Raines looked down at his boots and wiped them on the welcome mat before pushing the door open and stepping into the narrow hallway. It led to a small kitchen at the back of the house with a couple of rooms off to either side.

'Through here,' the voice shouted from Raines's right.

He pushed open the first door on his right and walked into the room, looking back to see if he was trailing any dirt. The man he had come to see was sitting by the fireplace. It was warm outside but the fire was roaring. The man turned to look at Raines. The pain never seemed to leave his eyes. Raines knew why.

★　★　★

Raines lay on the ground beside the dirt track watching blood soak through his combat

169

trousers. Andy Johnson kneeled beside him and tore at his trousers until the wound was exposed. Raines put his head back against the dirt and ground his teeth against the pain as it burned through his leg.

'It's okay,' Johnson said. 'You'll be okay, man.'

His voice was high and difficult to hear over the noise.

Raines felt sweat run back off his face and into his ears.

A British Chinook helicopter came in to land using the cover of the three Land Rovers to shield it from the enemy position. It settled on the ground quickly and heavily and a medical team rushed forward. One of the team came to treat Raines, but he shouted at them to get Horn first.

'Keep him alive,' he screamed at the medics as they fitted an oxygen mask over Horn's face and lifted him on to a stretcher.

The rotor blades of the Chinook continued to spin, blowing dust and grit into Raines's eyes. He closed them and held his hand up as a shield.

When he got back to the base, Horn was already in surgery. Raines leaned against a wall in the operating theatre while the British medics worked on Horn, oblivious to the blood soaking the field dressing on his own wound.

They told him he couldn't be there. Try and move me, he told them.

No one did.

They worked hard on Horn. He couldn't have asked for any more effort.

First thing they did was saw off what remained of his left foot. Tried to stem the blood flow from the stump where his right leg used to be by clamping arteries.

His heart still stopped.

They opened his chest and put paddles into the cavity.

Raines closed his eyes, certain that his man was not coming back.

★ ★ ★

But he did. Somehow. And now here he was in front of Raines.

'You don't have to like these people,' Raines told Matt Horn. 'They're a means to an end is all. A tool to help us get what we want.'

'I don't want to talk about it.'

'You need convincing at every stage. It's getting old real fast.'

Horn said nothing and looked out of the window at the front of the house. Raines hated the weakness he saw in his friend's eyes. He walked to the window and leaned against the wall beside it, his face set in a perpetual frown. The picture of Charlie Company that first day in Afghanistan was on the mantel above the fireplace. The same one Raines had in his office at the compound. Raines stared at it. Tried to reconcile the face of Matt Horn that he saw in the picture with the man he was now.

Horn turned his head and followed Raines's gaze to the photo. He stood awkwardly, pushing himself up with his arms, and walked in a stiff gait to look out of the window. Raines knew that Horn was still getting used to the new artificial legs.

'You heard about the latest one?' Horn said. 'The guy that died in Veterans Park?'

'I heard.'

'He was a soldier. Or at least he used to be.'

'I said I heard.'

'What about the others? And what about Stark?'

Raines moved off the wall, opening and closing his fists.

'If that was even his name.'

'Goddamnit,' Horn shouted at Raines. 'When did it get so easy for you?'

He turned and Raines saw his eyes glisten in the light from the sun. Horn wiped the sleeve of his shirt across his face. Raines bowed his head. Wondered if it would be easier for everyone if he killed Horn now. He would never have believed that he could have such a thought.

'It'll be over soon,' Raines told him.

'It won't bring any of them back.' Horn's voice trembled. 'Will it?'

'No.'

'And how many more will die?'

'I don't know.'

'You don't have anything else to say to me?'

Raines looked again at the photograph above the fireplace — thought about what he would do if he could rewind it all back to that day. Would he do it differently? Any of it? Never volunteer for that trip to the poppy field? He wasn't sure. His current mission seemed hard-wired into his psyche and nothing would turn him away from it. In quiet moments, he secretly relished it.

'I used to love this country,' he said.

'You still do.'

Raines looked at Horn again and smiled, shaking his head.

'And now I want it to burn,' Raines said. 'I mean, I love the *country*. But not the bastards that run it. They can rot in Hell for all I care. For all they did to us.'

He pointed at the photograph.

'We have to look after ourselves. That's what this is about.'

'And what about the people we hurt in the process?'

Raines turned to the window.

'I told you already. I'm tired of this conversation.'

'Can you at least tell me how this all ends?'

There was no answer.

2

Raines pulled up outside his building and looked in his mirror. He saw that he now had shadows. They were parked in an obvious Fed car across the street. They must have been waiting for him since this morning. Had to be expected after what happened to Stark. He was impressed that they had found him because he had rented the apartment under a different name but felt kind of insulted that they weren't very good at being covert, if that was their intention. Two young guys in suits sitting on the street in a Ford on a working day. Their ineptitude would have been funny if it wasn't for the fact that they were supposed to be the ones protecting the security of the country.

What used to be *his* country.

Raines decided on a direct strategy. They had nothing on him anyway. He reached under his seat, grabbed his Smith & Wesson nine-millimetre off the floor, stuck it into the rear waistband of his jeans and got out of his truck. He walked across the street towards the Ford, saw the men inside turn their heads to talk to one another. Their movements were fast and jerky.

Raines got to the car, leaned down to the driver's window and motioned with his hand for the man to lower the window. The man did what he was told, the window buzzing down, and stared at Raines through the narrow opening he had made.

'Let me in back,' Raines told him.

★ ★ ★

The driver turned to his companion who was entirely non-committal.

'We should talk.'

The driver turned back to Raines, stared at him for a while longer and nodded his head towards the back of the car. Raines heard the soft *click* of the car door being unlocked. He went to the rear door, pulled it open and sat inside.

'How old are you guys?'

The driver turned in his seat to look at Raines.

'What are you doing?'

'I asked first.'

The driver sighed and looked at the man beside him in the front passenger seat. They were both Hispanic men and looked to Raines like they were too young for the job.

'I mean, you don't look any older than, what, thirty?' Raines asked. 'Am I right?'

The driver looked at Raines again but said nothing.

'What did you do before you signed up for the badge and the gun? Or did you get into this straight out of college?'

'I was a cop,' the driver said.

His partner looked at him and shook his head.

'Why are we even talking to this guy?'

'What about you, chief?' Raines asked the partner.

175

The man faced forward again and ignored Raines.

'You've never fought for your country, have you? Never put yourself in harm's way for others. Because that's what it's about, you know. Self-sacrifice.'

'What is it that you want?' the driver asked him.

Raines snorted a laugh.

'What?'

'You're the first person to ask me that,' Raines told him. 'That's how we got to this.'

'What do you mean?'

'If someone like you, some government salary slave, had actually asked me what I wanted and been genuine about it, we might not be sitting in this car together today.'

'I don't know what you're talking about.'

Raines looked down.

'We can end it all if you want,' the driver said to him. 'Say the word and we'll take you in right now.'

'And charge me with what?' Raines asked, without looking up.

'We'll think of something,' the partner said, looking out of the windscreen.

'That's what I'm talking about,' Raines said, jabbing a finger at the man in the passenger seat. 'You guys are all the same, aren't you? So confident in your ability to always be right.'

'This is going nowhere,' the passenger told the driver. 'Cut him loose.'

'See,' Raines said, 'you can't even answer my question and so, instead of admitting that I've done nothing wrong, you treat me like a piece of shit on your shoe. Cut him loose, he says.'

The passenger turned to face Raines before he spoke this time.

'Don't get righteous with us now. We all know that it's only a matter of time.'

'Before what?'

'Whatever it is that you're planning on doing.'

Raines knew that they didn't have a clue. He'd kept Stark at arm's length the whole time, suspicious of his background story. Stark didn't know enough before he got on that plane.

'What is it that you think you're trying to stop me from doing? Has anyone even told you that, or do you get kept in the dark?'

'This isn't a game.'

'*I* know that. But I don't think you do. It's all just a game for you. There's no sense of responsibility for what you do in the name of this country.'

The passenger looked away. 'This is a waste of time.'

The driver sighed at his partner and looked at Raines.

'If there's nothing we can do for you right now . . .'

'There's nothing you can do for anyone at any time. That's what I'm trying to tell you.'

'This isn't anyone's fault except your own, sir. Don't try to convince yourself otherwise. You make your own decisions.'

'Are you even listening to what you're saying? I mean, some asshole with an inflated sense of his own importance told you to stake out my place and you accept blindly that he's right but you don't even ask why. Do you realise how stupid that sounds?'

The driver held Raines's gaze. 'Sir, I think you're the one that's confused.'

'How's that?'

'You were a soldier, am I right?'

'I was. I put *my* life on the line for the likes of you.'

'And why did you do that?'

'To serve my country.'

'I don't think I'm making myself clear enough. Let me try again. Why did you pack up your gear, get on a plane and go to a country thousands of miles away to fight?'

'Because I was ordered to do it by my Commander-in-Chief.'

'You mean the President?'

'Yes.'

'But that's not true, is it? I mean, the President himself didn't come down to your base and address you individually to give you an order.'

'That's not how it works.'

'Exactly. The President set the mission and you followed the orders of your superiors. You did it without question because the chain of command is important. Because it is necessary.'

Raines regarded the man, watching to see if he was being taunted. There was no trace of humour in his eyes.

'You're trying to tell me that we're the same?'

'Yes.'

'And what exactly are your orders?'

'We watch you. We report back. Simple as that.'

'And what is it that you think you've seen?'

'Nothing so far. But it's early.'

'I don't like being treated like a piece of garbage someone can throw away after it's been used up.'

'Look, sir. I don't know what your gripe is and, honestly, I'm not paid to care. I'm paid to make sure you don't do something that will hurt others.'

Raines wondered if he could get the drop on the two men — pull his weapon before they could. The thought of a gunfight in the close confines of the car got his heart pumping.

'Do we understand each other?' the driver asked.

Raines stared at him until the man looked away. You have no idea how close you are right now, Raines thought.

'Let's not do this again, okay? If you get on with your life as a respectful, law-abiding citizen of the United States, we can leave you alone. How does that sound?'

Raines put his hands on his lap.

'Maybe it's too late for that,' he said. 'Did you think about that?'

The man looked down at Raines's hands and back at his face. Raines saw the realisation dawn that they had allowed a man into their car, a suspect, without searching him. Neither of the two men in the front of the car had any idea whether he was armed or not.

'It's never too late, sir,' the driver said.

Raines let his hands drop to his sides. The driver shifted in his seat. Raines knew that he was trying to get into a position where he could reach his sidearm — figured he would have it in a shoulder rig like all the Feds do.

'Sometimes it is, son. That's why we go to war.'

The passenger seemed oblivious to what was going on and sat staring out of the windscreen. Raines wanted to do it so much it hurt. Take out some of his anger on these two men and all that they represented.

'Sir . . . '

'What?'

'I think you better leave now.'

The strain in the man's voice caused the passenger to turn to look at Raines. His hands stayed loose by his sides, palms now resting on the back seat of the car.

'Maybe I don't want to leave.'

The passenger's eyes flicked between the two other men.

'Some other time,' Raines said eventually, reaching out to open the door. 'It's been a blast.'

3

The apartment felt emptier than when he had left. Raines went to the kitchen and dropped his keys on the counter before getting a can of Coke from the fridge and popping the tab. He drank half the can in one go and went to the living room, sitting on the couch and flicking aimlessly through twenty or so channels before happening on news coverage of some new military initiative in Afghanistan. He watched for a while until the various senior officers being interviewed blurred into one indistinguishable whole.

Light from the setting sun washed over the living room before fading to dark. Raines muted the sound on the TV and closed his eyes, the flickering light from the screen playing across his face.

Fatigue settled down through his flesh and into his bones. He took another sip from the Coke, not tasting it. He'd noticed in the last two weeks how food no longer held any pleasure for him. It was fuel for his body and nothing more than that. He hadn't had a beer in weeks. Didn't know any more what it was that used to give him pleasure.

Raines left the TV on and went to the bedroom, going straight to the wardrobe and pulling down a box from the shelf above the hanging rail. He took it back to the living room and set the box down on the table, taking the lid off and lifting out a rag. It was smudged and well worn and smelled of metal and gun oil.

Setting the rag down on the table, he placed his gun on top of it and began methodically taking it apart and cleaning it like he had done a thousand times before.

Take care of your weapon and it will take care of you.

When he was finished cleaning the gun, he put it back together and made sure that the mechanisms were all working correctly, slipping the magazine out of the handgrip and racking the slide.

He took the magazine out again and held it up, looking at the exposed bullet sitting on top of the magazine. It looked innocuous, like it was nothing at all. How could something that small be capable of doing so much damage?

The metal of the magazine felt cool against his forehead when he pressed it there. It slid smoothly back into the handgrip with a satisfying *click* and Raines jacked a round into the breech.

Ready to rock 'n' roll.

That's what all the young guys said before they headed out on their first mission. Like it was a movie or something. Not real.

Then a mine took your leg off.

Your blood pumped out into the sand.

Real enough for you now?

And what happened when you got home? Thanks, son, for all your sacrifices. Here're your papers. Now go find a real job and pay your own medical bills.

Can't afford it?

Tough shit.

Suck it up, soldier. No one never promised you nothin'.

'You reap what you sow,' Raines said out loud, turning the gun and placing it at his temple.

He put his finger inside the trigger guard and touched it to the trigger. Felt it give.

Just a little pressure and it'll all be over. No Feds watching your every move. No more deals with the Devil. Just the quiet.

He applied more pressure to the trigger. Wondered if he'd hear the explosion as the gun went off. Would he be aware of that split-second as the tip of the bullet passed through the barrel of the gun before shattering the bone of his skull and shredding his brain?

Wondered if he would feel the pain.

His leg started to ache under the scar.

He pressed the trigger some more. Realised that it was more than he had ever done before. Wondered if this time he would keep going until all the lights went out.

The phone rang through in the kitchen. Raines waited for it to ring out.

It started again as soon as it had stopped. He sighed, released his finger from the trigger and placed the gun on the rag spread out over the table.

Went to the kitchen to get the phone.

'Sorry about earlier,' Matt Horn said. 'I didn't mean to upset you when you were here.'

'I wasn't upset.'

'What are you doing right now?'

Raines rubbed absently at the welt by his

temple where he had pressed the gun to his head.

'Nothing much, you know. Watching TV.'

'Anything good?'

'No.'

'Want to come over for a beer?'

He stepped into the doorway between the kitchen and the living room, looked at the gun sitting there on the table.

'We could watch a game or something,' Horn said. 'Like we used to. I mean, we haven't done that in a while.'

'Sounds good.' He hung up and went back to the table, looking down at the gun sitting there. He wondered if Horn was now a security risk and whether he should go over there again tonight and make sure he wouldn't talk to anyone. But he couldn't find it in himself to do that. Not after everything.

He switched off the TV, picked up his keys and went outside into the dark. The gun still lying on the rag on his table.

Part Seven:
Homeland

1

Wednesday

Wiping condensation from the mirror in her bathroom, Irvine leaned forward and looked at the side of her face. It looked worse than it had last night. She prodded gently at the stitches in the cut by her eye and winced at the pain.

She stood back a little and turned her face to the side so that she could see the full extent of the damage. The area around the wound was swollen and discoloured and her eye had closed a little overnight. A dull throb pulsed behind her eye so she took two painkillers from the drawer in the vanity unit beneath the sink and washed them down with water from the tap.

Irvine got dressed in her bedroom and was drying her hair when Connor wobbled into the room in his jammies and wrapped himself around her legs. She switched the dryer off and lifted her son into her arms.

'Hey, little man. How are you today?'

He grinned at her and buried his face in her neck, putting his hands in her still damp hair and twisting it around his fingers. He pulled back from her and put a hand on her bruised face.

'You hurt, Mummy?'

Irvine stroked his hair back from his forehead and kissed him.

'No,' she lied.

'Good.'

She hugged him again.

'Breakfast?' he asked.

'What do you want?'

'Toast.' His face contorted as he considered other options. 'Juice.'

Irvine admired his ability to communicate his precise needs in as few words as possible — thought it would be nice if little boys could grow into men and not lose that trait.

★ ★ ★

After dropping Connor at the childminder, Irvine looked up and saw a jet high above her, fumes trailing behind it. She checked her watch and guessed that Logan and Cahill were probably sitting around the lounge at Heathrow waiting for their connection to Denver right now.

She got in the car and her phone rang. It was Armstrong.

'How's the face? Bet it looks like you've gone ten rounds with someone.'

'I've looked better.'

'You coming in today?'

'Yes. Why wouldn't I be?'

'No reason. Just that after last night, you know . . . '

'Listen, why don't you speak to Jim Murphy. See if the forensics people have come up with anything yet. I spoke with him last night. He said they had found Lewski's clothes.'

'Where?'

'Not sure. Nearby somewhere.'

'Intact?'

'No. They'd been burned just like we thought. But there might be something they can get.'

'Blood results back yet?'

'Not as of last night. Ask him about that too.'

'I'll see if I can find him.'

Irvine started her car and tuned the radio to a news channel. There was a brief story about the body found in the river but there was nothing much to it. Basic information. She switched it off and drove into town.

★　★　★

Armstrong wasn't around when Irvine got to her desk so she called the CCTV centre again and spoke to the shift supervisor, hoping he would tell her that the stuff was on its way to her already.

'Dan Patrick,' the supervisor said when he came on the line.

'Dan, this is DC Irvine from Strathclyde CID. I'm looking to see if we can get anything from the last couple of days in connection with a murder investigation. I spoke to someone already about getting some recordings over here.'

'Okay. We're kind of short-staffed. But I'll help if I can.'

She got the impression that no one had done anything about looking at the footage yet. Irvine went through the circumstances of Joanna Lewski's death and the time periods that she thought would be crucial. Again.

'We should have some coverage that might

help,' Patrick told her. 'It'll take a while to go through it, though. I mean, that's a lot of hours.'

'I don't need you guys to go over it. And I need it now. Send it to DS Jim Murphy at Pitt Street. Today.'

There was a brief pause before he replied.

'I'll get someone on to it.'

2

After an hour, there was still no sign of Armstrong. Irvine picked up her desk phone and called his mobile.

'Kenny, it's me. How are you getting on? Any progress after the post-mortem yesterday?'

'I'm over here at the mortuary with the pathologist. He's finished with his report and I've got some samples from Lewski's body. I thought I'd pick them up and rush them over to the lab. Let forensics get a head start on things.'

'You should have told me you were going there.'

'Just trying to move things on, you know?'

'I told you that I'm fine, Kenny. You don't have to treat me like an invalid.'

He didn't say anything.

'What kind of samples did we get?' she asked.

'A swab of semen and also some hairs.'

'She had sex before she was killed?'

'That's what he says.'

'If we're lucky we'll get a DNA hit on it.'

'I'll get the stuff up to Pitt Street, to the lab, then meet you back at your desk. What you been up to?'

'I'm going to see the lawyer here, find out who owns Suzie Murray's flat.'

'It's not hers?'

'She said no.'

'Okay. Let's keep this thing moving forward.'

'Hey, how did you get on with Jim Murphy?'

'Yeah, they haven't finished with the clothes yet. Don't worry, I'm on it.'

★　★　★

Irvine went down the stairs to the ground floor of the building and through the main reception area to a corridor at the back. At the end of the corridor was a large, open-plan room with four desks. The force's only full-time in-house lawyer was a middle-aged woman with a fondness for green tea and blueberry muffins who sat at the desk nearest the door. The muffin habit had not been kind to her waistline. She looked up as Irvine sat in the chair on the other side of the desk.

Irvine smiled and introduced herself. The lawyer took her glasses off and fidgeted with a paper clip that she had bent out of shape, using the end of it to scrape under her nails. She brushed the resulting debris off her desk and on to the floor.

Irvine's smile faltered.

'What can I do for you?' the lawyer asked, boredom clear in her expression.

'I'm looking for some help. It's on a murder investigation.'

That caught her interest. She put the misshapen paper clip down and clasped her hands.

'What do you need from me?'

'I need to log into your Land Register account. For information on a flat.'

'What kind of information?'

'Who owns it? When they bought it? That kind of thing, you know.' Irvine smiled again. 'Can you log me in now?'

'Sure.'

Irvine followed her to a spare desk where the lawyer set her up to access the search function on the Register. She waited for the lawyer to leave her alone, entered the address of Lewski's flat and put in a request for the search results to be e-mailed to her. She thanked the lawyer and went back upstairs.

There was an e-mail already in her inbox attaching the search report on the flat. It was owned by a company — not an individual. From the name, 'ScotLets Limited', she assumed that it probably held a number of properties for rent.

Irvine opened the Internet browser on her own computer and went to the Companies House website — one that she could access directly without going through the lawyer. It had details of all companies incorporated in the UK. She found the search function and typed in 'ScotLets'.

The result gave her basic information, but not the details of who owned the shares in the company or who its directors were. She clicked on the 'print page' option and went to collect the sheet of paper from the network printer.

The registered office of the company was at the office of an accountancy firm in a commercial park north of the city centre.

Irvine went back to her desktop and clicked on an icon that allowed her access to more detailed reports on companies — for a price — and printed off the information she found for the shareholders and directors. She saw that there were two shareholders and that those same people were the only directors. They had listed their address as being the same as the registered office.

A quick Google search on the accountancy firm disclosed that it had two partners — and that they were the same people who owned and operated ScotLets. Nothing unusual in any of that, Irvine thought. Plenty of professionals put their money into property and did it through separate businesses, but she made a note to go and visit the accountants with Armstrong later that day.

She knew from experience that there were professionals out there who had no problem in dealing with dirty money.

3

There was a sandwich and a can of Coke sitting on Irvine's desk when she came back from a quick walk around the block to get some fresh air. It was just past twelve-thirty. She looked round and saw Armstrong in Liam Moore's room. Armstrong saw her looking and walked over to her desk.

'Thought you might be hungry,' he told her. 'I got chicken salad coz I thought it would be safe enough. Who doesn't like chicken, right?'

'Thanks.'

He sat on the edge of her desk.

'You know the boss?' she asked him.

Armstrong looked over at Moore's room.

'Not really, no. I mean, I'm kind of into boxing and I know he used to fight so we were passing the time.'

Irvine touched the swollen side of her face. 'You having a laugh at my expense?'

'No. Anyway, it suits you. Makes you look tough.'

Irvine opened the sandwich and the Coke and ate while Armstrong explained that it would be tomorrow at the earliest before the forensics lab would be able to create a DNA profile from the semen sample and check it against the national database.

'What do you want to do this afternoon?' he asked.

She told him about the accountants who appeared to own the Lewski/Murray flat.

'So let's go talk to them.'

'Should we give them a call in advance?'

'Nah. I mean, if they are scumbags it'll be best to catch them on the hop. Did you run the names to see if anything came up?'

'No prior convictions.'

'There's a first time for everything.'

★ ★ ★

Armstrong drove them to the office of the accountants Marshall Scott, picking his way through the city traffic and treating every amber light as an invitation to accelerate. Irvine tutted a few times but he didn't seem to hear. Either that or he was ignoring her.

'Which division were those guys from?' she asked him.

'Which guys?'

'The uniforms we spoke to about Lewski.'

'Stewart Street.'

Irvine called Pitt Street from her mobile and asked to be connected to the Stewart Street station. The duty sergeant came on the line and told her that the two officers were out on patrol.

'I'm looking for information on some working girls,' Irvine said. 'Who's the Super there?'

'Neal Pope.'

'Can you connect me?'

The line hummed and then another man spoke.

'Pope.'

'Sir, this is DC Irvine from CID.'

'What can I do for you?'

'I'm looking for some information on a couple of working girls in your division. Other girls they know, who their handler is, that kind of thing.'

'What's this about?'

'It's a murder inquiry, sir.'

'Who's the stiff?'

Charming.

'Joanna Lewski.'

'She one of the prozzies?'

'Yes.'

'What's the other one called?'

'Suzie Murray.'

'Right. Give me your number and leave it with me. I'll have someone call you back.'

'This is urgent, sir.'

'I appreciate that. We'll get right back to you.'

'Thank you, sir.'

Armstrong was smirking when she looked at him.

'What?'

'Did you write that book? You know, the one about making friends and alienating people.'

'I just asked him for information. What's wrong with that?'

'He's a Super.'

'So?'

'You told him it was a murder inquiry and that it was urgent he got back to you. I mean, I think he would have worked that one out for himself.'

Irvine closed her eyes.

'You need to relax more,' Armstrong told her.

The accountants' office was the smallest of seven two-storey units in a neat commercial park just off the M8. As they pulled into an empty parking space at the entrance to the unit, Irvine noticed two expensive German sports cars with vanity plates.

'Looks like they do okay for a small outfit,' she said, nodding at the cars.

Armstrong applied the handbrake and looked over. 'Let's not jump to conclusions.'

'I'm just saying.'

They pushed through double glass doors into the reception where an attractive young woman with a telephone headset smiled and asked them if she could help.

Armstrong took out his gold shield to identify himself. Irvine felt vaguely inadequate next to him with only the standard issue warrant card. That and the fact the woman was staring at the injuries to her face.

'We're looking to speak to . . . ' Irvine looked at the printout in her hand. 'Mr Marshall and Mr Scott.'

The woman's smile faltered.

'They're both here, right? I mean, we saw their cars outside.'

'I'll check if they're available. Can I tell them what it's about?'

'We'll explain it to them,' Armstrong said.

They stood in front of the woman's desk while she called through to each of the men in turn. The conversations sounded calm enough to

Irvine from what she could tell from the receptionist's side of it.

Irvine looked around the place and saw that the furnishings were expensive and that there were original pieces of art on the walls. She couldn't tell if they were worth anything or if they were junk. But it didn't look like the kind of place that hung any old rubbish up on the walls.

After a few minutes, a door opened to the right of the woman's desk and a slim man in his early forties walked over to them and held out his hand. His handshake was firm and he maintained eye contact the whole time. He had neat, fair hair, tanned skin and a navy suit that fitted him very well.

'I'm Paul Scott,' he said. 'Come on through and we can have a chat.'

4

The other accountant introduced himself as Lawrence Marshall. He looked a little younger than Scott, but not by much. He had the same air of health and prosperity about him, dressed in a charcoal pinstripe suit with thinning hair swept back on his head.

The two men sat together on the near side of a table in the office boardroom. It was on the ground floor and had two long windows which looked out towards the motorway in the distance. They were both doing their best not to look at Irvine's bruises.

'Can we get you anything to drink?' Scott asked.

'No thanks,' Irvine replied, sitting two seats away from them.

Armstrong walked around to the far side of the table and sat opposite Irvine. Scott looked from Irvine to Armstrong and back.

'What can we do for you?'

'You own a property company. ScotLets. Is that correct?' Irvine asked.

'Yes. Is there a problem with it?'

'Not that we're aware of, no.'

'You have a flat in Bridgeton?' Armstrong said. Both men looked at him.

'You rent it to a couple of women.'

Scott shifted in his seat. Marshall remained still.

'Is that what this is about?' Scott asked.

'You know what they do for a living?'

'I do now. But not when we rented to them.'

Irvine raised her eyebrows.

'Come on. Is that the best you can do?'

'It's the truth. I mean, we have an agency that rents all the properties for us. We trust them to get all the references and stuff.'

'So long as the money rolls in you don't care.'

'That's not what I said. It's a respected agency. We don't have the time to do all of that ourselves.'

'It's true,' Marshall added.

'But you know about these particular tenants. About what they do to earn a living and pay your rent?'

'We started getting complaints about them from one of the other tenants in the building,' Scott said. 'They got the company name from the lease and called here direct to complain rather than going through the agency.'

'And you didn't do anything about it?'

'We left it to the agency.'

'It's been tough in the property market,' Marshall said.

'So any tenant is a good tenant?'

'Something like that.'

Irvine believed what they were saying, didn't see any 'tells' to indicate that they were lying.

'Can you give us details of the agency?' she asked.

'Sure, I've got it here.'

Marshall reached into his jacket and took out a business card which he handed to Irvine. She looked at it briefly, saw that it was one of the big commercial agencies with an office in the city centre.

'One of the women died,' Armstrong said. 'Joanna Lewski. We're treating it as murder.'

'My God,' Scott said, his tanned face going pale.

'Is that why you're here?' Marshall asked. 'You think we had something to do with it?'

'We follow all lines of inquiry. This is one of them.'

'If we knew anything, we would tell you.'

'That's terrible,' Scott said, almost as though he was no longer listening.

'You seem awful upset about a woman you didn't know,' Irvine said.

Scott looked at her.

'It's just . . . I don't know.'

Irvine stood.

'We'll be speaking to your agency.'

★ ★ ★

Outside in the car, Irvine asked what Armstrong thought about Scott's reaction to the news of Lewski's death.

'Yeah, I saw that.'

'What do you think? Did he know her?'

'It's funny. His reaction. Those two uniforms we spoke to.'

'I know. This girl seemed to have an effect on men.'

'Difficult to tell why from the way we found her.'

'I didn't get the impression he was lying to us.'

'I agree. So what do you want to do about it?'

'It wasn't the reaction of someone who had anything to hide. More like he was shocked. Like he just found out about it.'

'Yeah.'

'If we can get the lab results and look at the CCTV recordings and then go see this agency . . . ' She waved the card Scott had given her. 'Something's going to break on this. I can feel it.'

5

Irvine put an elbow on her desk and propped her chin up on her hand. She could feel her lower lip pouting and tried to pull it back in. Armstrong was sitting beside her and tried his best to look sympathetic.

Jim Murphy was used to pouting detectives.

'You know how it is,' he said to Irvine. 'This blood stuff takes time. I've been up to the top floor twice already today but those lab guys can't be rushed. It'll be done when it's done.'

Irvine leaned back in her chair and rubbed at her eyes, suddenly feeling tired.

'What about CCTV? They delivered the recordings yet?'

'Oh, sure. I got an e-mail with all that stuff in digital format. Save me logging on to try to find it.'

'Anything on it?'

He looked at his watch. Stuffed his hands in his trouser pockets and looked back at Irvine.

'Came over less than an hour ago. So . . . '

'You haven't looked at it yet?'

'No.'

'But you know how to, right? I mean, you can read the angles, know where the cameras are pointed, judge distances.'

'Yeah, I can do that.'

'Any chance you can make a start on it today?'

He looked at his watch again. Now rubbing at

imaginary stubble on his clean-shaven face. He pushed his glasses up on to the bridge of his nose.

'Well . . . '

'It's a murder inquiry, Jim. Please.'

'Fine. But it'll just be a start. There's a lot of stuff on there and it's . . . ' He checked his watch. Again. 'After three now.'

'I appreciate it, Jim. I do.'

Irvine gave him her best smile: figured if she couldn't appeal to his sense of civic duty she'd try another route. Feminine wiles. Not subtle. Murphy didn't go for it.

So much for the killer smile.

'Let me know tomorrow morning how you're getting on?' Irvine said.

Murphy nodded, turned and walked away without saying anything else.

'That was . . . helpful,' Armstrong said.

Irvine watched Murphy pull open the door to the stairwell at the far end of the open plan area.

'Actually, he is very good,' she said.

Irvine looked at Armstrong, caught him staring at the injured side of her face. Realised that the pain was starting up again. She put her hand against her face and felt the swelling.

'I don't think we're going to accomplish much more today, do you?' Armstrong asked.

She knew where he was going with this.

'Before you say anything, I'm fine.'

'I'm not planning on contradicting you on that.'

'But you *are* about to suggest that maybe I should go home early. After all I've been through.'

205

She made quotation signs with her fingers as she said the last sentence. Remembered someone else who did that — Cahill. It was a sign that his particular brand of rough charm was starting to work on her.

'Something like that. We can pick up with him tomorrow,' he said, nodding his head to the side in the direction Murphy had gone.

'What about the rental agency for the accountants?'

She swivelled in her seat and lifted the card from her desk. 'We could go and talk to them.'

Armstrong took the card from her. 'I'll do that. I'm pretty sure I won't get attacked in their swanky office.'

Irvine narrowed her eyes at him, drummed her fingers on the desk.

'It would give me a chance to pick up Connor early from the childminder's, I suppose,' she said.

'Connor's your son.'

She nodded, though he hadn't asked it as a question.

'So go. Do it. Take a couple of hours off and swallow some painkillers.'

★ ★ ★

At home, Irvine made Connor his favourite dinner of spaghetti with cheese sauce and gave him a bath after watching a Scooby Doo DVD. He loved Scooby Doo. Maybe as much as she did.

She let him splash around in the bath with his

toys before taking him to his room and reading him a few pages of *Winnie-the-Pooh*. He listened rapt as she told him about Pooh's and Piglet's not-so-brilliant plan to kidnap Roo. She found herself vaguely disturbed — thinking that it was a little too much like a child abduction plot. Then Kanga gave Piglet a cold bath for his troubles. Order restored to the Hundred Acre Wood.

Crime and punishment.

If only it was that easy in reality.

After Connor was settled in bed, Irvine checked her mobile, hoping that Logan had called. He had not.

'Probably still in the air,' she told herself.

She ran a bath and looked in the mirror at the ever-expanding mass of black and purple bruising that seemed to be spreading across her face.

Undressing in the bathroom and leaving her clothes in a heap on the floor, she slipped into the hot water and dipped her head, soaking her hair and pushing it back. After that she doused a facecloth with cold water from the tap, put it over her face and lay back, trying hard not to remember the fear she felt back in Suzie Murray's building as the man who might have killed Joanna Lewski came at her.

6

Descending into Denver International Airport, Logan stared out of the window of the 747 jet at the vast expanse of the Great Plains. He knew that the city sat in the shadow of the Rocky Mountains and was surprised at how flat the land was.

Cahill was still dozing in the seat next to him. In fact, he'd slept for almost half of the flight while Logan tossed and turned for an hour before giving up on sleep and watching two movies and some episodes of *Seinfeld*.

The terminal building was visible on the left as they cruised in to land: a series of white peaks looking like snow-covered mountains. It was a unique design for an airport. Logan remembered Cahill telling him a while back that the roof had partially collapsed under the weight of snow one year.

The big plane touched down and the pilot engaged reverse thrust. Logan felt himself slide forward on the leather of his seat. Cahill stirred and opened his eyes, blinking away the residual sleep.

'We there yet?' he asked, smiling.

Logan tried to smile, but it felt more like a grimace. He rubbed at his own eyes and felt the early morning start beginning to wear him down. His watch was still on UK time and it showed just after ten at night, totally at odds with the bright sunshine outside.

'What's the time difference?' Logan asked Cahill.

'Seven hours.'

Logan fiddled with his watch until he got it to three. He stretched and yawned as the plane slowed and turned towards the terminal.

'Best way to beat the jet lag is to try to get acclimatised now. Stay awake as long as you can.'

Logan nodded, knew he was right. He also knew that he was going to struggle to make it much past dinner.

'Trouble with this place,' Cahill went on, 'is you've got the altitude to adjust to as well. You'll probably feel nauseous for a day or two till your body gets used to the thin air.'

'Great.'

Cahill clapped a hand on his shoulder and unbuckled his seatbelt. The plane was still moving. Logan had a thing about keeping his belt fastened till the light went off. Cahill was not so much one for the rules. He stood and opened the overhead luggage space, drawing a look from one of the female stewards at the front of the cabin. He smiled at her sheepishly, a look Logan guessed he'd perfected over many years. The woman shook her head and smiled. The benefits of looking a bit like Bob Redford.

All his friends call him Bob.

They trooped off the plane and walked with the other passengers through a series of long corridors. Logan noticed a lot of Native American images on the walls and heard chanted music. He asked Cahill what it was about.

'American guilt. Like all this makes up for everything that was done to the native population. You'll see when we get into town that a lot of the streets are named after tribes as well. Champa, Arapahoe and the like.'

The arrivals hall was like any other place: everyone was tired and desperate to get to their end destination. Logan was glad that they had packed carry-on luggage only as they walked towards the immigration lines.

'This is where we find out', Cahill said, 'if we are persons of interest.' He made quotation marks in the air with his fingers.

'Nice euphemism,' Logan said.

'You ready to be locked away in a room for several hours?'

'Not really. Unless there's a couch I can crash on.'

'There will be a floor. Beyond that, who can say.'

'Look forward to it.'

There were separate queues for US citizens and foreign nationals so Logan and Cahill split up and waited in line. Logan looked across at Cahill and saw that he would be at the desk before Cahill.

He stood nervously behind the white line, watching as a German family in front of him went through the process: the parents having their fingerprints scanned and recorded digitally. The young man behind the desk wore a navy blue uniform with Department of Homeland Security insignia and a sidearm in a belt holster. His shirt was tight on his muscular frame.

210

When the family was done, the officer waved Logan forward. Logan glanced quickly over at the US queue and saw that Cahill was third in line.

'Afternoon, sir,' the officer said as Logan handed over his passport.

The name badge pinned to his shirt read 'Whitaker'.

He looked at the passport and up at Logan. 'What brings you to Denver, sir?'

Unfailingly polite.

'I'm here with a friend. He's over here to see some family.'

Whitaker looked at the line of people behind Logan.

'He's an American citizen,' Logan said. 'He's in that line.'

Whitaker nodded and tapped something on the keyboard in front of him. He looked at a monitor screen hidden from Logan's view under the desk. After a moment he asked Logan to register his fingerprints on the digital scanner. Logan did what he was asked, noticing that the officer had kept hold of his passport. He tapped some more on the keyboard while Logan went through the fingerprint process.

When he was done, Logan looked over again at Cahill and saw that he was now at the immigration desk as well.

Whitaker handed Logan his passport.

'Welcome to Denver, sir. Have a nice stay.'

Logan smiled and said thanks, his heart beating hard enough to bruise itself against his ribcage.

He walked past the desk and over towards the US citizens desk to wait for Cahill. When he got there, Cahill looked over and winked. Logan was amazed that he looked so calm.

Logan went to the far wall and leaned against it, propping his bag up and closing his eyes. He felt exhausted, but knew Cahill was right about beating the jet lag. He couldn't afford to go to sleep now — or in the next few hours.

When he opened his eyes, Cahill was at the immigration desk. The officer was speaking into a radio mike attached to his shirt. Logan came off the wall and felt his pulse start to accelerate again. What if they took Cahill and left him? He didn't know much about US law — had visions of Cahill being transported to Guantanamo Bay in an orange jumpsuit and made to sit on the ground outside all day with a bag over his head.

But the officer finished his radio conversation, looked at Cahill and smiled before handing over his passport.

'See,' Cahill said as he walked up to Logan. 'Piece of cake.'

'I'm glad. Orange isn't your colour.'

Cahill frowned, not understanding.

'Never mind,' Logan said, grabbing the handle of his bag. 'Let's get out of here before they change their minds.'

7

There was more Native American art on the walls of the main terminal building when they came out of the customs hall. Cahill pointed to a sign suspended above them indicating the way out.

'Let's go find a cab,' he said.

Logan nodded and followed after Cahill. They went down a short, wide corridor to automatic doors leading out of the terminal concourse. Logan was suddenly aware of two DHS uniformed officers behind them. He couldn't be sure, but it felt as if they were being shadowed by the two men.

'Are we being followed?' he asked Cahill.

'Yeah. You just noticed?'

'For how long?'

'Since we left the immigration desks.'

'But why didn't they detain us there? I mean, wouldn't that have made more sense?'

'Maybe they want to wait. See what we're going to get up to.'

'You don't believe that.'

Ahead of them, a dark car pulled up outside the exit doors.

'No, I don't,' Cahill answered after a pause.

'So what's up?'

'I reckon it's the FBI that is involved with this thing with Tim. So the DHS guys are probably just keeping an eye on us until the Feds show up.

213

They'll want to take us to the local field office rather than get stuck out here. That's their comfort zone.'

The door of the car facing the terminal opened and a Hispanic man in his early thirties got out. He was wearing a dark suit. Another man got out of the other side of the car. They both had dark hair parted neatly on the side.

'And here they are,' Cahill said.

The men walked forward as Cahill and Logan stepped through the automatic doors. Logan could see the flat expanse of the land beyond the airport, with the sun still high in the clear sky. The air was pleasant, but with an underlying chill as the day wore on. Snow was visible on the Rocky Mountains to the west.

Logan turned to look for the DHS officers and saw them standing inside the doors.

'Mr Cahill?' one of the suits asked, stepping up to within a few feet of them.

'That's me.'

'You must be Mr Finch.'

Logan nodded.

The man reached into his jacket and took out a leather wallet. He showed his identification.

'I'm Special Agent Martinez and this is Special Agent Ruiz. We're with the FBI.'

'You don't say,' Cahill said.

Martinez cocked his head to one side, like he didn't understand what Cahill had said.

'Would you come with us, please?'

Ruiz opened the rear door of the car.

'What's this about?' Logan asked, stepping in

front of Cahill. 'I mean, we're not under arrest, are we?'

Martinez looked at Logan, then at Ruiz.

'No, sir,' Ruiz said.

'We're hoping you could help us with our inquiries,' Martinez said, turning back to face them.

Cahill stayed quiet, content for Logan to take the lead.

'Can you tell us anything else?'

'We can speak more comfortably at our office in town, sir.'

'I'm a lawyer and I'd prefer to know what this is about before I get into that car.'

Ruiz spoke again and Logan began to wonder if he was the more senior of the two agents, even though Martinez had taken the lead initially.

'I'm afraid we're not at liberty to discuss that with you right now, sir. But I'm sure it will all be clearer when we get to the office.'

Cahill looked at Logan and shrugged: it's up to you.

'We're not under arrest?' Logan asked Ruiz.

'No, sir.'

'And you have no plans to send us back the way we came on the first available flight?'

'That's correct, sir. You're welcome to stay here. Mr Cahill is a US citizen after all.'

'You just want to ask us some questions about Tim Stark?'

That got a reaction. Martinez drew in his breath sharply and stared at Logan.

'No one said that.'

'But that's what it's about, right?'

'As I said, sir,' Ruiz interrupted, an edge in his voice like he was annoyed with his partner for reacting. 'We can go over everything in town.'

'I guess we could do that.'

Cahill took his bag from over his shoulder and held it out to Martinez.

'Would you mind?' he said.

Martinez hesitated and took the bag. Logan left his on the concrete and followed Cahill past Martinez and into the back of the car. He looked up to see Martinez set his mouth in a thin line before picking up his bag and heading to the back of the car. He could've sworn that Ruiz smiled a little before he closed the door.

'Game on,' Cahill said, rubbing his hands together.

★ ★ ★

The air con was on full all the way in from the airport and Logan felt gooseflesh rise on his skin. Both agents wore aviator-style sunglasses like in the movies and Logan swallowed an urge to laugh. The journey along the interstate was uneventful and the traffic fairly light. The city looked compact to Logan, the real centre of it probably no bigger than Glasgow. High-rise buildings stretched up with the mountains looming in the background.

Logan did not know the geography of the city centre or the outlying suburbs so he was content to watch the world go by outside. They stopped at a set of traffic lights and two city cops on horseback stopped beside the car. Logan looked up at the men and saw that they wore dark-coloured Stetsons to match their uniforms. One of the officers looked down at Logan and raised a hand in greeting.

'Welcome to the wild west,' Logan said quietly.

'What?' Cahill asked.

'Talking to myself.'

They drove on for another few minutes before the driver, Ruiz, indicated to turn left and slowed the car. Logan looked out of his window as they drove through the entrance to an underground garage that lay below an eighteen-storey office block.

The agents said very little after parking in a bay next to an elevator and going round to the back of the car to retrieve the bags. Logan pulled at the handle on his door but it was locked.

'We'll have to sit tight and wait for them,' Cahill said.

Logan looked out into the garage and saw Martinez and Ruiz carry their bags over to another agent who had emerged from a door to the right of the elevator. He took the bags from them and went back through the door.

'They took our bags,' Logan said.

Cahill glanced out of his window as the agents walked back towards the car. Logan stepped out when the door opened and asked what they had done with the bags.

'Don't worry, sir,' Ruiz told him. 'We took them for safe keeping.'

His overly polite and officious language was beginning to grind on Logan.

'You don't have permission to open and search

the bags. You know that, right?'

Ruiz said nothing for a moment.

'Is there anything in the bags we should know about?'

'No.'

They stood looking at each other.

'Follow me please, sir.'

Ruiz walked towards the elevator while Martinez waited behind them.

Cahill motioned with his head for Logan to follow Ruiz, which he did. Martinez stayed five paces behind them until they got to the elevator. Inside, Ruiz pressed the button for the eighteenth floor and the doors slid shut quietly. No one said anything and there was no horrible muzak playing. Talk about uncomfortable silences.

The reception area of the FBI field office was decorated in muted earth tones with a representation of the shield on the wall behind a desk. A young black woman sat at the desk and smiled when they approached.

'Where are we, Martha?' Ruiz asked the woman.

'Meeting room four.'

'They in there already?'

'Sure are. Go on ahead and I'll let them know you're coming.'

Logan had no idea who 'they' were, but was intrigued to find out.

He and Cahill dutifully followed behind Ruiz again as he used a swipe card to open a secure, frosted-glass door and walked along a narrow corridor past a series of meeting rooms.

They stopped outside a room near the end of the corridor and Ruiz knocked on the door before swiping his card to open it. Inside, two men sat at the far side of a long table. The sun shone in through high, narrow windows.

Both men stood as Ruiz held the door open and motioned for Logan and Cahill to enter the room. When they were in, Ruiz pulled the door closed leaving the four men alone.

One of the men took the lead, walking around the table and holding out his hand. He was a fit-looking black man just under six feet tall. Logan found it difficult to judge his age. Looked like he ran a lot, his smooth skin tight against the contours of his face. Logan stepped forward and shook his hand.

The other man stayed on the far side of the table. He was taller, probably six-two, with greying hair and small, frameless glasses. He clearly kept himself in shape too and his black suit was cut to fit his long frame just so.

'Gentlemen,' the shorter of the men said when he shook Cahill's hand. 'I'm Special Agent in Charge Randall Webb, head of the Denver field office.'

Logan nodded at him.

'And this is Special Agent Cooper Grange. He leads the Joint Terrorism Task Force out of this field office. Have a seat.'

Logan wondered if Webb's use of the word 'Terrorism' was supposed to scare him. It was working.

8

'What brings you to Denver for the first time, Mr Finch?' Randall Webb asked.

'Tim Stark,' Cahill answered.

Webb's eyes flicked to Cahill but the smile stayed on his face. Grange continued to stare at Logan. Webb leaned forward, clasping his hands in front of him on the table.

'You prefer the direct approach, Mr Cahill, is that it?'

Cahill nodded.

'I do.'

'Fair enough.'

Webb sat back and turned to Grange.

'It's all yours, Coop.'

Grange took his time, showing them that he was in control of the room and would dictate the pace of the conversation. He reminded Logan of Tom Hardy in the power that clearly lay behind his languid surface.

'Gentlemen, I'm sure you will appreciate that there's very little information that we are able to disclose concerning matters under inquiry.'

'So there *is* an active FBI inquiry underway into Tim Stark's death?' Logan asked.

Grange regarded him like a lizard does an insect it's considering for breakfast.

'Perhaps I didn't make myself clear enough. I'm afraid you've wasted your trip if you came to find out what's going on.'

'Is that what we tell Tim's wife?' Cahill said, his tone even. 'I mean, that his death is not important enough for anyone even to tell her about it?'

'You keep talking about his death . . . '

'That's because he's dead.'

' . . . but no one here has confirmed that.'

Logan was concerned that Cahill would use the information they had got from DHS and land his contact in a disciplinary process. Or on the receiving end of a prosecution for revealing sensitive material.

'Why don't you confirm that now for us?' he said. 'Clear everything up, you know.'

'Like I said — '

'I get it. You can't say.'

Cahill stood and pushed his chair back. Grange watched him but did not move.

'I guess', Cahill said, 'that if we're not under arrest and you're not going to tell us anything, there's no reason for this meeting to continue. We're free to go.'

'Any time you like.'

Logan looked at Webb, noticed a tension in his body language that had not been there before.

'Look,' Logan interrupted. 'Why don't we all save some time and effort and talk about why you pulled us in. I mean, Alex and I are tired and pretty cranky after being on the go all day. I know I need a good night's sleep. So why don't you come out and say what you've got to say without all the dancing.'

Webb put a hand on Grange's forearm.

'You're a lawyer back in Britain, Mr Finch. Is

221

that right?' Webb asked.

'I'm sure you know it is.'

Webb smiled and nodded. Cahill sat back down.

'And you've done some business with our government?'

'Yes.' He was cautious now.

'So you know how we like to operate. Take our time. Check all the angles.'

Logan nodded.

'So why not let us get on and do that without upsetting everything? We do have a plan, you know.'

'I'm certain you do. But Alex here lost a good friend and that man's wife can't start the grieving process until she knows what happened. I mean, right now she thinks that her husband is mixed up in some bad business. And this was a man of the highest integrity as I understand it.'

Webb steepled his fingers and glanced at Grange.

'You are correct about that. He was a man of the highest integrity. Right to the end.'

'You're confirming that he is dead?'

Webb closed his eyes slowly and nodded.

'Thank you,' Cahill said. 'I know I can be a hard-ass, but I respect that you told us.'

'Now, can we agree that you leave well enough alone and let us get on with our job?'

Logan was about to say yes when Cahill cut across him.

'I want to know what this is about. Was Tim still on the government payroll? Did you have him undercover in something?'

'I can't tell you that.'

Cahill jabbed a finger at Grange.

'Why is the head of your terrorist team here for this meeting? Did someone bring that plane down on purpose?'

Webb sighed. 'I really can't say any more.'

'Can't? Or won't?'

'Take it any way you like,' Grange said.

Logan felt his shoulders sink. Jesus, why did it always have to become a dick-measuring contest with these guys? Cahill invariably won when they got slapped on the table.

'Coop . . . ' Webb said softly.

'If you won't tell us, we'll find someone interested enough to take this public,' Cahill said.

'You mean the press?' Grange snorted.

He was trying *way* too hard to be cool about this, Logan thought.

'Sure,' Cahill answered. 'The press.'

'We could have you arrested right now for making that threat. Both of you.'

Grange and his adherence to the rules.

Webb interjected. 'We know your background, Mr Cahill, and it's very impressive. There's no need for you to demonstrate your allegiance to this country any more than you already have.'

'So play straight with me. I know the rules of the game. What you tell me here does not go outside these four walls.'

'What about Mrs Stark?'

'I'll tell her that Tim is dead. That the FBI confirmed it. Beyond that, I'd like to be able to

223

tell her that he was still the man she loved right to the end. How we do that, I'm willing to try to agree with you. I have no desire to compromise an ongoing investigation.'

'I appreciate what you say. But . . . ' Webb opened his hands, palms out. *What can I do?*

'Freedom of information and all that,' Logan said.

'National security overrides any public interest,' Grange said.

'Interesting debate we'd have if we took it to the courts here. Quite big on free speech, I hear.'

Grange dismissed it with a wave of his hand.

Logan turned his attention to Webb.

'Maybe there's a middle ground that will allow us all to leave here content,' he said.

'What do you have in mind?'

'I'm sure that you could draw up some official papers which we could sign. Undertakings of confidentiality in the interests of national security. Under penalty of . . . whatever, if we breach it.'

'I could do that,' Cahill added. 'I've signed my fair share of gag papers working for the flag.'

Webb turned to look at Grange. Looked at Logan.

'The paper's only worth the integrity of the man who signs it.'

Logan looked at Cahill and back at Webb.

'You have any doubts about this man's patriotism or integrity? If so, it would be news to me.'

'And you?'

'I'm a lawyer.'

224

'He wants to be convinced, Logan,' Cahill said.

That brought a smile from Webb. Grange was impassive.

'This is really need to know, sir,' Grange said. 'I can't agree to what he's proposing.'

'Well, it's my call ultimately.'

Grange looked like he'd been slapped.

Webb stood.

'Gentlemen,' he said, 'let me have a few minutes to consider this.'

9

After Webb and Grange had left the room Logan asked Cahill if he thought they would tell them what had been going on with Tim Stark.

'Unlikely.'

'Why?'

'You heard them. All that national security stuff. Plus if this has anything to do with terrorists — '

'Then why is DHS not involved?'

'The Feds like to keep things tight. All law enforcement agencies do. Inter-agency cooperation is something that gets talked about more in the abstract than anything else.'

Cahill got up from his seat and went to the window.

'You weren't serious about going to the press, were you?' Logan asked.

'No. And they knew it.'

'So if they decide that they won't tell us anything else, where do we go from here?'

'I haven't thought that far ahead.'

Cahill turned back to Logan and leaned against the window sill. Logan shook his head.

'I love it when a plan comes together.'

Cahill laughed.

★　★　★

They had been waiting for a half-hour — Cahill starting to get restless — when Webb came in on his own. Logan took this for a good sign.

Webb made them wait, pouring a glass of water and flicking through a legal pad with handwritten notes before speaking.

'Mr Cahill. I checked with your former boss in the service.'

'Scott Boston?'

'Yes.'

'Scott's a good man.'

'That he is. And he spoke highly of you.'

Cahill nodded but didn't say anything. Webb toyed with a pen on the table, as though he were still trying to decide how much he was going to tell them.

'I'll try to answer some of your questions. But I can't reveal anything of operational sensitivity.'

'Sounds fair enough,' Logan said.

Webb leaned forward and looked at Cahill.

'I'm doing this out of respect and as a professional courtesy to someone who has a proud history of serving this country. Nothing more. I don't respond well to threats.'

Cahill met Webb's gaze.

'Do we understand each other?'

'We do,' Cahill answered.

Webb appeared to relax, sat back in his seat.

'The plane Tim Stark was on crashed due to an engine malfunction. That will be made public in the next day or two, which is why I can tell you.'

'Did you think originally that it might have been brought down?' Logan asked. 'Is that why Agent Grange was involved?'

Webb considered Logan for a moment in silence.

'I can't say much more about that right now, I'm sorry.'

'Tell us this,' Cahill said. 'Was Tim using an alias? The reason I ask is that his name was not on the passenger list.'

'He died on that flight. That's your answer.'

'He was working undercover?'

Webb said nothing, inclined his chin and brought it back down. Logan wasn't sure if it was a nod in confirmation and looked at Cahill.

'Okay,' Cahill said, apparently satisfied that it had been intended as an answer to his question.

'Is that enough?' Webb asked.

'It's enough for Tim's wife.'

'And for you?'

'I always prefer to know more than less.' Cahill smiled.

It was Webb's turn to stand and go to the window, looking down at the late afternoon traffic starting to build.

'We carry out background checks on all gun purchases in the country,' Webb said, still facing the window. 'I guess you know that.'

They took it for a rhetorical question and waited for Webb to continue.

'Some time ago a man who had previously come to our attention due to some minor anti-government activities — letter writing, things like that — started to buy up legal weapons. A background check was done automatically each time and because he had a clean record the purchases were approved.'

'But multiple purchases raised a red flag somewhere, right?' Cahill asked.

Webb turned to face them again and nodded.

'As you would expect it to,' he said.

'Then what?'

'He stopped. I mean, after seven purchases in the space of six months he just stopped.'

'So?'

'He also sold his house. Didn't buy another one that we're aware of. No record of him renting either. At least, not under his real name.'

'He was working?'

'He quit. Didn't take up another job.'

'Gets you thinking what is he up to?'

'Correct.'

'Then what?'

'We start working in the background to find out what he's doing. He's got our attention now. We start to look at some associates. Turns out a few of them have also given up steady, decent-paying jobs and don't seem to have replaced them with anything.'

'Associates?' Logan asked.

'All ex-military.'

'They served together?' Cahill asked.

'Afghanistan.' Webb nodded.

A thought occurred to Logan.

'These activities you spoke about,' he said. 'The stuff that initially brought him to your attention. Was it related to the conduct of the war over there?'

'Something like that.'

'So,' Cahill said. 'You manufacture Tim Stark

getting sacked. He has a legitimate anti-government gripe and can find a kindred spirit in this soldier. Ex-soldier.'

Webb nodded.

'Stark was brought in to infiltrate the group.'

Another nod.

Logan frowned. 'I don't get it,' he said. 'I mean, if Stark was fired to give him a reason to be pissed off at the Government so he could use his real name and background, why was he using an alias when he got on the flight?'

'To avoid detection,' Cahill said. 'Am I right?'

'Yes,' Webb said. 'The alias was to send us a message. To let us know that he had been compromised and was coming home. The op was being run out of our headquarters in Washington. That's where Tim was going.'

'So you knew that they were on to him,' Logan said. 'Which is why you thought the plane crash might have been deliberate. To kill Stark?'

'Correct.'

'Turns out it was just his bad luck,' Cahill said.

Webb sat down again. 'You can see why this is sensitive,' he said. 'These people are still out there. Still planning whatever it is that they are going to do.'

'Except now you're blind because your man on the inside is gone.'

'Yes.'

Cahill was quiet for a moment before he spoke again.

'Do you need a replacement?'

10

'You can't be serious,' Logan said to Cahill, sitting in the back of a taxi heading for their hotel.

'Why not?'

'Your life isn't exciting enough already?'

'Look, he said he'd think about it but he wasn't really serious.'

'Why not?'

'I haven't been in the States for a while and I've been out of any recognised agency for even longer. They don't want someone like me. Someone they can't control.'

'So what was that all about? I mean, him saying he'd think about it.'

'He was humouring me.'

'But we're done here, right?'

'We're booked in the hotel for three nights. Why don't we make the most of it?'

'You want to do something about this, don't you? I can see it in your face. Even if Webb wasn't serious about taking you on in some official capacity. You want to be involved.'

Cahill shrugged.

'Christ. You are unbelievable, Alex. You know that?'

'Calm down. I mean, Bruce still has to get back to us on the 'D. Hunter' thing that Melanie found, so why don't we at least check on that while we're here?'

231

'And we can feed whatever we find out into Webb, right?'

'Sure.'

'That was the single most unconvincing thing you have ever said to me. And that's saying a lot.'

* * *

They got to the hotel after six. It was a modern four-star affair with a restaurant on the ground floor and a spacious reception and bar area on the next level. They checked in quickly and went to the room — a decent-sized space with two double beds.

'Cosy,' Cahill said when they walked in.

Logan found a TV concealed behind doors in a unit opposite the beds and turned to a local news channel. They unpacked their gear in a few minutes, storing the bags in the unit beneath the TV.

'You going to call Melanie Stark?' Logan asked.

Cahill looked at his watch. 'Yeah, I guess I should.'

'At least it's good news.'

Cahill stared at him.

'I mean, sort of.'

'I suppose.'

'I'll go explore the hotel. Give you some time to make the call alone. Then we can grab some dinner.'

* * *

Logan went down to the ground floor and got a coffee to go from an outlet there. After that, he went to the reception level and saw signs for a shopping mall which he followed to a set of double doors that led directly on to the first floor of the mall. He wasn't sure if the mall or the hotel was there first.

He wandered along looking at the shops and went down to the ground level where he found a rent-a-car desk. He figured they would be better off with a car than taking taxis or being on foot.

He sat on a bench outside a fast-food outlet and felt the nausea that Cahill had warned him about. It was low level, but still unpleasant. He couldn't stand sitting there with the smell wafting out of the place so he walked back up the stairs, following the signs for the hotel. He pulled out his phone and saw that he had a voicemail message.

Ellie had left a short message telling him that she was fine and not to worry. That he could call her any time anyway. He smiled when he heard her voice.

* * *

Back in the room, Cahill was sombre.

'Tough call?' Logan asked, sitting on his bed.

Cahill nodded. 'How did you get on?' he asked.

'Other than feeling sick . . . '

'What did I tell you?'

' . . . I found a car rental place. I figured we should get a car while we're here.'

'Good idea. You can do that tomorrow after breakfast.'

'You mean *we* can do it?'

'No.'

'What are you going to do?'

'I've got an errand to run.'

'Alex . . . '

'It's nothing. Just personal.'

Logan squinted at him, unsure if he was being lied to. He decided to leave it for now.

'Oh, and Bruce sent me an e-mail.'

'Anything interesting?'

'Only four D. Hunters in the metro Denver area.'

'Bruce get backgrounds on them?'

'Of course. All pretty bland.'

'We're still going to give them to the FBI to check them out, though. Right?'

'Not right now. I mean, we can do some preliminary digging around now that we're here.'

Logan didn't have the energy to argue with him any more.

'Whatever. Look, I'm going to watch some TV and then get to sleep.'

Cahill looked at his watch.

'It's only gone seven. What about dinner?'

'If I make it to nine I'll be doing well enough. And I'm not in the mood to eat.'

'Suit yourself. I'm going to go for a walk. I'll grab a burger or something.'

Logan couldn't muster the enthusiasm to ask him if that was a casual walk or something else altogether.

Cahill saw the look on his face.

'Jesus, it's just a walk.'

11

Thursday

Irvine logged on to her computer at Pitt Street and checked her e-mails. There was one from Armstrong timed at six-thirty the night before telling her about his visit to the agents who handled the lettings for the accountants. It was short and to the point:

Dead end. Speak tomorrow.

Irvine took her file of papers out and went through what they had so far. It might not lead her anywhere, but at least it would focus her mind on things. Maybe it would allow her to figure out where they went with the inquiry now. She jotted down some brief notes on a pad as she read. When she was done, she looked over the notes she had made:

Fentanyl/Heroin — Russia?
Overdoses — bad drugs
Lewski body dump — dealer did it?
Dealer and Lewski involved — sex
Cops and Lewski?
Accountants and Lewski?
Suzie Murray — is she lying + does she know the dealer?

She leaned back in her chair and thought about the last point. In the aftermath of the encounter with the man on the stairs she had kind of rushed through the interview with Murray. She looked in the file again for the notes she had made after the interview and re-read them.

Murray had said that Lewski moved into the flat about a month ago and she was the one who knew the dealer — the man who had assaulted Irvine. According to Murray's story, Lewski had brought him to the flat a couple of weeks later. But Murray never used his gear. Lewski traded sex for her stuff. The stuff that had probably killed her.

A question nagged at Irvine's mind — if she was right in thinking it was the dealer who had dumped Lewski's body in the river, why had he gone back to see Murray the day after Lewski's death? He would have known that the flat would be checked out by the police and that Murray would be questioned. So it was a risk for him to go there. A big risk.

Irvine couldn't think what the reason might be. She looked down at the notes again. The only thing she could think of was drugs. That the dealer had left some of the bad gear at the flat and went to get it. But she couldn't convince herself that a small stash of the stuff — only enough for personal use — would be worth the risk to him. And he had not been carrying any large package when she had encountered him.

She called Armstrong. It rang three times before he answered.

'Kenny, I've been thinking about this Lewski thing again. It occurred to me that there might be something Suzie Murray hasn't told us. About her relationship with the guy who gave Lewski the drugs.'

'The guy who gave you the black eye?'

'Yes.'

'What about him?'

'Well, I mean, why would he go back to the flat the next day and risk a confrontation with us? He would know that we would go to the flat and try to speak to Murray. What was so important to him that he would risk that?'

'Drugs, probably.'

'I thought of that. But he wouldn't risk it for a small stash, would he?'

Armstrong was quiet for a while.

'I wouldn't do it if it was me. But I'm not him. These guys are not the smartest, you know.'

'The top guys are.'

'They *think* they are.'

'I don't know. It doesn't make sense to me.'

Armstrong sighed.

'Remind me what she said. Murray, I mean.'

Irvine went through it all again for him.

'What do you think?' she asked when she was finished.

'I don't know. Let me think about it some more and we can speak later.'

'When are you coming here?'

'I need to go to SCDEA in Paisley. Catch up on some other work. See you before lunch.'

Irvine hung up. She thought that Armstrong would be the best person to look for a discrepancy in the story. He knew the drugs scene and she did not. She blew out a breath and tapped her pen on the desk.

She decided that she would go and find Jim Murphy and press him again for progress on the blood results and the CCTV footage. They were the only live leads that were still to bear fruit.

★ ★ ★

'I'm going through it now,' Murphy said, pointing at the screen in front of him.

Irvine saw familiar images from the city centre cameras.

'Anything so far?'

Murphy tapped on a notepad by his mouse mat where he had written what looked like some kind of code to Irvine. She picked it up and looked at the random numbers.

'What's this?'

'Reference points on the film for where there might be something you want to look at. An individual or a vehicle. Something like that.'

'How much more do you have to go?'

Murphy opened another window on his screen and pointed at it. Irvine was none the wiser.

'Another file after this one. And I'm about halfway through it now.'

'Can you send that other file to me and I'll look at it. Speed things up.'

He nodded and clicked on the file, sending it to her e-mail address.

'Anything from the lab yet?' she asked.

He looked up at her from his seat.

'You are a pain in the arse, you know that.' He smiled.

He opened a drawer in his desk and handed her a report.

She scanned it quickly and saw the expected references to fentanyl and heroin.

Irvine thanked him again and went back downstairs to her desk, feeling a little more positive now that there was progress being made.

There was a message on her phone when she got there and she saw that she had a missed call from Armstrong. She dialled into her voicemail.

'It's Kenny. Look, I just got a call on something. Another body. It's unconnected to our thing but it's my case and I need to go to the scene. If you want to tag along and we can catch up that's fine. Give me a call.'

Irvine called him back and said that she had news to report and would tag along.

'I'll swing by and pick you up in five minutes,' Armstrong told her. 'It's on my way.'

Irvine said fine and hung up. She was getting far too used to the sight of dead bodies.

12

Armstrong was waiting out on the street in front of the headquarters building with the car engine running.

'You in a hurry?' Irvine asked as she got into the passenger seat. 'I mean, so far as I know, the dead guy probably isn't going anywhere.'

'You're funny.'

He drove away from the building and headed east out of the city centre. Irvine looked out of the car at the redevelopment that was going on — gentrification of poorer areas in the east end. Some property developers would likely make a bundle, even in a depressed market like now.

'Who's the body?' Irvine asked, turning to face Armstrong.

'Guy I've come across before.'

'You said that earlier. What's the story?'

'You really want to know?'

'Yeah.'

'You heard of Frank Parker?'

'The gangster? Of course. It's not him, is it?'

'One of his senior guys. Russell Hall. We think he's the one who runs Parker's drug operation.'

'Parker's the nightclub guy, right?'

'Yeah. He's got three in the city and is starting to expand his empire to bars and restaurants.'

'He owns a chunk of real estate on the south side too, I hear?'

'Correct.'

'Wasn't there some issue over a fire in a warehouse years ago?'

'Like, twenty years ago. Frank came out of it clean with over a million in insurance money. It's how he got to where he is. That was his stake money.'

'Torch job?'

'That was the rumour.'

'You got someone inside his operation?'

Armstrong looked sideways at her. 'No.'

'That the official answer?'

'That's the answer I'm giving you.'

Irvine knew better than to pry any further. She assumed that undercover operations required a small circle of knowledge to avoid leaks.

'Blood results came in on Lewski,' she said.

'And?'

'They found the same stuff as the others.'

'No surprise.'

'Any more thoughts on Suzie Murray?' she asked.

'I don't know. I had one idea.'

'Go on, then.'

'It's something I heard about when I was in Quantico a few years ago. I was over there . . . '

'The FBI place?'

'Yeah. A bunch of us went over to see how they do things.'

'And?'

'Impressive. The resources they have committed to the drug war is beyond anything that we can manage.'

'No, I mean what was the thing you heard?'

'Oh. Well, they busted an operation in South

241

Florida where the bad guys had used prostitutes as mules. The drugs came ashore, got transported to a car dealership and from there went to Miami on public transport. They sent the prostitutes down to the dealership from Miami on the bus and they took the stuff back in plain bags on the bus again.'

'Not very high tech.'

'That's the point. Makes it difficult to track.'

'So you think maybe our guys took a leaf out of the Americans' book, that Lewski and Murray are mules?'

'Maybe. Was the only thing I could come up with.'

'Would explain her attitude. Not wanting to speak to us.'

Armstrong slowed the car. 'Here we are,' he said, pointing at an area of waste ground opposite an industrial park.

The Scenes of Crime team were there and had erected a portable white tent around the body. The area had been cordoned off with tape and uniformed officers patrolled the perimeter while the forensic technicians scoured the area on their hands and knees looking for evidence.

Armstrong stopped his car at the edge of the ground where a crowd of locals had gathered to see what was going on. It was more interesting than anything on daytime TV.

'You coming?' he asked, unclipping his seatbelt.

'Why not.'

They walked together across the grass and showed their badges to get inside the cordon.

Irvine saw a man standing at the entrance to the tent and recognised him as Paul Warren, the SCDEA Director General.

'Kenny,' Warren said as they approached. 'And DC Irvine. What brings you here?'

'I'm tagging along with Kenny. We were discussing Joanna Lewski.'

'Right. You'll want to see this, Kenny.'

Warren turned and pulled aside the entrance flap to the tent. The three of them stepped inside.

A man dressed in a grey suit and a pale blue shirt lay on his back, all colour drained from him — his skin an unnatural, waxy grey. Irvine stared at the multiple stab wounds on his abdomen and neck, the ground around him drenched in blood.

'That's him all right,' Armstrong said. 'What do we know so far?'

Warren was about to answer when Irvine looked at the man's face and inhaled sharply, bringing a hand up to her injured eye.

'What?' Armstrong said, turning to her.

'That's him.'

'Who?'

'The man who attacked me at Joanna Lewski's flat.'

13

They stood by Armstrong's car, looking at the tent in the middle of the waste ground.

'You're certain it was him?' Warren asked Irvine.

'Yes. I mean, I only saw his face briefly but it's definitely him.'

'Where does this take us, Kenny?'

Armstrong stared at the tent before looking at Warren.

'Russell Hall was Frank Parker's enforcer for a few years before Parker put him in charge of the drug business that he runs out of his clubs. We've been looking at putting a case together now for the last eighteen months.'

'What's the connection with Joanna Lewski?'

'I don't know. All I can think is that Hall met her, maybe in one of the clubs, and that either he was using her as a mule to bring drugs into the city from wherever they came into the UK or he was using drugs to buy sex from her.'

'Could be both,' Irvine added.

Armstrong nodded.

'So we think this whole thing goes back to Parker?' Warren asked. 'Maybe he even had Hall killed because of the screw-up with Lewski. That would be beautiful. If we could hang a murder on him . . . ' He smiled and shook his head.

'I think I should go see Parker now,' Armstrong said.

'Why now? We should wait till we have it all tied up. Then we go in with the rams and take his door down.'

'We don't have anything like enough evidence for that. And I don't think we'll get it any time soon either. I'd prefer that we go talk to him now.'

'Risky.'

'I could take the lead,' Irvine said. 'Explain that I'm investigating Lewski's murder and we think this guy Hall might be connected to it. We know that he works for Parker so . . . '

'I can sit in the background and stay quiet,' Armstrong said. 'If he doesn't think it's linked to the drug investigation, he might be a little less on guard.'

'Might work,' Warren said. 'Do it.'

* * *

They drove back towards the city centre, that sense of excitement building when a case is starting to take shape.

'Where do we find Parker?' Irvine asked.

Armstrong looked at his watch.

'He usually has lunch at one of his own places so we'll try there first.'

'Does he know you? I mean, that you're with the SCDEA?'

'He knows me all right.'

It sounded to Irvine as though there was something more to Armstrong's comment than being on opposite sides of the law. It sounded personal. She decided not to push it for now.

245

Armstrong drove to the Merchant City area and parked at a meter opposite an expensive-looking restaurant. There were some professional types sitting at the tables by the window: sharp suits and good haircuts.

'That it?' Irvine asked as they got out of the car.

'This is the flagship place. Opened six months ago. His favourite place for lunch.'

'I assume he won't be alone?'

'Correct. Gangster types like their entourages. He'll have some heavies with him.'

Irvine nodded and they jogged across the street when there was a gap in the traffic. Armstrong pulled the door of the restaurant open and motioned for Irvine to go in. They stood at a sign that told them to please wait to be seated and Irvine spoke when a maître d' type in a black wool suit and an open-necked white shirt came over.

'Is Mr Parker in today?' Irvine asked, producing her warrant card and holding it out close to the man's face.

He took a step back, looked at the card for a while and then at Irvine.

'You've had your hair done,' he said. 'Wait here.'

Irvine turned the card to look at it and saw that she had her blond bob when the picture was taken. She looked a lot younger than she remembered.

'Nice picture,' Armstrong said.

The maître d' came back after a couple of minutes.

'Is it Mr Parker Senior or Junior that you're looking for?'

'Senior,' Armstrong said.

The maître d' looked at him for a moment.

'I don't believe that I saw your identification, sir.'

Armstrong took out his SCDEA gold shield and showed it to him.

'Mr Parker thought that it might be you. Please follow me.'

Irvine glanced at Armstrong but his face was impassive. She wondered again what it was between him and Parker. It seemed like maybe she would find out once the two of them were in the same room together.

The maître d' led them through the restaurant, past a central bar area and into a private room at the back of the building. He left the room and closed the door.

The room was dark, lit subtly and decorated in sombre tones of black and deep burgundy. There was a large round table set in a half-moon booth with a curved, padded leather seat. An immaculately clean white tablecloth covered the table.

Two large men sat off to the side under a window and stared at Irvine and Armstrong. There were four other people in the room — three men and a woman — and they were all sitting in the booth, sipping wine.

The woman was a young blonde who immediately got up and walked past Irvine to leave the room. She teetered by on monster stilettos and her teeth flashed white in a deeply tanned face. Parker was a little obvious in his taste for women.

The oldest of the three men at the table was also well tanned and had dark, curly hair swept back and gelled in place. Grey flecked the hair at his temples. The youngest of the men looked like he could have come from the same gene pool and Irvine made them for father and son: the Parkers.

The other man was thin and wore glasses on his narrow nose. Weaselly was a word tailor made to fit him.

'DS Armstrong,' Parker Senior said, standing and holding out a hand for Armstrong to shake.

Armstrong stared at him but made no move to accept the greeting.

'Frank,' was all he said.

'Mr Parker, I'm DC Irvine with Strathclyde Police CID.'

Parker nodded and sat down.

Irvine walked forward and pulled out a chair from the table. She sat down. Armstrong stayed standing behind her.

'Can you tell me what you know about Joanna Lewski?' Irvine asked.

'Don't know her. Who told you that I did?'

'What about Russell Hall?'

Parker's eyes flicked to Armstrong. 'I know Russell,' he said, his eyes remaining on Armstrong's face.

'How do you know him, Mr Parker?'

He looked back at Irvine. 'He used to work for me.'

'Used to?'

'Yes.'

'And now?'

'Now he doesn't.'

One of the goons sitting off to the side laughed.

'Do you mean because he's dead?'

This took Parker by surprise. He leaned forward, his hands coming up on to the table. 'What?'

'I asked you if the reason he didn't work for you any more is because someone killed him last night.'

Parker Junior stiffened next to his father.

'This Joanna person,' Parker Senior said, 'I take it that she's also dead. I mean, that's why the CID is here, right?'

'That's correct.'

'Did Russell kill her?'

'What makes you ask that?'

'He had difficulty controlling his impulses. Back when I knew him.'

'Which was when?'

'Russell hasn't worked for us for the last three months,' Junior said. 'I run the clubs now.'

Irvine could have sworn his chest puffed out as he spoke. A look of annoyance passed across his father's face. The message wasn't lost on Irvine and she knew that Armstrong would have picked it up: Frank Parker Junior was now in charge of the Parker organisation's drug trade.

14

'So you're saying that you fired Mr Hall, is that correct?' Irvine asked, looking at Junior.

'Yes,' his father answered. 'It wasn't working out.'

'He'd been with your organisation for some time?'

'Nothing lasts for ever.'

'So it would seem.'

Junior smirked. Irvine had taken an immediate dislike to him. She wondered if he would be quite so confident if his father wasn't here.

'When was the last time you saw him?'

'Haven't seen him since we . . . let him go,' Senior answered.

'Can you account for your whereabouts last night? All of you.'

Irvine made a point of looking around the room and making eye contact with everyone.

'Yes. Let us know what you need.'

Senior reached into his jacket and took out a business card. He leaned across the table and held it out until Irvine took it from him. He knew the police had a job to do and he understood the rules of the game. Irvine wasn't so sure that Junior would look at it in the same way.

Armstrong moved forward and sat next to Irvine, across the table from the Parkers.

'What was it, Frank?' he asked. 'Russell not making enough money for you or something?'

Parker Senior looked at Irvine and smiled.

'Your colleague doesn't think that I'm a legitimate businessman.'

'I'm not in a position to comment,' Irvine said. 'And right now I don't really care. There are two murder inquiries ongoing and that's my only concern.'

'We had nothing to do with them,' Junior said loudly, leaning forward. 'So why don't you fuck off.'

Irvine stared at him.

'Everybody out,' Parker Senior said sharply.

No one moved.

'I mean now.' His voice was even but firm.

The goons got up and shuffled to the door, followed quickly by the weasel in the glasses.

Junior stayed put, but shrank back in his seat.

'You too, son.'

Junior glared at his father for a long moment before sliding across the leather seat and out of the booth. He slammed the door as he left.

'I apologise for my son's ignorance,' Parker said. 'That's not how I like to do business.'

'Frank,' Armstrong said, 'cut the bullshit, okay? You're not impressing anyone here.'

Parker shrugged.

'Who was Russell working for after he left you?'

Parker flicked at an imaginary piece of fluff on the lapel of his suit jacket.

'If you tell us, we'll be going after them hard. Maybe help take out some of the competition.'

'I don't know what you mean by competition.'

Armstrong sighed. Irvine felt that his intervention was proving counter-productive.

251

'Mr Parker,' she said. 'I'm sure you would be just as pleased as we would be to take a killer off the streets. Make it safer for everyone. That's my aim here. Nothing else.'

She maintained eye contact with him, hoping that Armstrong would stay quiet.

Parker looked from Irvine to Armstrong and back. 'I appreciate what you're trying to do,' he said eventually. 'If I can help I will.'

Irvine nodded.

'Do you know who Mr Hall was working for after he left your employment?'

'I heard it was someone . . . new to the business scene.'

Armstrong turned his face away from Parker and snorted.

'Anything you can do to help us would be appreciated,' Irvine said.

Parker regarded her silently for a moment. 'Andrew Johnson,' he said finally.

Irvine wondered if he was joking.

'The Andrew Johnson who's dead? Murdered. I mean, it was all over the newspapers. I'm one of the investigating officers.'

'Yes, that Andrew Johnson.'

'So what are you telling us? Did Russell Hall kill Johnson and take over his organisation?'

Parker smiled benignly.

'I would be very surprised if Russell had big enough balls. I mean, Johnson was out of his league. A proper psychopath.'

'I'm not following what you're telling us.'

'Russell worked for Johnson until his unfortunate meeting with a bullet. Now he works for the

252

man who succeeded Johnson.'

'And is this man still alive, or do I have another body to discover?'

He laughed this time.

'I don't know his name. But I understand that he is very much alive.'

'I'd appreciate it if you would let me know if any of your sources of information can identify this man.'

Parker looked at her for a long moment without blinking.

'I'll see what I can do,' he said. 'But whoever he is, I'd stay well clear, you know. Anyone crazy enough to take out Johnson is deserving of respect.'

Irvine took a business card from her pocket and placed it on the table in front of Parker. She stood and waited for Armstrong to do the same.

'Thank you for your assistance, Mr Parker,' Irvine said as Armstrong started to rise.

★   ★   ★

'I know how to deal with these scumbags,' Armstrong said, his voice rising.

Irvine stared at him from the passenger seat of the car.

'And you don't treat them like that.'

'Like what?'

'Giving them any respect or legitimacy.'

'I didn't.'

'He's a drug dealer and a gangster.'

'Did we advance the investigation?'

'That's not the point.'

253

'Maybe not to you. Look, it's obvious that this guy has done something to get at you in the past. I don't need to know about it. But he gave us a lead. The rest of it I'll leave to you SCDEA boys to take care of. You brought me in to look at the deaths. That's what I'm doing.'

Armstrong looked ready to argue but the fight seemed to drain out of him. He started the car and put his hands on the steering wheel.

'Ask me about him again when this is all done.'

'Okay.'

'But for now you're right.'

'What he gave us, if it's correct, is good stuff. We can link the Johnson case to Hall and Lewski. Get all these cases closed. This is real progress.'

'Let me see if I follow,' Armstrong said. 'Hall goes to work for Johnson. Johnson's outfit is the one selling the bad gear. For whatever reason, Johnson gets killed and the new boss takes over.'

'Right. And this new guy must be the one who killed Hall.'

'It's a safe bet that Hall gave the drugs to Lewski for sex and then when she died he dumped her body to get rid of the evidence. Or, at least, that was his plan. Then what? Hall's boss has him taken out for making such a mess.'

'Seems like he covers his tracks in extreme ways. The boss, I mean.'

'I agree.'

'This new guy is obviously a very serious individual.'

15

Armstrong dropped Irvine off before heading over to the SCDEA HQ in Paisley to see if he could find out anything more about a new face on the scene — either from his colleagues or from street contacts. He said he'd call if he got anything concrete.

Irvine opened the CCTV file from Murphy's e-mail and settled down for a long afternoon. She started watching, fast forwarding through stretches of film that were clearly of no help.

After more than an hour, she noticed a silver Mercedes saloon that she had seen on the film before. She moved backwards and forwards through the film, following the car as best she could. It went south towards the river and out of sight for about twenty minutes before reappearing heading north.

'What were you doing down at the river?' she said aloud.

Dumping Joanna Lewski's body.

She reviewed the film again until she found a clear shot of the car's licence plate and wrote it in her notes before calling DVLA. When she got through to the section she needed she explained who she was, gave her warrant card number and asked for confirmation of the registered keeper of the Mercedes.

She wrote down the name that the operator gave her: Russell Hall.

She called Armstrong and told him what she had found — asked if he had heard anything from his colleagues.

'Nothing so far. Most of the guys here didn't even know that Hall had left Frank Parker's organisation. He's covered his tracks well.'

'You coming back here today?'

'Probably not. There're still some people I can talk to. Maybe hit the streets as well, to find some sources.'

Irvine looked at her watch. It was approaching four in the afternoon.

'I guess we've done what we can today,' she said. 'It all starts again tomorrow with the lab results from Hall's scene.'

'We're a step closer than we were. That's something.'

'Sure,' she said, not convinced.

'You heard from your new best pal yet?'

She didn't know what he was talking about and said so.

'Frank Parker.'

Irvine sighed. 'No. And get over it.'

Part Eight:
Brothers in Arms

1

Seth Raines dressed in a pair of Khaki Dockers and a black shirt. He was watching TV when his mobile phone rang. He recognised the number as being the passenger that he had taken up to the compound.

'Everything is checked out at my end,' the man on the other end of the line said. 'Now it's up to you. When do you want to exchange?'

'I need to speak to my team.'

'I appreciate that there's a lot to prepare.' The man paused. 'Do you have any security concerns?'

Raines wondered if the man was also having him followed and knew about his FBI shadows. Whatever. Honesty was how he liked to do business.

'The FBI are following me.'

'That's unfortunate.'

'They don't have anything on me. It's harassment.'

'Why?'

'In the past I've had occasion to put some things in writing that may have upset some people. Given them a false impression of who I am and what I might do.'

'False impression?'

'Yes. Plus, we think that one of them was trying to infiltrate our team.'

That brought a long silence. Raines said

259

nothing for the duration.

'This is the first I have heard of this.'

'It's sorted now. And, anyway, he never got close enough to know what we were planning.'

'But they suspect something?'

'They don't have a clue what this is about.'

'In my experience, they are not lateral thinkers.'

'I agree. We're safe.'

'Do you have a contingency for dealing with the current FBI interest in you?'

'Yes.'

They both knew what he meant.

'Good. You'll be in touch when the final timing is set?'

'Yes.'

The man ended the call without saying anything else.

Raines knew that he needed to make at least one final trip up to the mountain compound before he finalised the arrangements with the man. That would prove awkward with the FBI tail. He wondered if it might be possible to go part of the way by bus or train and get one of the team to pick him up at the other end. That might be enough to get them off his tail.

He dialled Matt Horn's number.

'How's your head after last night, Seth?'

'I'm fine. I didn't have much anyway.'

'Can't say the same. What's up?'

'I got a call from the guy this morning.'

'And?'

'He's looking to finalise things. You're okay with that now?'

'Yes. But it doesn't mean I have to sing and dance about it.'

'No one's asking you to. Listen, I need to go to the mountain to wrap things up. You have to be there as well.'

'I know. When?'

'Tomorrow.'

'What about your friends at the FBI?'

'I'm still thinking about how to deal with them. Leave it with me.'

2

Cahill left the hotel room after seven on Thursday morning with Logan still asleep. He went down to the bar area and sat by the window before calling Tom Hardy. It was mid-afternoon back in the UK.

'Tom, it's me. I'm going to need to visit that contact you were arranging over here.'

The gun.

'Sure. Want me to e-mail you the details?'

'Yeah. You got it now?'

'I do. I'll hang up and send it.'

'Who is he?'

'She. It's a woman.'

'How do we know her? I mean, what's her background?'

'I didn't enquire. She runs a legit gun shop. Does a sideline for those in need of something untraceable. I'm told that she is very careful to ensure that it's only those with right on their side that she deals with.'

Cahill smiled.

'Use my name,' Hardy said. 'That'll be good enough.'

* * *

Cahill took a taxi to a suburb in the predominantly white South Denver area. The city was like a lot of the big metropolitan centres

262

in the US — the neighbourhoods were divided largely by race. In Denver it was African Americans in the east, Hispanics on the north and west sides and whites in the south. There were always exceptions and, as the cab drew up on the opposite side of the street from the gun shop, Cahill saw a black woman behind the counter. It was eight-thirty and the shop was already open.

He got out of the cab and spent a little time checking out the area. It was unremarkable. Neither particularly affluent nor poor, and the houses were clean and tidy with small, well-kept front yards. It was a good place for wanting to go unnoticed.

Cahill walked across the street and went into the shop, a bell above his head ringing as he pushed the front door open. The woman behind the counter looked over at him and smiled. She was serving a man in a checked shirt wearing a Broncos cap.

'Be with you in a minute,' she said to him in a Boston accent — all elongated vowels. 'Have a look around.'

Cahill nodded and said he would. He didn't know if she recognised him as one of her *other* customers.

He walked around the small shop, marvelling again, now that he was home, at the availability of such destructive weapons to members of the public and seeing posters advertising gun clubs and shooting ranges. He was a trained soldier and knew how to use these things, but any idiot could walk in here and buy one if they checked out okay.

Cahill was at the back of the shop when he heard the bell ring again as the other customer left. He walked over to the counter and smiled at the woman, offering his hand in greeting. She shook it.

'I'm Elizabeth Holmes. Call me Lizzie. What can I do for you?'

She had a firm handshake and wore a white T-shirt with a Smith & Wesson logo. Cahill could see the slender, well-toned muscles of her forearm as she shook his hand. Her hair was short and she had wide-set brown eyes. He made her for late forties.

'Tom Hardy said I should come see you if I was in town,' Cahill said.

She held his hand a moment longer then released it, putting both her hands on her hips. It was a girlish pose, but she pulled it off.

'I'm always happy to meet new friends,' she said.

'Likewise.'

'You an ex-cop or what?'

'Army then Secret Service.'

'You get around. What you up to now?'

Getting to know you.

'Close protection. Corporates, politicians. That kind of thing, you know.'

Her eyes opened wider. 'Any celebrities?'

'Sometimes. I mean, try to avoid them.'

'Very sensible. Bet they pay well, though.'

'That they do, Lizzie.'

She looked at him for a moment and walked around the counter, heading for the front door.

264

'Give me a second to close up and I'll take you downstairs.'

She turned a lock on the door and put a sign in the window telling her customers that she'd be back in a half-hour.

'Follow me,' she said as she went towards a door at the back of the counter area.

He went through the door behind her and down a narrow set of stairs. There was another door at the bottom with three heavy-duty locks which she opened. The door swung inwards and Cahill could tell from the way she held it that it was armoured — the wood fascia intended as a disguise.

He walked past her into a large, well-lit basement. It was a workshop with a couple of long benches and shelving racks on two walls. There was a large metal cabinet on one of the other walls.

'What's your story?' Cahill asked as she picked a key from a chain attached to the belt of her jeans.

She looked back at him from over her shoulder.

'Boston PD. Twenty years.'

'Why this now? Why Denver?'

She shrugged. 'Why not?'

Cahill walked over to the cabinet as she opened it, displaying a number of handguns arranged on metal pins. There were two shelves at the bottom filled with boxes of ammunition.

'Before we go any further,' she said, turning to him and putting a hand firmly on his chest, 'I know that you've been vouched for, but what's

265

your intention with my stuff?'

'Defensive only.'

She looked hard at his eyes.

'Okay, soldier. I had to ask, you know.'

It came out like: *Okay, Soul-jah. Hadda ask, y'know.*

Cahill nodded. 'Of course.'

'What are you after?'

Wotcha ahftah.

'Something reliable, like a Glock.'

'I got plenty of them bad boys. Take your pick.'

Cahill looked at the guns and pointed to the one he wanted. She told him to go ahead and he lifted it from its mount and checked it out.

'Good for you?' she asked.

He nodded. 'It'll do.'

He reached down and grabbed an identical weapon.

'And this,' Cahill said. 'Just, you know . . . '

She nodded. 'Can never be too careful. Ammo?'

She was Cahill's kind of person. Direct. No words wasted.

He paid cash and took a box of bullets and two nylon holsters to go with the weapons. When they were done, she led him back up the stairs and into the main part of the shop.

'You be careful out there, soldier,' she told him as she unlocked the front door. 'Bad people around, you know.'

3

Logan swung his legs out of bed and on to the carpet, scrunching his toes up and releasing them again. He saw that Cahill's bed had been made up, the cover pulled military tight. A note on hotel paper was lying on the pillow. It was from Cahill: said he had gone out on an 'errand' and that Logan was to organise getting a car — 'something with a big engine in case we need it.'

Need it for what?

He went for a shower and towelled dry, dressing in jeans and a plain navy T-shirt. He didn't feel tired and was glad of getting a long period of uninterrupted sleep. He also felt hungry, so grabbed a lightweight Merrell walking jacket and went down to the restaurant to get something to eat.

He checked his phone after breakfast but he had no messages. It was too early back home to call Ellie so he stuck the phone in his pocket and left to find the rental car place that he had seen in the mall last night.

There wasn't much foot traffic in the mall. It was a standard working day for most people and the city wasn't exactly built as a holiday destination — not unless you were staying there to use it as a base for the nearby ski resorts.

He spent an hour in the rental place, most of that time stuck behind a large American woman who insisted on telling the sales agent every detail of her flight down from Chicago and how she was visiting her sister who was ill and how her sister's no good husband . . .

Logan zoned out.

After a brief attempt by the agent to sell him a convertible, Logan rented a Cadillac sedan with the biggest engine that they had. It sounded to Logan like it would be powerful enough for whatever Cahill had in mind. The agent gave him directions to the rental parking lot, where the cars were stored, and all the paperwork in a branded folder.

Logan walked the short distance to the lot in the crisp morning air and found the car with the help of one of the attendants who looked about as bored as a person could. He started the car engine and it came to life with a satisfying growl. He spent fifteen minutes getting used to the car's controls and driving around the lot to acclimatise himself to the automatic gearbox, and also turning left and right from the 'wrong' side. When he was happy, he looked in the car's Sat Nav for a local landmark to give him on-the-road-driving experience and settled for the Denver Broncos' stadium — Invesco Field at Mile High — because it was a little outside the centre of the city.

The sky was clear again today and it was a pleasant drive to the stadium. He parked the car and went to the small museum to look around at old photos of the football team and learn about its history.

When he was back outside, his phone rang.

'You get a car?' Cahill asked.

'Yeah. A Cadillac.'

'Sounds good. Where are you?'

'Out at the football stadium.'

'Why?'

'No reason. Just went for a drive. What about you?'

'Back at the hotel. You coming here now?'

'Sure. You get your errand done?'

'Yes.'

'Probably best if I don't know what it was.'

'You got it. Listen, I want to go see if we can speak to these people this afternoon.'

Logan was about to ask what he meant, then remembered it would be to check out the D. Hunter list that Bruce had e-mailed over last night.

'Okay. I'll head back now. Ten, fifteen minutes.'

Logan parked on the street near the hotel and bought a local newspaper — *The Denver Post* — before walking back to meet Cahill.

'You should drive,' Logan told Cahill. 'You're the native after all.'

'Sure.' Cahill nodded. 'Think you can handle being my passenger?'

Logan looked at his friend and, not for the first time, wondered if there was a tiny spark of madness inside his head — the kind of spark that marked men like Cahill out as different from everyone else.

Men capable of going into battle and coming out the other side.

4

'We got a hit on the semen sample,' Murphy told Irvine, perching on the edge of her desk.

'You sure know the way to a woman's heart.' She smiled.

He looked so pleased; Irvine didn't want to burst his bubble by saying that she knew it would belong to Russell Hall. Let him have his moment.

'Russell Hall,' he said.

'We know him. His name surfaced already.'

'Is he in custody?'

'Sort of.'

'What does that mean?'

'Depends on whether being in the care of the pathologist counts as being in custody.'

'He's dead?'

She nodded.

'Killed some time last night or this morning out in the east end. I guess he made someone unhappy when he killed Lewski.'

Murphy put the DNA result on her desk and left. She felt kind of bad.

She went back to her notes from the review of the CCTV footage. Looked again at the licence number for Hall's car. A thought struck her: how does a drug dealer finance a luxury car purchase? Probably not cash. That would arouse suspicion at the car dealership.

What if he had an outstanding lease or finance contract?

She accessed the force's credit reference database and entered the details for the car. The search result told her that there was a loan on it for £10,000 through a little-known finance company. And that the loan was in the name of a company.

She checked out the company. Its registered office was located at an accountancy firm: Marshall Scott.

She was still for a beat. Then she called Armstrong and told him the news.

'Can you get over here and we'll drive up to see them?' she said.

'What about getting a warrant and doing a proper raid?'

'We don't have enough evidence for that yet. Let's see what we can get by dropping in unannounced again.'

'I'm leaving now.'

* * *

'Run it all past me again,' Armstrong said to Irvine as he drove. 'So I've got it clear in my head, you know.'

'Okay. So, Russell Hall used to run Frank Parker's drug operation.'

'I got that.'

'But he left three months ago to join up with Johnson and now this as yet unidentified new boss. This new boss is probably the real owner of the flat that Lewski and Murray lived in — not the accountants.'

'Why do you say that?'

'Well, it's all supposition at this point, but Hall was running around in a high-end car which was financed through a company with links to the accountants. Which probably means that they *are* dirty.'

'You mean that they launder money for the organisation that Hall's boss runs?'

'Correct.'

'And they are committed enough to their client's cause to even use some of the money to buy flats for prostitutes and put the flats in their own names.'

'That way the money looks even cleaner. I mean, it's not even connected to Hall or the boss in any way.'

'Right. And if they're doing stuff as basic as organising finance for cars, it probably means that they have access to all of the financial information for the organisation.'

'Sounds like we can probably break the whole thing open through their records.'

'Maybe.'

They parked outside the office and saw immediately that the cars they had seen on their previous visit were not there. Irvine looked at Armstrong.

'Think maybe they're on the run after what happened with Hall?'

Armstrong shrugged.

'Let's see what we can find out here first.'

The receptionist looked nervous when they walked in.

'Remember us?' Irvine said, showing her warrant card.

The woman nodded.

'They're not here,' she said. 'Haven't come back since late yesterday.'

'Is that normal?'

'Not really. I mean, they missed some meetings this morning and they never do that without telling me.'

'You called them?'

She nodded again. 'At home, on their mobiles. I sent them e-mails and texts.'

'And you haven't heard from either of them?'

'No. Is something wrong?'

Irvine felt sorry for her. She had probably received her last ever salary slip from these guys.

'I think it probably is, yes,' was what she said. 'Do you have their home addresses?'

The woman stared straight ahead. 'I can't give you those,' she said.

Armstrong placed his hands on her desk and leaned forward. 'Look . . . ' He glanced at her name badge. ' . . . Mary. It's very likely that your bosses are mixed up with some bad people and are now getting ready to run. If they are not already running. So the sooner you give us the addresses the easier it will be. I mean, we can find them on our own but that will just waste time.'

He stood up to his full height.

'You want to be seen to be helping us, don't you? Who knows who will get dragged into this investigation, you know.'

The woman caught the insinuation, her face going two shades paler in an instant. She tapped on her computer and a printer under her desk

273

hummed and spat out a sheet of A4. She handed the sheet to Armstrong.

'Thanks,' he said.

'What should I do now?' she asked, her eyes filling and her voice wavering.

'I suggest you lock up, go home and start looking for a new job,' Irvine said. She reached over and put her hand on top of the woman's. 'You'll be fine. But call me if you hear anything.'

Irvine put a business card in front of her on the desk. The woman looked at it as though she had never seen one before in her life.

Back in the car, Armstrong asked Irvine what she thought was going on.

'I have a bad feeling,' she said.

'Me too.'

'I mean, if this guy killed Johnson and Hall, he'll have no problem taking care of a couple of accountants as well.'

'Especially if these guys have the keys to his money.'

'You want to call and get some uniforms over to the houses?'

Armstrong waved the sheet of paper that the receptionist had given to them.

'No, they're not far,' he said. 'Both in the west end.'

'We can be there in less than half an hour. You ready for what we might find?'

'Not really. But what's that got to do with anything?'

5

Marshall's car with the vanity plate was sitting in the driveway of his modern home. It looked as though he had bought an older house and demolished it to build something in glass and steel. Something very expensive.

'I don't care how well you're doing as an accountant,' Irvine said. 'There's no way that a two-partner firm operating out of that office makes enough to allow him to buy something like this.'

'You're right.'

'We should have checked them out more thoroughly.'

She looked at Armstrong and felt the skin on her face stretched tight across her bones.

'They brought it on themselves,' Armstrong told her, opening his door and stepping out on to the pavement.

Armstrong walked ahead of Irvine up the driveway, stopping to cup his hands on the driver's window of the car and looking inside.

'Nothing,' he said, turning to Irvine as she came up behind him.

She walked past him to the front door of the house. It was a heavy, oak door — double the size of a standard door. There were glass panels on either side and Irvine looked through one of them into a wide entrance hall. There was nothing immediately out of place

275

that she could see.

'Looks normal,' she told Armstrong.

A metal intercom panel was installed on the wall to the side of the door. It looked to Irvine as though it was a video camera device to allow the occupiers to see who was at the door. She pressed a button on the panel and heard a chime inside.

Waited.

Pressed the button again.

Waited.

'No one's going to answer,' she said to Armstrong.

He grabbed the door handle and pulled it down. The door clicked and Armstrong pushed it open. He looked at Irvine. Unsaid between them: not a good sign that the door was unlocked.

They stood together looking inside the house and listening for any sound. It was silent.

'Does he have a family?' Irvine asked.

'Don't know.'

'It's too quiet.'

'Do you want to call for support?'

'Armed response?'

He nodded.

Irvine looked inside the house. It felt empty. Or, at least, devoid of life. Whatever that would turn out to mean.

'No. I don't think we need to worry about anyone who might be in there.'

He got her meaning. Irvine walked inside.

There was an open staircase at the back of the hall leading up to a first-floor balcony with a glass guard along it. They went through each of the rooms on the ground floor and found nothing until they got to the kitchen at the rear of the house.

It was a high-end installation in black and grey with a central island and the best in appliances that money could buy. Marble-tiled steps led down to a dining area that had a glass roof.

Irvine walked around the island and stopped. She motioned for Armstrong to join her and pointed at the floor.

There was a dark smear of blood on the floor and a splash of it on one of the lower cabinet doors.

'Looks like it was contained here,' he said. 'I mean, there's no blood trail anywhere else down here.'

Irvine walked closer and saw that a drawer at the end of the island had been left open. There was a collection of towels in the drawer.

'Probably took a towel from here,' she said, pointing at the open drawer. 'And applied it to the wound.'

Armstrong nodded.

'Either he took him upstairs or outside.'

'Let's go upstairs.'

★　★　★

There was a trail of blood on the wooden floor of the first-floor balcony leading to a room at the far end of a long hallway. They walked carefully along the hall to avoid stepping in the blood and contaminating the scene.

The door at the end was closed. Irvine felt her heart thudding and blood rushing in her head. She reached out and opened the door.

It turned out that Marshall did have a family.

A woman was on the floor inside the door and her body prevented Irvine from pushing the door all the way open. Her face was discoloured from the beating she had suffered and her throat had been cut so deeply that her head was almost severed.

The room smelled of blood and evacuated bowels and Irvine put a hand to her nose when the stench hit her.

Marshall's body was on the bed. She noticed straight away the mess of his right hand: two fingers were missing and the remaining ones were horribly disfigured. There was a pillow over his face. Or what was left of the pillow: shredded and soiled by blood from so many thrusts of a knife.

Irvine walked around the foot of the bed and found Marshall's son lying on the floor on the far side of the bed. Armstong stood in the doorway staring at Marshall.

The boy was in his early teens, from what Irvine could tell from his clothes. It was impossible to know based on the mess where his face used to be.

Something burbled in Irvine's stomach.

Hold it in, Becky.

She turned from the boy's body and looked at Armstrong.

'There's another one here. He's just a boy.'

'He tortured them.' Armstrong continued to stare at Marshall. 'Why?'

'Looks to me like he did it because he enjoys it. Which makes him extremely dangerous.'

6

DS Ewen Cameron called Irvine from the other accountant's house an hour later. She was standing in Marshall's driveway as the Scenes of Crime team pulled up to the house in a van. Cameron was a fifteen-year street veteran and still his voice wavered.

'They're dead,' he said.

'How many?'

Please, no more kids.

'Two. Husband and wife.'

'Were they tortured?'

He made a sound. Irvine wasn't sure what it was supposed to have been.

'Yeah, you could say that,' he managed to say eventually.

'Did they have any children?'

'Looks like it from the photos in the house. A daughter. We're still trying to track her down.'

'But she's not in the house?'

'No.'

'Good.'

Armstrong came out of the house and stood beside her.

'They found Scott and his wife,' she told him. 'Same story over at that house.'

'Shit.'

'Yeah. But doesn't sound like their kid got caught up in it. At least, not yet.'

Armstrong shifted from foot to foot. Irvine

looked at him. It was clear he wanted to say something.

'What is it?' she asked.

He stopped shuffling and met her eyes.

'This is what the Frank Parkers of the world do, you know.'

'Kenny, I'm not some bimbo straight out of school. I mean, I spent my time on patrol and I earned the right to the job I have now. I know what these people are like.'

'Do you?'

'I do. I've seen . . . ' She turned away from him as the first of the forensics team walked past her to enter the house. 'I've seen enough,' she went on. 'To know what people are capable of.'

'And you still treated him like he was worthy of respect.'

She turned to face him, angry now.

'That's bullshit, Kenny, and you know it. I was doing my job. Following a line of inquiry and trying not to let my personal feelings get in the way of that.'

He started shuffling again. Didn't look at her.

'I'll quite happily snap the cuffs on him if the time comes for it. But right now he might be able to help us find out who did this. Because we're no closer now than when we started.'

'He's poison,' he said, looking at her now.

She decided to ask him straight out. It felt like he wanted to tell her anyway. 'What is it with you and him?'

Armstrong watched as more forensics drew up at the kerb.

'I had a good mate who was undercover.

281

Maybe three years ago now. Anyway, Parker found out and stitched him up. Made him look like a dirty cop and he went inside for eighteen months. Lost his job, his pension and his wife.' Armstrong looked down the street, seeing something much further than the house at the end of the road. 'He killed himself when he came out. First day, in fact.'

'How do you know it was Parker?'

Armstrong gave her a look.

'I'd take him over a thousand Frank Parkers.'

He left her and went back into the house.

* * *

The day dragged long. Time stretched out interminably. Irvine left Armstrong on scene at around five-thirty, he not saying very much to her now after the argument about Parker. She could do without his mood.

Back at Pitt Street she was surprised to see Liam Moore still at his desk. She told him that they were getting exactly nowhere: every witness smeared from the face of the planet.

'You've got to give him credit,' Moore told her. 'I mean, he is committed to this scorched earth policy of wiping out everyone and anyone who can connect him to the bad drugs. It's impressive in its singular purpose.'

'Impressive?'

He shrugged his massive shoulders.

'It's all relative.'

'I suppose.'

'What about this Parker guy? Think he can

282

come up with anything?'

'I don't know. I only met him the once.'

'Keep an open mind. Armstrong will get over it.'

'Yes, boss.'

Moore snorted, leaned back in his chair and stretched. Irvine waited for the chair to break under his bulk. She was grateful it held out.

Moore looked at his watch and then out at the almost empty office outside. Most everyone had gone home already. 'Getting late,' he told Irvine.

She looked around at the office then at her own watch. 'I hadn't noticed.'

'Go home. Nothing more to do tonight.'

She stood and opened the door of Moore's office.

'And Becky,' he said behind her. 'We *will* get this guy.'

She turned back to look at him and nodded. Not sure that he was right.

7

It had been a frustrating morning for Logan and Cahill. The four D. Hunters that Bruce had tracked down turned out to have no remote connection to either Tim Stark or the FBI. They were a housewife in Broomfield, an attorney who worked for the public defender's office, a construction worker who was holidaying in Vegas for the week and a fifteen-year-old high school student. They had known the details of the individuals from the information Bruce had given them. And it turned out that they were exactly what the records showed.

'Dead end,' Cahill said as they got in the car after the last house call with the teenager's mother.

'What did you expect? That it was some sort of code name?'

Cahill gave Logan a pained look.

'So, *now* are you going to tell the FBI about it?'

'Why? It's a dead end.'

'It is in Denver. But maybe it wasn't supposed to be restricted to the city?'

From the look on Cahill's face, Logan figured that the thought had not occurred to his friend.

'I hadn't thought of that,' Cahill said.

Logan shook his head.

'Jesus,' Cahill went on. 'How stupid do I feel.'

Logan told him not to worry about it.

'But we've done what you came to do. You got an answer on Tim and Melanie can rest a bit easier now. Let's go home.'

Cahill gripped the steering wheel.

'Maybe we should talk to Webb again,' he said. 'Tell him what we found out.'

'I think that would be sensible.'

Cahill started the car up and pulled out from the kerb. Logan checked his phone and saw that he had two voicemail messages: one from Irvine and one from Ellie. He listened to both and wanted to be back home with them.

'What time is it?' Cahill asked him.

Logan checked his watch and said it was after three.

'Okay, let's get back to the room to get freshened up, then we'll grab an early dinner. We can go see Webb tomorrow.'

'And arrange flights back home?'

'Maybe.'

Logan wasn't convinced.

★ ★ ★

Logan took the laptop from his bag and went to the bar in the hotel to wait for Cahill to finish up in the bathroom. He ordered a bottle of locally brewed wheat beer — Easy Street — and sat at a table by the window, looking out on to the street. The beer was good.

He put the laptop on the table and opened it, settling back in his seat to read the newspaper he had bought that morning while he waited for the computer to boot. The first couple of pages were

285

taken up by some story about illegal campaign donations in a local election. Seemed to Logan like politicians were the same the world over.

The computer beeped, waiting for him to input a password. He typed it in and connected to the Internet via the hotel's Wi-Fi connection.

He was annoyed by the futility of their search today for the elusive D. Hunter, so he found a local phone directory and typed the name into the search box.

The search returned two of the people they had checked out today, a whole bunch of other, plain old 'Hunter' entries, one Dr Hunter and a law firm — Dutton Hunter Green. He thought that the law firm might be more of a possibility than the others so searched again for its own website and then scrolled through the names of all the lawyers. Nothing jumped out at him.

He tried a new Google search: 'Hunter, Denver'. It returned over a hundred pages of results. He skimmed through the first fifteen pages before he saw one that caught his attention. It was an article from the same newspaper ten years ago — about a young police officer injured in a bank robbery which had descended into a gunfight. It had been an FBI operation that he stumbled into before his very first shift as a uniformed cop. His name was Jacob Hunter.

Logan read the story twice, something nagging at his mind. There was a quote from the Chief of Detectives about the investigation into the shooting.

Logan had a thought: if Hunter started in the

force ten years ago, maybe he was a detective now.

D. Hunter — Detective Hunter.

That would make sense. What if Tim Stark had seen something that meant this Hunter was somehow involved in whatever the gang he had infiltrated was up to?

He ran a search on 'Detective Hunter, Denver', found a recent news story about a disabled veteran who had been found dead in one of the city centre parks. There was a quote from a homicide detective about some potentially related deaths in recent weeks. As usual, the cop was non-committal.

The cop's name was Detective Jake Hunter.

* * *

'What do you think?' Logan asked Cahill back in their room. 'Maybe it's him.'

Logan waited while Cahill read the articles Logan had found.

'I don't know,' Cahill said when he was done reading. 'I mean, why would an undercover FBI agent have an interest in a city homicide detective?'

Logan thought for a moment.

'Maybe he's dirty. The detective. Involved with whatever Stark was investigating.'

Cahill scanned the stories for the third time.

'We need to tell the FBI, right?' Logan said.

'Let's not get ahead of ourselves.'

'What do you mean?'

'We don't know what his part is in all of this.

Or if it's really his name that Tim sent to himself. If he is involved, could be Tim was simply reminding himself that he was someone he needed to speak to about the case. I mean, you remember what Webb said. Tim was using an alias on the flight because his undercover status had been compromised. He must have known the bad guys were after him and maybe he didn't know how much time he had or whether he'd make it out alive.'

'Webb didn't exactly say that, Alex.'

'He said as much.'

'If you're thinking what I *know* you're thinking, it's a bad idea. Let the professionals handle it.'

Cahill put the paper down and stared at Logan.

'After everything we've been through over the last couple of years, you can say that to me without a trace of irony? You've seen the so-called professionals at work. Does that give you the confidence to hand something over to them?'

'Not the FBI.'

'Same thing so far as I'm concerned. I mean, I'm not about to trust something like this to those guys. I owe it to Tim to do more than that.'

8

'We're coming up tomorrow,' Raines said into the phone.

He was talking to his second in command at the mountain compound.

'What time?'

'After breakfast. Around nine.'

'Fine with me.'

'Listen, we need picking up. I've got an FBI tail and I don't want to drive myself. I can lose them easier on foot in town.'

'Tell me where and when and I'll come get you myself.'

'No. You stay put. Send one of the others.'

'Just one? I mean, what if you get into a tight spot with the Feds?'

Raines thought for a moment. He didn't want to get into a war in the city. But how did that Rolling Stones song go? You can't always get what you want.

'You're right. Send two and make sure they come loaded for bear.'

'Copy that.'

'I'll be at the diner. The one we usually meet at.'

'The Fried Egg on Seventeenth and Market?'

'That's the one.'

'You want the boys to come into town and you can call them when you're set? They won't be far away. That way you can make

289

sure the Feds aren't on to you.'

'Yeah. Let's do it that way.'

'Does this mean we're doing it now?'

'It does.'

'Looking forward to it being over.'

'Me too. Stay sharp, soldier.'

★ ★ ★

Raines wasn't sure if he would be coming back to the apartment from the compound so he packed a bag with enough clothes to last him a week. Then he called Matt Horn.

'We're going to get picked up in town early tomorrow. Can you meet me at the diner for breakfast?'

'Sure. What time?'

Raines was glad that he didn't have to put up with any crap from Horn this morning. They could probably finish this thing off without him, but it would be safer if he was still on board. No loose ends to worry about.

'No second thoughts now?'

'No.'

Raines had expected some hesitation from him and was happy that there had been none.

'Good. Meet me at eight-thirty in the diner. I need to shake the Feds who are sitting on me first. Shouldn't be too hard. They're amateurs.'

'Don't underestimate them, Seth.'

'I've estimated them exactly. And they won't give me any trouble.'

'What do you want me to do if you're late?'

290

'Order breakfast. I'll call your cellphone when I'm on my way.'

Raines felt that he should say something more than just giving orders.

'Look, Matt, this'll be done soon.'

'You keep saying that.'

Raines sighed.

'You're the one who got fucked over,' he told Horn.

'I know.'

'And I got you out of that shithole hospital.'

'I said I know.'

'Nobody else was going to do anything for you. Not the army and not the Government.'

Horn stayed quiet.

'So this is where we get ours. You understand?'

'I don't need a lecture, Seth.'

Raines was surprised by the anger he heard in Horn's voice.

'I said I'm in,' Horn went on, his voice getting louder. 'So let's get it over with.'

'That's the plan.'

9

The hotel concierge gave Logan and Cahill directions to the police headquarters building and they went out on to the Sixteenth Street Mall to catch one of the free shuttle buses that traversed the mile-long street in both directions. They got on a southbound bus and stepped off at the last stop at the corner of Broadway.

'State Capitol Building is over there at the east end of the park,' Cahill said, pointing to a grand-looking building with a gold-domed roof as the bus pulled away. 'We need to go to the west end, behind the City-County building.'

They walked the short distance to the park and Logan saw another imposing building opposite the Capitol Building, with granite columns and a clock tower above.

The park itself would have been an impressive sight had it not been for the large numbers of vagrants who called it home. Some lay sprawled in groups under trees drinking alcohol of unknown origin while others wheeled shopping trolleys along the pathways piled high with blankets and the rest of their worldly possessions. Logan saw that some of them wore army issue coats and trousers.

Cahill surveyed the park in silence.

'It's worse than it was last time I was here,' he said eventually.

They walked until they were past the

City-County building and turned left on to Cherokee Street where the police headquarters were situated. Two buildings forming an L-shaped pedestrian plaza, five storeys high and constructed from brown brick. The windows were heavily tinted.

The two buildings had signs above the entrance doors: one read 'Administration Building' and the other 'Pre-Arraignment Detention Facility'. Logan pointed at the first one and they walked over to the glass doors.

Inside the foyer of the building was a public desk with two uniformed cops sitting behind bullet-proof glass. Cahill walked over to the desk and Logan wandered around looking at some of the history of the department displayed in glass cases on the walls.

'We're looking for Detective Jake Hunter,' Cahill told the sergeant behind the desk.

'Your names?'

Cahill told him.

'What's this about?'

'We might have some information to share.'

The sergeant had been writing on a pad in front of him and now looked up at Cahill, a vertical line creasing between his eyes. You might have called it a frown but his eyes were devoid of emotion. He was a large man, probably nearing the end of his career, with wispy grey hair and a round face. He wore glasses and did that thing where he looked over the tops of the glasses in a quizzical manner. Vaguely condescending. Like he was talking to a child.

'Is he in?' Cahill asked. 'Detective Hunter.'

The sergeant stared at Cahill and shifted his gaze to Logan as he came up and stood beside Cahill. Logan couldn't tell how the conversation had gone so far so adopted a non-threatening look and said nothing.

'What kind of information?' the sergeant asked.

'Well, we're not very sure but it's about the death of a federal agent.'

The sergeant paused for a moment to look at them some more. When he was done looking he wrote in his pad, told them to have a seat and picked up the phone on his desk.

They sat in the seats in the middle of the foyer and watched the sergeant speak into the phone. They couldn't hear what he was saying from this distance. He put the phone down and waved them over.

'Someone will be down to talk to you shortly,' he told them.

'We should sit down again?' Cahill asked.

'If you like.'

They sat and waited for a half-hour or so before a man in his late twenties wearing a navy suit and with fair, almost blond hair came through a door to the left of the main desk. The man looked at the sergeant who pointed at Logan and Cahill.

'I'm Detective Collins,' the man said as he came over to where they were sitting. 'I understand that you've got some information for us?'

He stood there as though he wanted to hear what they had to say quickly and then leave again. Like he was used to dealing with time wasters that way. He hooked his hands into his belt and Logan saw the holster clipped on his right hip as his jacket pulled back.

Cahill stood.

'It would be better if we spoke in private.'

'Why's that?' Collins asked.

'It's kind of sensitive.'

Collins looked down at Logan, who was still sitting, then back at Cahill.

'Who are you guys?' he asked.

Logan sensed that Cahill was going to struggle getting anywhere with this guy if he took his usual approach so he stood to speak instead.

'My name's Logan Finch,' he said, holding out his hand. 'And this is Alex Cahill.'

Collins shook his hand.

'You're not from around here.'

'No. I'm a lawyer and we're here at the request of the wife of a federal agent in connection with his death.'

Collins tilted his head to the side. He appeared unimpressed by what Logan had said. Probably dealt with lawyers all the time and no doubt had a low opinion of most of them.

'The Feds know about this mission of yours?'

'We're only asking to speak to Detective Hunter in private for a few minutes. We'd rather not discuss this out here.'

Collins blinked.

'If you think we're wasting your time, you can show us the door,' Cahill added.

'And who are you again?' Collins asked Cahill.

'He's a retired US army NCO and former

member of your Secret Service.'

Collins looked at Cahill again for a moment and told them to follow him.

They went through the same door that Collins had used to come into the reception area and a metal detector beyond that. From there, Collins led them along a narrow corridor to an interview room. Collins held the door open for them and waited till they were seated at the small table in the room.

'Wait here,' was all he said before closing the door, his footsteps echoing as he walked away.

'At least we got past the first line of defence,' Logan said. 'Though I still think we should have spoken to Webb about all of this first. I mean, Tim Stark was his guy. He wasn't a cop.'

'Let's see where this takes us. I want to see Hunter's reaction to all of this.'

'But we're going to tell Webb after this?'

'Sure.'

Cahill had a way of saying 'sure' that meant: let's wait and see how this pans out first before we make a decision.

10

They waited for around fifteen minutes before the door opened again and Collins came in followed by a slightly older man about Logan's height with close-cropped dark hair. He wore black trousers and a white shirt with a plain red tie and no jacket. He had a holster on his belt like Collins.

'I'm Detective Hunter,' he said, extending his hand to shake Logan's.

Hunter's shirt cuffs were rolled up on his forearms and when he shook his hand Logan noticed a pale scar running up his right arm: the wound from the bank robbery. He looked serious. In fact, he looked like he was always serious.

Cahill shook hands with Hunter and they sat looking at each other across the table. Collins stood leaning against the wall just inside the door. He folded his arms across his chest and crossed his feet.

'Danny . . . I mean Detective Collins said this was something about the death of an FBI agent.'

Logan nodded.

'What does it have to do with me?'

'We don't know that it has anything to do with you yet. That's why we're here.'

'I don't understand,' Hunter said.

'Maybe we should start at the beginning.'

'That usually helps.'

Logan looked at Cahill.

'Detective,' Cahill said, 'so that you are aware of who we are and that we can be taken at our word, I'm a retired US army soldier and former Secret Service agent. Now I run a close protection business over in the UK. In Scotland.'

Hunter looked closely at Cahill as he spoke but said nothing.

'I'm a lawyer,' Logan told him. 'I work in-house with Alex.'

'We'll try not to hold that against you,' Collins said, smiling.

Hunter continued to look at Cahill.

'You can check us out if you like,' Cahill told him. 'Go do it now and we'll wait.'

'Already done, Mr Cahill. You checked out.'

'I used to work in the Secret Service with a guy called Tim Stark,' Cahill said. 'He was a Fed before he joined the service. A real all-American, you know?'

Hunter nodded.

'And a friend too. Anyway, I got a call out of the blue this week from his wife Melanie. She said he was on that plane that crashed here but no one would tell her anything and his name wasn't on the passenger list that the airline had.'

Logan could tell from Hunter's face that he had no idea what this was all about but he let Cahill continue without interrupting.

'I did a bit of digging on Melanie's behalf. Cut a long story short, Tim was working undercover here in Denver on behalf of the FBI.'

'How did you find out about that?'

'We asked the FBI chief here.'

'And he told you? Just like that?'

'Yes.'

Hunter raised his eyebrows, turned and looked at Collins who remained impassive. Logan guessed that they were partners. They seemed at ease with each other and able to communicate non-verbally.

'Which brings us to you,' Logan said.

'Go on.'

'Tim Stark sent himself an e-mail before he boarded the plane. Before he died. It said 'D. Hunter, Denver'. That was all.'

'And you think that's me? Sounds slim.'

'We don't know. It's no one else in town, that's for sure.'

'You checked them out?'

Logan nodded.

'Bit of a long shot,' Hunter said. 'I mean, I don't know this guy Stark. Never heard of him until you said his name.'

'You know anyone in the FBI?'

Hunter paused for a moment. Something passed across his face — something that Logan couldn't read. He wondered if Cahill noticed it.

'I've had some dealings with them, yes,' Hunter said. 'But nothing to do with whatever this might be.'

'Are you dirty?' Cahill asked.

Logan's head snapped to the side to look at Cahill. Hunter leaned back in his chair but held Cahill's gaze. Collins came off the wall and stepped forward.

Hunter stayed calm, looked at Logan.

'Your friend is very direct,' he said.

'Tell me about it.'

299

'To answer your question, no, I'm not dirty. Why do you ask?'

'It would explain why Tim thought that you were someone of interest.'

'If it really was me that he identified.' He leaned forward and put his hands on the table.

'Did the FBI tell you what Stark was working on? The details, I mean.'

'Not really.'

'What did they tell you?'

'They were looking at a group of ex-soldiers up to no good. They were hazy on the details of what exactly the no good part was. I don't think they know.'

Collins walked forward and sat in the chair next to Hunter. Logan took it as a sign of interest in the subject of ex-soldiers.

'How did they come on to the FBI's radar?' Hunter asked.

'The main guy, I don't know his name, put some stuff in writing that got him red flagged. Probably some anti-government crap. Then he gave up his job, started buying weapons. Legal guns. Sold his house. Went off the radar.'

'That kind of behaviour usually means he's up to something, that's for sure,' Collins said.

'You said it was a group,' Hunter said. 'How many?'

'Don't know. They never told us. All they said was that this guy had some associates who did the same thing. Gave up their jobs, I mean. For no apparent reason.'

'Sounds like prototypical domestic terrorists,' Collins said.

'I know, right. But I'm not convinced.'

'Why do you say that?' Hunter asked.

'Well, I mean, how would they finance something like that with no jobs and no capital behind them?'

'Could be they hooked up with an existing group that had cash?'

'I don't think so. Unlikely there's two groups operating in the area and the FBI hasn't heard of either of them until now.'

Hunter got up abruptly and said he was going to get some water. He asked them if they wanted anything and they both said yes. Hunter left, motioning for Collins to follow him.

'What do you think?' Cahill asked after they left.

'I believe him when he says he's not dirty.'

'Me too.'

'Yeah, and thank Christ for that. What the hell were you thinking coming out and asking him like that?'

Cahill shrugged.

'I got a feel for him, you know. He seemed like a good guy.'

Logan puffed his cheeks and blew out a breath.

'I swear, Alex. Working with you is taking years off my life expectancy.'

'But they were definitely interested when I mentioned the soldiers, did you see that?'

'I did. I expect the water was an excuse to make them leaving look casual when they really wanted to talk about it before going any further with us.'

'Yeah, no doubt.'

Hunter and Collins came back with cardboard cups for Logan and Cahill and sat at the table sipping at their own drinks.

'So what are you guys working on?' Cahill asked. 'Anything with a military connection?'

'You know that I can't say much about an ongoing investigation.'

'So that's a yes. The Feds would be interested.'

Hunter smiled for the first time. It changed his face, made him look much younger.

'We represent the family of a victim possibly connected to your investigation,' Logan said. 'I mean, leaving aside how you feel about lawyers, you'd normally keep the family advised. Am I right?'

'Tenuous,' Collins said.

'If there is something in this,' Hunter added, 'we *will* need to speak to the FBI. Even if I'd rather we kept it all here.'

'You said you've dealt with the FBI in the past,' Logan said. 'I take it that didn't work out so well?'

Hunter rubbed absently at the scar on his right arm, caught himself doing it and tugged at his shirt cuff as if wanting to pull the sleeve down and cover the scar.

'I have the highest respect for some people in the Bureau. One of my closest friends works out of Quantico. It's just that . . . '

Collins looked at his partner.

'We all have our scars to bear?' Cahill asked.

Hunter held his gaze.

'Yes, we do.'

11

'We've had a number of deaths in the city recently from drug overdoses,' Hunter said.

'Not our regular gig,' Collins added.

'You're homicide, right?' Logan asked.

'Yes.'

'Anyway,' Hunter added, 'we had a relatively large number of overdose deaths. Concentrated in the park over at the Capitol Building.'

'How many?'

'Three to start with. Two more in the last week.'

'Doesn't sound so big.'

'It was also noticeable for the type of drug. A heroin derivative. Fentanyl and heroin, to be exact. Definitely not run of the mill.'

Logan recalled hearing about something similar recently but couldn't quite remember what it was.

'Why was that so noticeable?' Logan asked Hunter.

'Heroin is not a product of desire in the US. We don't get so much of it here. Crack cocaine is the big thing.'

'So a sudden increase in heroin-related deaths means what? That you've got someone new in the area trying to make his mark with a new product?'

'Most likely, yes.'

'What does this have to do with soldiers?' Cahill asked.

'We checked in with the DEA,' Collins said.

'To see if they had anything going on in Metro Denver or in our vicinity.'

'I take it that you got a hit?' Cahill asked. 'Something with a military angle.'

'We did.'

'Can you tell us about it?'

Hunter stood and paced to the door and back.

'Guys, this is getting kind of to the point where I think it's best handled between law enforcement agencies. No offence, but I don't feel comfortable saying too much more.'

Logan knew that wouldn't sit well with Cahill. Hunter must have seen that in Cahill's face.

'I appreciate your background, Mr Cahill, I really do. And that this agent was a friend of yours. But we're getting into potentially very sensitive areas here. Beyond law enforcement confidentiality.'

'You mean national security?'

'Yes.'

'I've still got clearance. You can check that out as well.'

Hunter sat back down and stared at Cahill.

'I've got permanent clearance. Comes with the job.'

'From the Secret Service?' Collins asked, frowning. 'I never heard that one before.'

'Another agency.'

Collins's eyes widened a little. 'You get around some.'

'I've seen and done a lot in my time, gentlemen. Let's leave it at that.'

Hunter clasped his hands on the table and leaned forward.

'That never showed up on your records when I checked before. The other agency thing, I mean.'

'It's not supposed to. That's kind of the point.'

'So how do we know that you're cleared for this kind of thing?'

'I can tell you who to call.'

Collins took a pen and a small notepad from inside his jacket.

'Go ahead,' he said.

* * *

'You checked out,' Collins said to Cahill when he came back into the room five minutes later. 'But what about him?'

He pointed at Logan.

'He's my lawyer.'

Collins looked at Hunter who turned to Cahill.

'We're going to have to talk to the FBI after this,' Hunter said, ignoring Collins's question about Logan.

'I'll make the introductions personally,' Cahill replied.

Collins sat at the table.

'You know that the cocaine trade originates in Colombia?' Hunter asked.

Logan and Cahill nodded.

'Well, the Mexicans have also got in on the act. In fact, most of the US drug trade comes through there now, not Colombia. And one drug lord in particular has taken to hiring ex-soldiers as security.'

'The DEA told you this?'

'Yes. Turns out that one of these soldiers is now a high-ranking lieutenant in a Mexican cartel and he's been tracked entering the US three times in the last six months.'

'Entering here, in Denver?'

'Correct. The DEA has a watch list on known or suspected cartel members and footsoldiers. So they can track their movements if they come into the US. Sometimes it's better to see where they go and who they talk to rather than arresting them on entry.'

'I can see how that would work,' Cahill said. 'Do they know why this guy has been in the US?'

'Nothing concrete. Snatches of intel gathered from intercepted communications.'

'And?'

'They think that the cartel is trying to establish links with a group here in the US.'

'Let me guess,' Logan said. 'Also ex-military?'

'You win the watch.'

'But you said that the overdoses here have been from heroin. What's the connection to Mexico if they deal in cocaine? Expanding their product lines or something else?'

'That part we don't know for sure. And neither does the DEA. But heroin trade does also come in via Mexico.'

'Sounds like you only have pieces of the puzzle and can't see the whole picture yet.'

'That's about right, yes.'

'Did the DEA get any names of the people here that the Mexican was in contact with?'

'No. They traced some calls but they were to illegal, cloned mobiles. Nothing they could use.'

'You know,' Logan said, stretching his arms above his head, 'I can see why the FBI would be focused on terrorism since nine eleven and I have no doubt that's what they thought Stark was working on. They as much as told us that. But what if this group that Stark was trying to infiltrate had nothing to do with anything like that? I mean, maybe they're just good old-fashioned capitalists.'

'Drug dealers,' Cahill said.

'Yeah. Maybe Stark was getting close to the truth and they got suspicious. If he'd seen the stories about the overdoses and finally joined the dots to the crew he was with it would explain why he wanted to speak to you, Detective.'

Hunter folded his arms.

'It makes some kind of sense. But right now it's just a theory. Nothing more.'

'I think you need to talk to the FBI,' Cahill said.

Hunter looked at his watch, saw that it was now almost six.

'Those FBI types work late?' he asked.

'Oh, yeah,' Cahill said.

'I got a date,' Collins said, looking almost crestfallen.

Hunter turned his head to look at his partner.

'What?' Collins said. 'It's the blonde. You remember?'

Hunter shook his head and raised his left hand, waggling his wedding ring.

'Doesn't mean you don't remember what it was like.'

'You go if you want. I'm going to see if we can

set something up with the local Bureau guys tonight. Sounds like we have a lot to talk about.' He looked at Cahill who nodded.

'Crap,' Collins said. 'Count me in.'

'Make the call,' Hunter told Cahill.

12

Irvine got home at six, made pasta with tomato sauce and ate it with her son at the kitchen table while he regaled her with his adventures from the childminders. She listened patiently as he tried to express himself using his limited vocabulary and wiped his face every minute or so as the sauce spread ever outward. She felt numb all over.

After Connor was asleep, she went down to the living room and sat on the couch with her feet curled up under her. She couldn't get rid of the smell from Marshall's house, not sure if it was real or just a sensory memory. A few hours of TV didn't help.

Irvine grabbed the phone and dialled Logan's mobile number. It rang once and went straight to voicemail. She left a short message telling him that everything was fine and that he should call her when he got the chance.

She hung up and reached down to the floor to pick up the remote control for the TV. As she did, she thought that she saw a shadow flit across the blinds of the window that looked out on to the street. She froze, her hand hovering above the remote. Images from Marshall's house flashed in her head. She saw Connor's face on Marshall's dead son, shook her head to wipe the image from her brain.

She strained to listen for movement outside.

She heard a car door open and shut not far from her house then low male voices. She couldn't tell if they were moving towards her or away.

Standing up, she padded quietly out to the hall where she grabbed her extending baton. There was no light on in the hall and Irvine stood there, listening for any sound from outside. She heard the male voices again. This time there was no doubt that they were coming closer.

The voices grew louder until they were outside Irvine's door. She looked upstairs, knowing that her son was up there alone. Thought about pulling the door open and going out to meet them head-on. Catch them by surprise.

She almost jumped out of her skin when the doorbell rang. Irvine caught sight of herself in the full-length mirror in the hall, standing in a pink velour tracksuit with her hair up and a steel baton in her hand.

The bell rang again.

Irvine hesitated, then went to the door and looked through the peep-hole. Frank Parker was standing there with one of his bodyguards.

'I only want to talk,' Parker said loudly.

Irvine hesitated, then dropped the baton and kicked it to the side where it clattered into the skirting, taking a chunk of paint off. She opened the door.

Parker was dressed in another immaculately tailored suit. One of the big men from the restaurant was standing behind him.

'Detective,' Parker said.

Irvine felt anger begin to bubble. Parker must have seen it in her face and held his hands up.

'Look,' he said. 'I'm sorry that I had to come here. I didn't mean to upset you or anything. It's just that — '

'You're crossing the line, Mr Parker. I think you know that fine well. In fact, I think you're doing it deliberately.'

Parker dropped his hands and turned to the man behind him.

'Wait for me in the car.'

The man looked from Parker to Irvine before turning and walking towards the car parked not far along the street. Irvine watched him until he was in the car.

'What's this about?' Irvine asked.

'Can I come in?'

Irvine stared at him. Parker's face was difficult to read.

'You're pushing it.'

'If you get to know me, and I'm a helpful guy to know, you'll understand that I'm a little bit old school, Detective.'

'What does that mean?'

'It means that I like to conduct business on a personal basis. You might not believe it, but trust and honour go a long way with me.'

'Honour amongst thieves,' Irvine said.

Parker looked disappointed.

'If that's how you want to play it, I'll leave you alone. But we won't speak any further about Russell Hall's murder.'

Irvine hated having to deal with Parker on his terms, but she had backed herself into a corner now and regretted the cheap jibe at him.

'Let's get this straight,' she said. 'I'm a police officer and you . . . ' Parker watched her closely. 'You seem like a gentleman on the face of it, I'll give you that.'

'But . . . '

'But, you're also a person of interest to the police authorities in this city.'

'That's a nice euphemism.'

'So any contact we have will be strictly business.'

'Understood. That's my intention.'

'Why not call me first? Or set up a meeting somewhere in town. We don't have to conduct business at Pitt Street, you know. This is . . . inappropriate.'

'I apologise. But, like I said, I find business relationships work best if there's an element of trust.'

'So why are you here?'

'To demonstrate that I am not a threat to you. We can have a pleasant, professional communication in your home and you'll see that I am a man to be trusted. I show the police due courtesy and respect.'

'What about Kenny?'

'It's Mr Armstrong who has a problem with me.'

Irvine wanted to hear what he had to say, but still found it difficult to come to terms with the notion of letting the man in her house at this time of night.

'I saw some things today I'd prefer not to have ever seen. What people can do to one another.'

312

Parker pursed his lips.

'I saw that on the news. You were on TV.'

'I've got used to that.'

'It wasn't me,' he said finally.

'I know that.'

'That's not who I am.'

'I can't comment on who you are.'

Parker sighed. 'Let me offer this,' he said. 'If you allow me to come in and we have a conversation, we can put that in the favour bank in your credit. I mean, I have information that will be of interest to you as regards Russell's employer, so ordinarily that would put you in my debt.'

Irvine raised an eyebrow. She knew that having contacts in the criminal world was all part of the game, but this guy was too slick for his own good. She hesitated and stepped back to allow Parker to come in.

* * *

'You've got a nice home,' he said as he sat on the couch in her living room.

She got the impression that he meant it.

'I understand that these relationships can be beneficial,' Irvine said. 'But I want to be clear that next time we arrange a meeting in advance, okay?'

Parker nodded.

'And any future meetings will not be at my home. In fact, I don't want you anywhere near here again.'

He paused to look at her and nodded.

'What's this about, Mr Parker?'

'You want to get right to it?'

Irvine nodded.

'Well, I asked around like I said I would. Regarding Russell Hall's current employment status.'

'Uh-huh. And?'

'I heard a name mentioned in passing.'

'You heard it, or you knew it already but kept it to yourself until now?'

'I thought that we agreed to be courteous?'

She said nothing, not prepared to apologise to him.

'Do you want the name?'

'Yes.'

'Butler.'

'That's it?' she asked. 'No first name?'

Parker shook his head.

'Do you know any more than that? His background or where I can find him?'

'There's a limit to how much I can say. I mean, you understand that, don't you?'

'The favour bank has strict withdrawal limits, obviously.'

Parker stood and laughed.

'That's a good way of putting it, yes.' He turned and went to the door. 'Don't get up,' he told her.

Irvine hadn't moved.

'Oh,' Parker said, turning to her as he opened the door to the hall. 'I think that this Butler may have worked with Johnson before. That both of them were soldiers or something in a past life.'

Irvine stared after him as he closed the door softly.

13

'It's been a while, Jack,' Seth Raines told the man on the other end of the telephone line when his call was answered.

Jack Butler grunted.

'How are things over there? Business is good?'

'Uh . . . '

'Are you drunk?'

'No, I'm not drunk. I'm tired. It's been a rough few days and it's nearly three in the morning here.'

Raines looked at his watch which showed that it wasn't quite eight at night. He always forgot about the size of the time difference.

'Sorry.'

'Never mind. What do you want?'

'We're getting out of the business.'

Raines felt like it would be best to tell Butler straight up. No preamble. He knew that Butler would not take it well. Not after Raines had ordered Butler to kill Johnson.

'What?' Butler asked, sounding more confused than angry.

'We got an offer we couldn't refuse from the Mexicans. We're cashing out.'

'You mean you got scared of them. The competition. They threatened you and you chickened out.'

Raines couldn't tell if Butler was joking or not.

'You know me better than that.'

Butler grunted again; Raines was unsure if it was anger, derision or something in between.

Raines didn't know Butler well. Had trusted Andy Johnson's recommendation. Johnson had been the one to float the idea that grew into the business conducted out at the compound and in the UK. Johnson had spent all the money he earned after he got out of the army — as a private security consultant in Iraq and Afghanistan — and was getting desperate for cash. Butler had worked with Johnson in Afghanistan and had contacts in the drug trade there — which he had revealed to Johnson on one particularly drunken night.

Johnson had stayed in touch with Raines. He heard about Matt Horn's problems from Raines. Knew that he, too, was desperate for money.

For Raines it was a matter of the end justifying the means. Getting enough money together to get Horn out of the hospital and finding him a pair of artificial legs he could at least walk on. The ones he'd been given at the hospital rubbed his skin so badly that he'd been bedridden with infected blisters for weeks. And then the real infection had set in — almost killing him.

But Raines had grown to believe now that he had much more in common with Butler than with either Johnson or Matt Horn: that this line of work fed the need they both had to express themselves through violence.

In quieter moments, Raines wondered if he had always been a man who lived for violence and the adrenalin rush of it. And whether the

316

war, the events that day after they left the poppy field and the indignities suffered by Matt at the hands of his so-called country had simply unleashed the real Seth Raines, free from the restrictions that society sought to impose.

'Where do I get my gear now if you're getting out — from the Mexicans?'

'That's up to you.'

'You're abandoning me, is that it?'

'Hardly. You'll work something out.'

'Couldn't be any worse than the fucking mess Horn has made of it,' Butler snorted. 'Your little buddy with the chemistry degree who was supposed to run the manufacturing end of things. And look at us now. See how that turned out.'

'You've had more ODs too?'

'Yeah. And I had to cover my tracks.'

'What do you mean?'

'You know what I mean. I had to leave some cold ones behind and the cops are sniffing around.'

Raines pulled at the collar of his shirt. It felt like things were close to being out of control. First Johnson was killed for skimming profits, then Stark and now Butler was losing it. They were all at risk.

'I worry about Matt,' he told Butler.

'He never did have the stomach for it. Not after he was out and hobbling around on his new legs.'

'We had an undercover FBI agent trying to infiltrate us.'

'What?' Butler shouted. 'Because of Matt?'

317

'No. I mean, I don't think so. I don't know.'

'So why are you worried about him? You're not making any sense.'

'He's depressed. About the overdoses we had here. I don't think he can take it any more.'

'So do what I did.'

Raines wasn't sure what he meant and said so.

'Take him out. It's the only way you can be sure he won't turn you in.'

The thought had passed through Raines's mind more than once. But it seemed like such a waste. This whole thing got started to get Matt out of the hospital. To get him well. It was only after that, when the operation grew, that they hatched the notion of doing something more with it.

'Look,' Butler said. 'Fuck him. And fuck the FBI. You do what I did. You take out anyone who is a threat. A weak link. Don't even think twice about it. Doesn't matter if they are civilians or if they wear a badge. There's only two types of people: soldiers and all the rest. And the rest of them don't matter.'

'What about you?'

'Don't worry about me. You do what you have to and I'll do the same. I can take care of myself.'

'Okay. We won't speak again.'

'It's been . . . interesting.'

★   ★   ★

Raines drove to Matt Horn's house and sat in the car parked along the street. It was still light outside. His gun was in a holster under the front

318

passenger seat. He leaned down and grabbed it, taking the gun out and sitting it on his lap. Closed his eyes. Saw it all play out.

Matt in the hospital screaming. Wanting to know why him.

The overbearing arrogance and lack of interest among the hospital bureaucrats: only interested in how much money they could make from the treatment.

Matt fading away as the multiple infections took hold and ravaged his body.

Him lashing out in the hospital waiting area, trashing the place.

The condescending replies to his letters.

Drinking himself into a stupor and making the threats.

Then, at the bottom of his despair, the thought of exploiting the contacts Johnson and Butler had made back in Afghanistan. Those men seemed like magnets for others soaked in violence and blood.

Raines tried to remember how he justified what he'd done in his own mind. He couldn't have contemplated such a thing before the war. Before Matt. Wondered if his mind had snapped. Maybe it was Matt reminding him of his own son and the pain and suffering he endured before the leukaemia finally took him far too young.

He wondered if he'd ever been truly sane since his son had died. Thought that probably he had not.

Raines's attention was drawn to a taxi pulling up outside Horn's house. The front door of the house opened and Horn walked stiffly out to the taxi and climbed awkwardly into the back seat.

'Where are you going, Matt?' Raines said aloud.

Raines started his car and followed the taxi.

14

'Cooper Grange,' Danny Collins said for the third time in as many minutes. 'Sounds like a cowboy.'

He turned in the passenger seat of the car being driven by Jake Hunter and looked at Logan and Cahill in the back seat.

'Does he wear a Stetson?'

'Not last time I looked,' Logan told him.

They had called Webb at the FBI field office and arranged to meet him and Grange there. Webb told them to park on the street outside the building and Grange would meet them to take them to the office on the top floor. Hunter and Collins had not said much about their investigation to Webb on the phone except that there was a link to a group of ex-soldiers with a possible connection to a Mexican drug cartel. That was enough for Webb.

Grange was standing on the pavement and walked to the car as Hunter pulled up at the kerb. His suit still looked immaculate after what had obviously been a long day for him, judging by the smudges of dark skin under his eyes.

Logan and Cahill hung back while Hunter and Collins introduced themselves and shook hands with Grange. Grange gave Cahill a look but said nothing, ushering the four of them forward and into the building lobby where they walked to the bank of elevators.

Webb was waiting for them in the conference room next to his office at the end of the hall. His jacket was draped over a chair and he had loosened his tie and his shirt cuffs. Hunter introduced himself and Collins.

'We should get down to business,' Webb said as he sat.

Hunter and Collins took seats side by side.

'What about these two?' Grange said, looking at Logan and Cahill. 'They can't be here for this.'

Webb looked from Grange to Hunter.

'What do you think, Detective?'

Hunter turned in his seat to look at them.

'It's fine with me if they stay. I mean, they're the ones who put us together.'

'By withholding information,' Grange said.

'You want to lock them up in your basement?' Collins asked.

'Danny . . . ' Hunter frowned at his partner.

Grange still wasn't happy.

'He's got clearance,' he said, jabbing a finger at Cahill. 'But the lawyer doesn't. He shouldn't be here.'

'The lawyer stays,' Cahill said.

'No,' Logan answered. 'I don't want to get in the way of this happening. Show me where I can get a drink and something to eat and I'll wait for you guys.'

Cahill opened his mouth to protest but Logan cut him off.

'We're all supposed to be on the same side,' Logan said.

'Coop,' Webb said to Grange. 'The least you

322

can do for the man is get him comfortable. It might be a long night.'

Grange huffed out a breath and opened the door, waiting for Logan to step out into the hall. From there, he led Logan back to the reception area and through a secure door behind it into an open-plan office area. Logan figured that this was where the regular agents went about their ordinary business. The place was largely empty apart from a female agent at a desk by a window and the two Hispanic agents who had picked them up at the airport — Martinez and Ruiz. They sat at desks facing one another and looked over as Grange came in.

'Look after this one,' Grange told them. 'Get him a coffee or something.'

He turned and walked back out the same door without waiting for an acknowledgement. Logan stared at the two agents who looked at one another. Finally, Ruiz got up and came over to where Logan stood.

'So, is it coffee? Or do you English types like tea?'

'I'm not English.'

Ruiz frowned.

'Scotland's a different country.'

'Whatever. What's it to be?'

'Coffee is fine.'

* * *

Grange came back into the conference room, walked around to the far side of the table and sat next to Webb. He kept his suit jacket on. Hunter,

323

Collins and Cahill were on the other side of the table.

'I don't buy into any of that inter-agency competition,' Webb started. 'We're all chasing the same goal so why don't I explain where I'm coming from.'

'Go ahead.' Hunter nodded.

Webb placed his hand on a file that sat on the table in front of him and slid it across to Hunter.

'Seth Raines came on to our radar maybe a year ago,' Webb said, pointing at the file which Hunter opened.

'He was a platoon sergeant in the Marines. First Recon Division. That'll mean something to you, Mr Cahill.'

Cahill nodded.

'Anyway, he was nearing the end of a tour in Afghanistan around two years ago when he was caught in an ambush in Helmand Province. The vehicle he was travelling in was hit by an IED, a mine, and came under heavy fire from entrenched enemy positions.'

Hunter flicked through the file till he found a photograph of Raines. Cahill leaned in and looked at the photo. It showed a man in a typical military pose: upright and composed. He had a cartoonishly square jaw and eyes that were almost black. The tips of tattoos showed on his neck above the collar of his shirt.

'Casualties?' Cahill asked, looking at Webb.

'Four dead including a female British army officer. Multiple wounded.'

'What about Raines?'

'He took a round through the leg. Anyway,

Raines and one of his men, Matthew Horn, were in a small convoy that had been monitoring the eradication of an opium poppy field and were returning to base when they got hit. It was a fierce encounter according to the official reports. Raines and a British soldier . . . ' Webb opened another file on the table and ran his finger down a report. 'Corporal Andrew Johnson of the Royal Military Police, distinguished themselves in the action. Saved a lot of lives according to this. Johnson suffered a gunshot wound to his head. He survived it but had to be discharged from service. He became unstable. Violent. Badly injured a couple of civilians in a fight.'

Webb tapped the report in the file on the table.

'So what went wrong with Raines?' Hunter asked.

'Raines's man, Matthew Horn, received severe injuries. Double leg amputations. He suffered very badly in hospital when he got back here. Infections and that type of thing. Almost died.'

'What about Raines's injuries?'

'He recovered fairly quickly.'

'And psychologically?'

'I guess we wouldn't be here if the same could be said for his mind.'

'Tell us the rest.'

'Okay, so Raines is released from hospital but starts to make some noises about Horn's treatment. Showed up at the hospital and wrecked the place one time. He got arrested for that. Then he starts writing letters to just about everyone. Around the time Horn was at his worst he started making veiled threats in the letters.'

'Like what?'

'How this country wasn't fulfilling its obligations to its servicemen and that someone would have to pay for that. Nothing too specific.'

'And this is how you get involved?'

'Yes,' Grange said. 'We take that kind of threat very seriously.'

'You think the arrest sent him over the edge?' Cahill asked Grange.

'Maybe. Who knows.'

Cahill was not warming to Cooper Grange.

'Anyway,' Webb went on, 'we sent a couple of agents to talk to his ex-wife and to Raines. He didn't respond to the interview at all. Pretty much ignored them.'

'And it's after this that he starts buying up weapons and goes off the grid?' Cahill asked.

'Correct. And it looks like he recruited some other like-minded veterans.'

'So how does Tim Stark get mixed up in all of this? I mean, he was still with the Secret Service.'

Grange leaned forward and spoke.

'We wanted to infiltrate covertly and we needed a back-story that would stand up to scrutiny. Someone with a tale to tell of anti-government sympathies. Stark had applied to come back to the Agency and with his previous background here it struck us as the perfect opportunity to manufacture him getting sacked and that being the cause of his unhappiness.'

'Raines never bought it,' Cahill said. 'That much is obvious now, right?'

'We think so,' Webb said. 'Tim was using the name John Reece on the flight to Washington. That was a cover identity set up for him so that he could get out quickly and it was supposed to be untraceable.'

'He never got close enough to know what they were doing?' Hunter asked.

'He was doing okay for the first few months,' Grange said. 'We got regular reports. Then they got less and less frequent. It was getting risky for him.'

'Which brings us to you, Detective,' Webb said to Hunter. 'What's the story with your case?'

15

Logan looked at Ruiz and Martinez when his phone rang. He took it from his pocket to turn it off and saw that it was Irvine calling.

'Hey,' she said when he answered the phone. 'It's me.'

'Becky? What time is it there?'

'Late. Or maybe it's early. Depends on how you look at it.'

'What's wrong?'

'Nothing. I can't sleep. This case I'm working on, you know. So I thought I'd call.'

'I'm glad you did.'

'What you up to? Alex keeping you out of trouble?'

'Uh, not really. Believe it or not I'm sitting in the Denver field office of the FBI.'

'What?'

'Long story. And before that we were at the police headquarters.'

'Sounds like a typical Alex Cahill holiday plan.' Logan laughed.

'Tell you about it when I get back. But what's up with your case?'

'I don't know. It was a tough day. We were at a scene. Multiple deaths. One was a boy, just a teenager.'

'Sounds bad.'

'It was. I hate this drug stuff. Give me a robbery any day.'

Drug stuff.

'But I'm already feeling better,' Irvine went on. 'I mean, talking to you.'

Logan was only half listening. The other part of his mind was rewinding to an earlier conversation with her. Something about heroin overdoses that CID was asked to look at. He stood and walked out into the reception area out of earshot of the agents.

'You said something before,' he said to her. 'About drug-related deaths.'

'Yeah, it's this case. The thing today. Why?'

'I don't know. Maybe nothing, but the reason we're here, at the FBI, is kind of similar.'

'What?'

'I guess I'm not making much sense. Sorry. Must be the jet lag.'

'Similar to what?'

'I mean, drug overdoses. They've had a few here as well. Seems like there's something going on with ex-soldiers.'

There was a pause.

'Becky . . . '

'Somebody told me today that there are former soldiers involved in my case. You remember the murder I told you about — the one in the newspapers? Guy got shot dead in a Range Rover. Andrew Johnson. He's one of them. Not that the guy who told me is all that reliable a source and I haven't had a chance to check it out yet.'

Logan sat at the receptionist's chair and grabbed a pen, twisting it in his free hand.

'You're jet-lagged and I'm up in the middle of

the night,' Irvine laughed. 'We're making a lot of sense.'

Logan put the pen down and ran his hand up, through his hair. He leaned back in the chair as the female agent came out into the reception area. She glanced at him as she walked past and went out to the elevators.

'Where's Alex?' Irvine asked.

'He's locked in with the FBI chiefs and the cops right now talking about this stuff.'

'How come you're excluded?'

'Nobody likes lawyers.'

'I kind of like this one.'

He smiled. 'Nice of you to say.'

'Listen, I'm going to go back to bed. See if I can't get some sleep before the alarm goes off. I expect I'll be up to my neck in paperwork tomorrow. It'll be a nightmare.'

'Okay. I'll see you when I get back.'

* * *

Irvine sat the phone handset down on the kitchen table and sipped at a cup of tea. It was comforting in the middle of the night when the darkest kind of man was still out there.

She thought about Frank Parker and his son. They were so secure in their place in the world. No matter how reasonable Parker seemed, or how desperately he wanted to be considered some kind of old-fashioned gentleman, he still ruled by violence. People died on his say. He sold drugs that ruined lives. And what now?

Soldiers turned drug dealers shot in the head.

330

People laundering drug money tortured and killed in their own homes.

Parker had shaken her with his visit. No doubt that had been part of his strategy too. Letting her know that it didn't matter that she was a cop — he could still get to her whenever he wanted to. Business would be done on his terms.

She drained her cup, rinsed it in the sink and went upstairs to her room. She used to love getting into bed and pulling the quilt up to her chin, safe in the womb-like warmth. But tonight she couldn't get warm, the cold ingrained in her bones.

And when she closed her eyes all she could see were the faces of the dead.

16

Hunter took his time explaining his investigation from start to finish, giving a lot more detail than he had to Cahill and Logan back at the police headquarters building. He spoke in depth about the information that the DEA had shared with him and the intercepted communications.

'If Tim Stark was here he might be able to tell us if this Mexican had been in touch with Raines,' Webb said when Hunter was finished.

'Maybe he heard something and that's when he put it all together,' Cahill said. 'And was going to get in touch with you, Detective Hunter.'

Webb nodded, looking thoughtful.

'It's plausible,' he said. 'But there's absolutely nothing concrete to back it up, is there?'

'No,' Hunter said. 'You're right.'

'But you're going to do something about it, right?' Cahill asked, feeling a little exasperated.

'Of course,' Webb answered. 'We're going to treat it as a line of inquiry. Try to find out if there really is a link.'

'But it's obvious.'

'No,' Hunter said. 'I know it kind of sounds like it might be, but it's not. Look at what we have. The only thing actually linking the two investigations is your e-mail. It might have been a reference to me, or it might have been something else altogether.'

'And because Tim Stark is dead we can't know for sure,' Webb added. 'So we have to treat it like any possible lead. Run it down properly.'

Cahill knew they were right, but still fought against it. He wanted Stark's death to mean something. To lead somewhere.

'So what now?' he said.

★ ★ ★

Logan's eyes were starting to close when a phone in the office rang. It pulled him from his near sleep, the ring tone slightly different from the other phones he had heard go off since he had been there.

Martinez got up from his desk and went to a phone on the wall next to the door out to the reception area. He spoke into it for a moment and listened for what seemed like a long time, though it was probably no more than a minute or so.

He hung the phone up without speaking again and went back to his desk. He spoke quietly to his partner, Ruiz, and they both put their suit jackets on and left the office in a hurry. Logan followed them out and saw that they headed up the corridor to where the meeting was.

★ ★ ★

Webb stood as if to signal that the meeting was over.

'Let's speak again in the morning,' he said to Hunter. 'Work out where we go from here.'

Hunter nodded.

'And who does what,' he said. 'I mean, we can't just hand our investigation over to you guys. You know that, right?'

'Of course.'

There was a knock at the door. Agent Martinez opened it and walked in, followed by Ruiz.

'What is it?' Grange asked.

'There's a man downstairs says he needs to speak to the agent in charge.'

Everyone looked at Webb. He was impassive.

'Well,' Webb said. 'Is that all the information he gave you? Because I'll tell you right now, it's not much to go on.'

The more he saw of Webb, the more Cahill liked the man.

'Uh, sorry,' Ruiz said. 'He says his name is Matt Horn and he has information about Seth Raines and Tim Stark.'

17

Raines knew straight away what Horn was doing at the building on Stout Street. Knew that the FBI had their office here. He wanted to feel something about it. Felt nothing. He looked again at the gun sitting on the passenger seat beside him.

Raines watched as Horn climbed out of the back of the cab and went to the intercom at the side of the main entrance to the building. The place was locked up tight at this time of night, but there was a security guard inside in case anyone came around. He guessed that happened a lot. Given the FBI's line of business.

The cab pulled away, leaving Horn alone with one hand pressed on the glass of the building's door while he leaned in to speak to the guard through the intercom.

Raines grabbed his gun, opened the door of the car and stepped out. He walked around to the front of the car leaving the door open. He stopped at the edge of the sidewalk, thought about running over there and taking both of them out in an instant. No witnesses.

Horn leaned back from the intercom and Raines saw the guard inside get up from his desk. He looked like a retired cop. Carried himself that way.

Raines took a step forward into the road.

He tightened his grip on the pistol.

But the moment passed as the guard opened the door and ushered Horn inside. The guard looked over at Raines before turning to go inside the building.

Raines went to the car, sat inside and dropped the gun on the seat.

He picked up his mobile and dialled the number for the compound.

'Change of plan for tomorrow morning,' he said when his call was answered. 'Bring everyone.'

Part Nine:
Grace

1

Logan was alone in the main part of the office when Cahill came in through the door from the reception area. Cahill walked over and sat on the edge of the desk beside him.

'What's up?' Logan asked. 'Looked like something was causing excitement.'

'Yeah, you could say that. One of the soldiers in the group showed up. Guy called Matt Horn.'

'Seriously?'

Cahill gave him a look.

'What are you, a sixteen-year-old girl?'

'What?'

'*Seriously*,' Cahill repeated, shaking his head.

Logan stood and went to the window. He looked down on to the street and saw a car parked on the other side of the road. He watched it for a moment before it drove away, then turned to Cahill.

'So what's the story?'

'Well they're still no closer to knowing if their investigations are on the same thing. The cops and the Feds, I mean. Maybe this guy who's coming in will clear it up.'

'Why is he here?'

'Who knows? Guilty conscience.'

'What did you find out?'

'I don't know if I can tell you.'

Logan frowned. Cahill played it straight but couldn't hold it together long enough to be convincing.

'Screw that. I didn't sign anything in there.'

'You always were trustworthy.'

'This guy Horn and his sergeant, Seth Raines, apparently got caught up in an ambush over in Afghanistan a while back. Horn got injured real bad. Lost his legs. Almost died in hospital.'

'And how do we get from there to here?'

'Seems Raines wasn't happy at Horn's treatment when they got him to hospital back here. Bottom line, this Raines guy went postal.'

'They still don't know if it's drugs, though?'

'Right.'

Logan sat down again. Cahill stretched his arms above his head, joints popping as he did it.

'They were all in the ambush?' Logan asked. 'The other soldiers who dropped off the radar?'

'Don't think so. But there was a Brit caught up in the thing.'

Logan stared at Cahill.

'What?' Cahill asked.

'I don't know. Maybe nothing.'

'Spit it out.'

'It's Becky. I mean, she's been pulled into some drug squad operation back home.'

'I'm not following.'

'I don't know if I am either.'

Cahill frowned.

'Listen,' Logan said. 'Becky told me about this the other day and it was in my head when Hunter was going over his investigation earlier. But it didn't mean anything at the time. But then Becky said tonight that she got information about soldiers being involved in her thing.'

'So?'

'I'm not making myself clear. She got pulled into the drug squad case like Hunter did. Unexplained overdose deaths in suspicious circumstances.'

Cahill rubbed at his eyes.

'What was the soldier's name?' Logan asked. 'The British one.'

Cahill closed his eyes, thinking.

'Johnson,' he said. 'Andy Johnson.'

'He's one of them. I mean, in Becky's case. Or at least he was.'

'Was?'

'He's dead. Murdered.'

The door to reception opened again and Webb came in with Grange. They came over to where Cahill was sitting.

'We're going to speak to Horn alone,' Grange said.

Cahill looked at Webb who nodded.

Cahill was half inclined to have a fight with Grange and Webb because, well, just because he enjoyed it and it would wind Grange up. But he was sick at the thought of what appeared to be happening. He couldn't quite comprehend how soldiers, people like him, could start up some sort of drug operation that spanned the Atlantic.

But if there was one thing he had learned over the last few years it was that human beings are capable of anything in extreme circumstances.

'We need to speak to Becky about this now,' Logan said after the others had left.

2

Randall Webb and Cooper Grange sat patiently at the table in the conference room while Ruiz helped Matt Horn into a seat. When Horn was settled, Webb nodded at Ruiz who went out of the room but left the door open. Hunter and Collins came into the room, closed the door and sat at one end of the table. Horn looked at them until Webb spoke, introducing everyone at the table.

Horn said nothing.

'What can we do for you, Mr Horn?' Webb asked.

Horn shifted in his seat and grimaced. He looked at Hunter and Collins.

'Shouldn't you, like, read me my rights or something?'

'Why would we do that?' Grange said.

'I don't know. Isn't that how it's done?'

'Why don't you tell us your story and we'll see where we go from there,' Webb told him.

Horn shifted again. Everyone waited for him.

'I killed those men. The drug addicts. It was me.'

Some opening gambit.

Webb leaned forward and clasped his hands on the table.

'Why don't you start at the beginning, Mr Horn. I find that usually helps.'

'How far back do you want me to go?'

'That depends. When did it start?'

'In Afghanistan.'

His voice wavered, phlegm at the back of his throat.

'I lost my legs there.' He looked down and rubbed his thighs.

'You were ambushed?'

He narrowed his eyes and looked at Webb. 'You know about that?'

'Yes. Is that where it started?'

'I suppose it is. If we hadn't been caught up in that . . .'

'Tell us about it,' Webb said.

'It was Seth and Andy. Until Andy got killed. But mainly Seth. He lost it after I got sick.'

'Andy?' Grange asked.

'Andy Johnson.'

Grange flipped through the file in front of him on the table.

'The Scottish RMP corporal?'

'Yes. He wasn't the same after he got shot. Losing part of your skull will do that.'

'I'm not following,' Webb said. 'Johnson is dead now?'

Horn nodded.

'Take it back a step and tell us what's going on,' Webb said.

'I needed money for treatment and Seth didn't have it. Andy had been back in Afghanistan working private security after the army discharged him. He made some contacts over there — through another soldier, guy called Jack Butler. Drug contacts. Heroin. Saw a way to make some money. Seth told him no the first time he mentioned it. But he got so desperate, so angry at everyone and

343

everything, that he would have done anything.'

'For you?'

'Yes.'

'Why?'

Horn cleared his throat.

'He had a son. He died when he was real young and Seth split from his wife after it. I don't think he ever recovered from it. He saw me as a replacement.'

'He told you that.'

'Not in so many words.'

'Which is why you getting sick . . . '

'I nearly died. Technically I was dead for a minute or so before they revived me.'

Webb sat back again, looked over at Hunter.

'You have any questions, Detective?'

Horn looked at Hunter.

'You said that you killed them,' Hunter said. 'What did you mean by that?'

'I'm a chemist. I came up with the idea of mixing the heroin and fentanyl. I wanted to be useful. Didn't want to get on the wrong side of Seth and Andy. That's not a good place to be.'

'But you didn't get it right.'

'Actually I did. I knew what I was doing.'

Hunter frowned.

'I don't understand. If you got it right, why are people dying?'

'I changed it. Didn't tell Seth.'

'You wanted people to die?'

'Yes.'

Horn showed no emotion now. As though he had stamped it down to where he couldn't feel it any longer.

344

'Why?'

'So that it would stop. So that we would get caught.'

'Why did you want to get caught?'

'The Mexicans.'

Hunter was starting to see it all fit together now.

'They were going to take you out,' Hunter said. 'For muscling in on their trade?'

Horn smiled, but not like it was funny.

'No, not like that. They wanted to buy us out. It appealed to them mainly because they would have a manufacturing facility right here inside the US border. They wanted to flood the market.'

'Would certainly avoid the need to get the product across the border.'

'Exactly. And they were soldiers too. Or at least the guy we dealt with was.'

'Brothers in arms crap,' Grange said.

Horn shrugged.

'This is still my country and I couldn't sit by and let it happen.'

'One thing I don't understand,' Hunter said. 'Where does Johnson fit into this?'

Horn made a face like he thought it was a dumb question.

'He ran the UK operation. Or at least he did before Seth found out he was taking half the profits for himself. Seth told Butler to kill him.'

Webb looked at Hunter who put his palms up indicating he was done asking questions for now.

'So, Matt,' Webb said. 'What was this all about? I mean, why raising all this money? Are you planning to attack your own country?'

Horn frowned and shook his head.

'Is that what you think?'

He laughed.

'What?' Grange asked.

'It started off because we were all broke and desperate. After that, they got used to the money. That's all it was. That's why they're selling out to the Mexicans. We're getting five million dollars in cash.'

'This is all just about money?'

'Is there anything else?'

Grange sat back in his seat looking disgusted.

'So, Matt, what is it that you want from us?' Webb asked.

Always the pragmatist.

'To stop it. All of it. I thought I said that already.'

'But you want a deal. Immunity. For helping us. Am I right?'

'Whatever. I don't care any more what happens to me. Just stop it.'

'How do we do that?'

'I'm meeting Seth tomorrow morning in town for breakfast. I'll tell you where and when and you can pick him up with minimum fuss. And I'll tell you who the others are and where we make the stuff. It's up in the mountains.'

'You'll give us everything?'

'Sure. I mean, if you want it.'

There was a knock at the door. Grange stood and pulled it open. Cahill was there with Logan.

'Uh, there's a detective in Scotland that you guys might want to talk to,' Cahill said.

3

Detective Superintendent Liam Moore was a creature of habit. He liked being a Super. It meant that he didn't have to do the legwork any longer. He could work a solid nine to six most days and leave the late nights to his team. He'd put his shift in when he was younger. He was respected and maybe a little feared. Fear was a good thing for a boss to instil in his team.

Which is why when his wife shook him awake in the middle of the night and stuck the phone on his ear he was not happy. He was less happy when he heard DC Irvine's voice.

She was such a hard charger. Which was good. And bad.

Bad like now.

'Sir, I'm sorry to wake you but — '

'Get to the point.'

'I have a situation with this drug case.'

A situation. This didn't sound good. Not one little bit.

'The thing is, the stuff here looks like it might be the other end of a bigger operation. Run out of Colorado.'

'The Colorado in America?'

'Yes.'

'How did this come up?'

'It's kind of a long story.'

'Can't you just tell me?'

'The FBI are involved.'

Moore sat up in bed, pulling the covers off his wife and causing her to grunt at him.

'Have you spoken to the SCDEA about this?'

'No. I only just found out.'

Moore looked at the clock by his bed. Whatever time it was, and he wasn't quite sure, it was too early.

'The FBI are meeting about it right now.'

'How do you know this?'

'Uh . . .'

Moore waited.

'That's part of the long story, sir.'

'Becky, just tell me, okay? I'm going to find out eventually.'

She told him.

'We're not doing anything about this right now,' he said when she finished.

'Sir?'

'It's the middle of the night and it sounds like the Yanks have their end of things under control.'

'What about ours?'

'We can do it better in the morning. I mean, the real morning. When normal people are awake.'

'Shouldn't we at least make contact with the FBI? I mean, like, now.'

'No. I want the SCDEA on board first.'

'But — '

'No. Meet me at the office at seven-thirty. Then we'll work out what to do.'

He didn't wait for a reply.

4

Cooper Grange glared at Logan and came back to his seat, Logan thinking: *What did I do?*

'Have you been holding back any other information?' Grange asked Cahill.

'Were you not listening?' Logan replied. 'We only just found out.'

'That's what you say.'

'What? You think there's some conspiracy of silence?'

Grange leaned forward to speak again but Webb held up a hand, cutting him off.

'The important thing,' Webb said, 'is that we have the information now. We've got an opportunity to break up an international operation so we need to make sure we're all on the same page as to where we go from here. If one of us goes too soon it might tip them off.'

Logan nodded.

'Can you call over there now?' Webb asked. 'So we can make some kind of contact.'

Logan picked up his mobile to dial.

'No,' Webb said, pushing the conference phone on the table over to Logan. 'Use that. The speaker will be much better than on your cell.'

'Hello?' Irvine's voice sounded hesitant when she answered the call.

'Becky, it's me again,' Logan said.

'Hi, listen — '

'I'm with the police and FBI agents here in Denver.'

'Detective Irvine, this is Special Agent Randall Webb of the FBI. I head up the Denver field office.'

'What can I do for you, Agent Webb?'

'Mr Finch has explained the connection between our investigations and I thought it would be appropriate if we co-ordinated our activities.'

'I agree. But the drug investigation isn't my thing. I mean, I'm just helping out over here.'

'I see. What do you suggest, then?'

'I'm going to head into the office now. My boss, Liam Moore, wants me to brief him and then we'll talk to the SCDEA. The drug squad.'

'I should probably speak with Detective Moore.'

'Detective Superintendent. Yes.'

Webb looked at his watch.

'It's early for you, Detective Irvine. When should we arrange to speak?'

'If it's early for me, it's late for you.'

'We work as long as we have to. As I'm sure you do.'

'Of course. I'm going to get ready and go see my boss. Can I speak to him first and call you back to set something up? We need the SCDEA to be in on the call as well.'

'Of course. We've got, ah, other things to occupy ourselves with in the meantime. Speak soon, Detective.'

The room was quiet after the call. Webb sat back in his seat and looked at Hunter and

Collins and then across the table at Logan and Cahill.

'I'm afraid I'm going to have to ask both of you to leave again,' he said, fixing his gaze on Cahill. 'You understand.'

Logan knew for sure that Cahill would *not* understand. He waited for his friend's retort.

'I mean,' Webb continued, 'we have an operation to plan for first thing tomorrow morning and we don't have much time.'

Cahill stood and Logan thought that, for the first time, his friend was going to go quietly. He started to get up and felt Cahill's hand on his shoulder pressing him back down into his seat.

So much for that thought.

'You're going after a soldier, am I right?' Cahill asked Webb.

'Correct.'

'Do any of you have military training or experience?'

No one answered.

'That's what I thought.'

'We don't need military training to plan an arrest operation in town,' Grange said. 'We do this all the time.'

'I'm sure you do. I wasn't offering tactical advice.'

'Then what?'

'I can tell you how he thinks. What he'll be looking out for. What he might do if he thinks something is up. So that it goes down as smooth as possible. I mean, that's what we all want, isn't it?'

351

'What exactly are you saying, Mr Cahill?' Webb asked.

'Keep me in the loop on this. I'll help you get inside this guy's brain.'

'Sort of like a consultant?'

'Whatever you want to call it.'

'I can see how that might be useful.'

Cahill grinned.

5

Friday

There was no record of any current address for Jack Butler that Irvine could find. She checked all available sources but nothing turned up. She was alone in the office at Pitt Street at seven with only her desk lamp and light from her computer monitor illuminating the place.

She didn't want to wait for Moore to arrive before giving Armstrong the heads-up about Johnson's death, Butler and the Colorado connection. It didn't matter how they had left things yesterday, he deserved to know what was going on.

Except maybe Frank Parker's late-night house call. That might not go down so well with him.

Armstrong sounded wide awake when she called his mobile.

'Where are you?' she asked.

'At home.'

Sounded like he was still pissed off.

'I need you to get to Pitt Street now.'

'Why?'

'New lead. Something big. You should get the DG here as well. He'll want to be in on it.'

She knew that would get him interested.

'What's going on?'

'I don't have time to get into it right now. I've got to speak to the Super.'

353

'What time do you want us there?'

'Soon as.'

'I'll call the DG. This better be worth it.'

'It is.'

★   ★   ★

Liam Moore arrived at the office fifteen minutes later. He was still taking his jacket off when Irvine came into his room.

'I called Armstrong,' she said. 'The SCDEA guy. He's going to come in with the DG.'

'You work fast. As always.'

'I thought, you know, it was the right thing to do.'

'It was. When will they be here?'

'As long as it takes to get organised and drive over.'

'Okay. I suppose you'd better bring me up to speed on everything before they get here.'

Irvine nodded, walked to the chair across the desk from Moore and sat down. She had her file and put it on the desk. It was overflowing with new material so she ordered it as best she could and told him what she knew.

She did the same thing for Armstrong and the DG, Paul Warren, half an hour later.

When she was done, Warren looked at Moore before he spoke.

'It's just the one guy running things here?' he asked Irvine.

'So far as I'm aware, sir, it is now. But the FBI may know more.'

'Do we have an address on him?'

354

'No. But I've got this.' Irvine took copies of a photograph of Butler from her file and passed them around.

'I got this from the MOD this morning. It's maybe four or five years out of date but it's the best I could do.'

'Priority number one has to be getting this guy in custody,' Moore said. 'Are we agreed?'

Warren nodded.

'We can't have him running around out there killing everyone who can identify him. It's bad enough already. The last thing we need is more bodies piling up.'

'What should we do?' Irvine asked.

Moore pointed at the file in her lap.

'Go through everything on him. I mean, service history, family, previous addresses. Everything. Run down every lead. If you need more bodies to do it, let me know. I'll authorise the manpower for it.

'Do you want me to speak to press relations?' Irvine asked. 'You know, to get his name and picture out there?'

Moore leaned back, clasping his hands behind his head. 'What do you think?' he asked Warren.

'My inclination is not to do it. Not just yet anyway. I mean, if he sees it, he might go right off the deep end. Could be a bloodbath.'

Moore nodded.

'Isn't it a bit late for that?' Armstrong said. 'Look at what he did to Johnson, to Russell Hall and the accountants. How much worse is it going to get?'

'We don't know,' Moore said. 'That's the

problem. We have no idea how many more people he's likely to target. So let's not give him a reason.'

'Who's going to speak to the FBI?' Irvine asked.

'I'll handle that,' Warren said. 'Can you give me the names of the agents over there?'

Irvine nodded.

'Okay, people,' Moore said. 'Let's get to work and get this bastard locked up.'

6

Irvine went back to her desk and shuffled through her file again. She focused on what little information she had on Butler, but it was insubstantial and led nowhere, no matter how many times she went over it. The guy was a ghost.

She went back through the file one last time from the start. After ten minutes she came across the handwritten sheet of notes she had made when trying to get her head around the case earlier in the week. One line jumped out at her:

Suzie Murray — is she lying + does she know the dealer?

It wasn't so much the content of the note, but the thought process that it triggered: about working girls and where they lived. She picked up her desk phone and called the Stewart Street police station.

'Stewart Street,' a male voice answered.

'Superintendent Pope, please,' Irvine said.

'Who's this?'

'DC Irvine with CID.'

'Hold on.'

She did. A minute stretched to two, stretched to three.

'Pope,' a voice said.

'Sir, it's DC Irvine from Pitt Street.'

'I know. What's this about?'

'We spoke earlier this week. About a murder inquiry.'

The line went quiet. Irvine heard Pope breathing but he said nothing.

'Sir?'

'Is this about the prozzies?'

'That's correct, sir.'

'You wanted information on other girls, that kind of thing. Connected to your stiff.'

'Yes.'

She heard the sound of papers shuffled on a desk.

'Two names and an address,' Pope said after a little more shuffling.

Irvine wrote down the names he gave her and the address of a flat in the east end of the city, not far from where Russell Hall's body had been found. She wanted to ask how long Pope had been sitting on the information, bit her tongue instead and thanked him. He hung up without replying.

She thought about going over to the address on her own. Remembered the last time she had done that and put her hand against the bruised part of her face. Decided to find Armstrong and go over together.

Armstrong was still in with Moore. Warren was nowhere to be seen. She stuck her head around the door.

'Kenny,' she said.

He turned, slightly startled. She held up the piece of paper with the names and addresses on it.

'I got an address for other girls that Joanna Lewski and Suzie Murray worked with.'

Armstrong frowned.

'From the Super at Stewart Street. I called him before, remember?'

'He called you back now?' Armstrong asked, looking at his watch.

'No. I called to chase him.'

Armstrong turned from her to look at Moore, who said nothing.

'Okay,' Armstrong said. 'I need to be in on the call with the FBI in an hour. Then we'll get over there.'

Irvine stared at the back of his head after he turned to Moore. She went back to her desk and looked at her computer monitor as the screensaver came on. Someone had been on to her computer and changed it to a topless shot of some Z-list female celebrity.

She found it kind of funny. Wasn't sure why.

Strange days.

7

'I think they let us in on the bare minimum to keep us happy,' Logan told Cahill as they rode the elevator down from the eighteenth floor at close to midnight.

'What do you mean?'

'Allowing us to sit in on the preliminary stuff and then telling us to get lost when they were going to have the call with the cops back home.'

'You're probably right.'

Logan was surprised that Cahill was so calm.

'That doesn't piss you off?'

Cahill turned to him, flicked his eyes above and to his left and said 'no'. Logan looked in the same direction quickly and saw a camera in the corner of the elevator car. He said nothing else until they were in the car and driving back to their hotel.

'What's going on?' Logan asked.

'I got everything that I needed from those guys already.'

Logan concentrated on the junction ahead, the traffic system still feeling alien to him. After safely negotiating a left turn, he glanced at Cahill.

'Alex, this is serious stuff and we need to back off now. Leave it to the FBI.'

'Like at Ruby Ridge? Or Waco?'

Logan had never heard of Ruby Ridge and thought that WACO was an ATF operation so far as he could remember. Not that it mattered.

'So what? This isn't our fight. We got to the truth about your friend. Let's go home.'

'I can't.'

'Can't you let it go for once?'

Cahill said nothing. Didn't look at Logan.

'What is it with you and this thing?' Logan asked, almost shouting now.

Cahill sighed.

'It's just me.'

'What does that even mean?' Logan said, pulling the car to a stop at the side of the road.

Cahill turned in the passenger seat to face Logan. In the harsh light from the streetlamps outside he looked older to Logan than he had before. The lines on his face more prominent. A roadmap of his life in service.

'What I mean is, it's who I am. I don't back away from anything. I never will.'

Logan held his friend's gaze.

'A good man died. Maybe not directly at the hands of this Raines and his crew, but close enough. And not just a good man, but someone who put his life on the line for others and for his country. Who served with me. If it had come down to it, we would have died together defending what we believed in.'

'But . . . '

'And I know that Webb and Grange and Hunter and the others are the same. But that doesn't matter to me. It's personal for me. And that means that I can't let it go.'

Logan twisted his hands over the steering wheel.

'You've been through enough with me now to understand.'

'I don't think I'll ever understand, Alex. I guess we're just built different.'

'If I ask you to stay in this with me, to cover my back, will you do it?'

'You know that I will.'

Cahill put a hand on Logan's shoulder.

'Not so different,' Cahill said.

★　★　★

When they got back to the hotel, Logan called Ellie's mobile. He knew she would be up, getting ready for school.

'Hey, Ellie. How's things there?'

'Okay. But I miss my own room. I mean, having my own stuff around.'

'I know. Me too.'

'When are you coming home?'

'Soon. Probably tomorrow.'

Assuming I'm not in jail. Or dead.

'Cool.'

Do kids still say that? he wondered.

'We'll do something when I get back, okay. Go out for dinner or whatever.'

'Shopping?'

He laughed.

'If you like.'

'I like.'

'Okay. Look, it's late here so I'm going to go to bed now.'

Cahill was watching him when he ended the call.

'That sounded nice,' he said.

'It was.'

'You miss her.'

'Of course.'

'Then make sure you get back to her. That girl needs you.'

'I'm not quitting on you, if that's what you're saying.'

'I wasn't saying that. We've all got families.'

Nothing bonded one human being to another like blood.

Logan went to the bathroom and splashed cold water on his face. It had been a long day. He dried his face and went back out to the main part of the room. Cahill was sitting at the small table by the window looking at the TV. Logan was sure he wasn't taking in what was on. There were two handguns on Cahill's bed, nestled tightly in nylon holsters with a box of bullets beside them.

'This was your errand?' he asked. 'When I went to get the car.'

Cahill looked at him and nodded.

'Are they legal?'

'No.'

'Where did you get them?'

'I can't tell you that.'

'I mean, it wasn't from a criminal or anything, was it?'

Logan heard how stupid the question sounded even as the words formed in his brain and left his mouth. Wished he could have it back.

Cahill laughed. It sounded genuine, not like he was mocking Logan.

'Stupid question,' Logan said.

'I know what you meant,' Cahill told him. 'She's an ex-cop.'

'And how did she get into the business of selling illegal weapons?'

Cahill shrugged.

'She wanted to do some good.'

Logan shook his head and sat on the bed.

'One of these is mine?' He picked up one of the holsters and slid the gun out, feeling the weight of it in his hand. 'And you loaded them already.'

'Not much use to anyone otherwise.'

Logan put the gun back in its holster and replaced it on the bed.

'So,' he said. 'What's the plan?'

8

'Why did you support Hunter when he was pressing Webb to have the SWAT team on standby for this Raines operation tomorrow?' Logan asked Cahill.

They were sitting at the table in their room with the TV on mute. The guns were still on the bed.

'You've heard that cliché?' Cahill asked.

'I'm a lawyer. I've heard lots. Which one in particular?'

'That failing to prepare — '

'Is preparing to fail. Yeah, I've heard that one.'

'Webb said Horn told them that he was meeting Raines alone, right?'

'Uh-huh.'

'But if Horn's story is true, he's been thinking about coming in for a while now. And he deliberately messed up the drug cocktail to draw attention to their operation.'

'You mean killing people? There are other ways.'

'You're missing the point, Logan.'

'I get your point. I was making a different one. What you mean is that his behaviour might have rung an alarm with Raines. Who obviously isn't stupid.'

'Correct.'

'So Raines might be suspicious of Horn now and not tell him everything.'

'Go on.'

'Which means we should be ready for him coming to the meeting with back-up.'

'I knew all that training you've been getting wouldn't go to waste.'

'Trouble is, I don't think that Webb or Grange were buying into what you were telling them. Why else would the SWAT team be on standby at the police HQ instead of on site?'

'A mixture of institutional arrogance — which is standard for the Feds from what I can gather — and a desire to keep it low key. They figure if Raines doesn't see an army coming for him his reaction might be less . . . '

'Extreme?'

'Good word. Yes.'

'What's your take on that? I mean, Hunter was definitely on your side.'

'According to what you read about that Fed bank robbery job he got caught up in, he's got reason to be cautious. Every new screw-up by the Feds that gets someone killed demonstrates a certain resistance to anyone's perspective but their own.'

'I think Grange said no because it was the opposite of what you said.'

'You might be right. Great tactical thinking, huh?'

Logan smiled, though the knot of tension in his stomach was tightening with each minute that passed. He glanced back at the guns.

'You know, you can still say no,' Cahill said, seeing the anxiety in Logan's face. 'And I'll go it alone.'

Logan stood and walked to the window, looking out into the city.

'Tell me what we're going to do,' Logan said.

He turned to Cahill and leaned back against the window sill.

'Webb and Grange will be across the street in the building opposite the diner where Raines will meet Horn. It's a three-storey residential apartment building. They'll put the occupants of the second-floor apartment at the front up in a hotel and use that as their forward command post. They'll have comms links to their agents on the ground and to the SWAT team.'

'Hunter and Collins will be in the diner at separate tables,' Logan added. 'Dressed like regular guys getting breakfast before going to work.'

'Correct. There will be two female agents and a male agent in there also posing as the owner and serving staff.'

'No civilians?'

'Never. Too risky.'

'What about ordinary customers. How do they deal with them?'

'Turn them away at the door. Make up some story about why they can't serve anyone else. Regular people will swallow anything if you say it with enough conviction.'

'We're regular people.'

Cahill looked blankly at him.

'Never mind,' Logan said. 'So, that's a total of five law enforcement personnel in the diner and two across the street.'

'Plus Ruiz and Martinez in a car around the

corner on Seventeenth Street.'

'And we're just going to walk right into the middle of this operation and order breakfast.'

'While wearing our illegal weapons.'

'I forgot that part.'

Logan shook his head.

'The Feds are going to go mental when they see us in there, so how do we get past the first line of defence? I mean, won't they turn us away as well?'

'They know me well enough by now and won't risk compromising the operation by getting us out of there.'

'Sounds easy.'

'It's not. And you stay as far out of harm's way as possible if Raines decides to light it up, okay.'

Logan nodded.

'Leave that shit to me.'

'You can count on it.'

'If you have to put him down, though . . . '

'I've done it before.'

9

They took Armstrong's car to the flat in the East End occupied by the two prostitutes Pope had identified. Armstrong drove out of the city centre along Duke Street while Irvine stared at the old photograph of Butler, trying to see something in his eyes to explain everything that he had done. But it was just a digital facsimile of the man: coloured ink arranged by a computer on glossy paper. The more she stared at it, the less real it became. She put the photograph in the door pocket and looked ahead.

'How did it go with the FBI?' she asked.

Armstrong glanced at her then back at the road.

'Not much for us to tell them. We don't have anything to go on with this guy Butler yet.'

'What about them?'

'They were cagey about giving away too much. All they said was that they were close and planning for an operation.'

'An operation?'

'They didn't elaborate.'

'We're co-operating with each other, right?'

'As much as we can at this point. But they'll want to keep it to themselves.'

'You mean take all the credit.'

'I suppose.'

They fell into silence again. Irvine checked her

watch. It was around nine. She thought that the two prostitutes would likely be asleep after a long night shift. Might be good to catch them a little off guard. Maybe they would say something that ordinarily they would try to hide, whether out of fear or a general mistrust of the police.

'I need to tell you something,' Irvine said.

Armstrong didn't look at her or say anything.

'About how I got Butler's name.'

'I was wondering.'

She took a quick breath.

'Frank Parker told me.'

She saw his fingers tighten on the steering wheel, the skin stretching and turning white.

'He came to my house last night.'

This time Armstrong turned to look at her. There was something hard in his eyes.

'There was nothing to it,' Irvine said quickly. 'He wanted to give me information.'

'Such a gentleman.'

'Kenny —'

'He'll want something in return eventually. You know that?'

'Yes.'

'Fine. It's between you and him. Nothing to do with me. But watch your back.'

She sensed that her interaction with Parker both at the restaurant and last night had changed her relationship with Armstrong. Had soured it for him. He would never be able to view anything Parker did objectively, no matter how positive it might be for this case. There was nothing she could do about that.

'This case will be over soon,' he said. 'Now

that we know who Butler is, he can't stay hidden for ever.'

Unspoken: *and we won't have to be partners any more.*

Irvine didn't regret how she had dealt with Parker: it was part of the job. Armstrong would have to carry his own personal demons.

10

Four men occupied the seats in the twin cab pick-up truck. A heavy-duty canvas sheet was strapped over the truck bed, covering two automatic rifles and four handguns. Behind the truck was a nondescript, five-year-old sedan. There were two men in the front seats with another two automatic rifles in a bag in the trunk of the car.

The six men travelled silently in the tension that builds before a battle. They were all veterans and used to the stress of such situations. It did not matter to them that their adversaries this time would be their fellow countrymen and officers of the Federal authorities.

These men were now on the other side of the line. And the pay-off that awaited all of them was all that mattered now. No one was going to take that away from them. Not one of their own and not the FBI.

The enemy was the enemy, no matter what flag they operated under.

The cars moved on through the night, ten miles from Denver city centre.

11

The flat was at the top right of a block of four. It was a familiar local authority property probably built sometime in the fifties or sixties. The entry door was located at ground-floor level beside the door for the lower flat. The stairs up to the first floor were internal.

Armstrong pulled up to the kerb outside the block and switched the engine off. Irvine looked up at the windows of the flat facing the street.

'Curtains closed,' she said.

'Maybe no one's home.'

'Probably still asleep. Let's go wake them up?'

Two young children, no older than seven or eight, were playing alone in the front garden of the neighbouring house on the left. Irvine smiled at one of them and got a two-fingered salute in reply.

'Nice,' she said under her breath.

Irvine stood behind Armstrong as he knocked on the door of the flat. They waited for thirty seconds and Armstrong tried again — harder this time. Third time, he banged with his fist until they heard movement on the stairs inside. A woman's voice, groggy from drugs or sleep or something else, asked who was there.

'Police,' Armstrong said. 'We need to speak to you.'

There was the sound of the woman ascending the stairs and a muffled conversation with someone. They couldn't make out the voices from behind the closed door.

Armstrong turned to look at Irvine and she raised her eyebrows at him.

'Probably trying to work out where to hide their gear,' he told her, turning back to hammer on the door again.

They heard the lock being fiddled with and the door swung inwards. A woman of about twenty stood in the lower hall in a dirty bathrobe. Her eyes were hooded and her jaw muscles slack.

'Come on,' Armstrong said, stepping into the hall and taking the woman by the elbow to lead her upstairs.

Irvine followed, smelling ripe body odour and marijuana smoke. The carpet on the stairs was worn at the edges and threadbare. It looked like one of those patterned efforts that had been popular thirty years ago.

Armstrong reached the top of the stairs with the woman and pushed at the door leading to the hall inside the flat. He went through the door. Irvine was two steps below him when the first gunshot sounded.

The brain takes a little while to react when encountering something unexpected. Irvine stopped where she was at the sound of the shot.

Another one sounded.

A woman screamed.

Another shot.

Irvine ran up and into the hallway.

12

The woman who had answered the door was slumped on the floor with her back against the wall. Her eyelids fluttered. The wall above her was streaked with blood and matter where she had slid down it. An entry wound below her right collar bone pumped blood out, soaking the front of her robe.

Armstrong was not in the hall.

The door at the end of the hall opened and another woman of about the same age came out of the bathroom. She was wearing panties only. She saw Irvine kneeling by the other woman. Irvine wasn't sure what her eyes registered, but the woman stepped back into the bathroom and closed the door.

'Kenny,' Irvine shouted.

Armstrong's hand appeared out of the first doorway on Irvine's right. She ran into the room at a crouch.

Armstrong was in a bedroom in a similar position as the woman out in the hall, sitting inside the door with his back against the wall. He raised his other hand and Irvine saw that his pinkie and the finger next to it were missing. Ragged stumps leaked blood. He was in shock, his skin pale.

Irvine pulled a pillow from the bed, took the cover off and wrapped it tight around his wound, tying it as securely as she could. The material was immediately soaked in blood.

She put her hands on his cheeks.

'Butler?' she asked.

Armstrong closed his eyes. She shook him and they opened again.

'Kenny. Was it him?'

He shook his head. Irvine wasn't sure if he was telling her no or that he didn't know. Not that it mattered. There was someone in the flat with a gun.

Irvine turned and crouched in the doorway. She looked quickly out into the hall. The woman was now unconscious. Otherwise, it was empty.

She pulled her phone from her bag, dialled nine nine nine and explained the situation to the operator as quickly as she could.

'I need an armed response team here now,' she said.

The operator was good. Most of them were. She got right on it and kept Irvine on the line until she could confirm that the message had been relayed and would be actioned.

'Do you want to stay on the line, Detective?' the operator asked.

'Yes. I'll keep it open. That way you'll have a record of anything that happens. But I don't want to talk any more.'

Irvine set the phone against the open door so that the sounds from within the house would be heard over the line.

She took a breath and shouted, 'Jack Butler!'

No reply.

'I'm a police officer. There is an armed response vehicle on its way here now.'

She wasn't sure what else to say so stayed quiet. There was no use trying to talk him out of any further violence. He was already in line to be charged with multiple murders.

A door opened down the hall and footsteps sounded, running towards Irvine's position. She moved back from the door, tripped over Armstrong's outstretched legs and fell on to her behind as the footsteps reached the door to the bedroom.

13

The woman from the bathroom hurtled past the door, still dressed in her panties and nothing else. Irvine heard her go down the stairs and out the front door where she started to scream incoherently.

More movement sounded from within the flat. Irvine held her breath.

'Does that mean you're not armed?' a man's voice shouted from somewhere down the hall. 'That there's an ARV on the way?'

'Mr Butler?' Irvine said loudly.

'How's your partner doing?'

'He's alive.'

'Pity. But I can fix that, you know.'

She heard him moving again. It sounded closer than the first time but she couldn't be sure. Armstrong reached out with his good hand and tugged at Irvine's sleeve. She looked at him. He pointed behind her. Irvine turned her head and saw an aluminium baseball bat resting against the wall by the bed. Self-defence for the criminal fraternity.

She stood and backed away from the door, reaching down to grab the handle of the bat. She went forward again and stood beside the doorway with her back against the wall. Her breathing felt hot and shallow, as though she couldn't get enough oxygen into her lungs. Sweat formed on her forehead and her heart

378

thumped loudly in her chest.

Irvine put both hands on the handle of the bat and raised it in front of her. She saw that it shook in her unsteady hands, adrenalin buzzing through her system.

She bent her knees and pulled the bat around to the side, readying herself to swing at anyone who appeared in the doorway.

'You're out of options, Butler,' Irvine shouted.

She heard him laughing.

'I think you're the one without options.'

The door frame splintered above Irvine as two bullets ripped into it. She turned her head away from it, feeling wood splinters bite at her cheek and head. She held that position as another shot sounded, the bullet thudding into the plaster of the wall outside the door.

He's trying to shoot me through the wall.

'You counting bullets?' Butler shouted.

She had not been. Tried to remember how many times he had fired now.

'Don't bother,' he called out. 'I've got plenty more.'

The woman who had gone outside was still screaming. Irvine thought that she heard distant sirens. Then nothing. Maybe she had imagined it.

Three more shots sounded, the plaster of the wall outside exploding under their impact.

Irvine looked at the window. It was front-facing. She could climb out and lower herself down, dropping the rest of the way. There was a risk she might break an ankle or leg in the drop and she would be a sitting target for Butler. Plus it would mean leaving Armstrong there alone. She decided against it.

Where's that damned ARV?

14

The pick-up truck and sedan stopped outside Union Station at the north end of Seventeenth Street in Downtown Denver. The big sign on the building — 'Travel By Train' — loomed above them.

It was close to four in the morning.

The driver of the truck got out and walked across the road. He looked down the street, three blocks from the diner at the corner of Market Street where Raines was going to meet Matt Horn. There was little traffic on the streets and the air was cool on his skin.

The man went to the sedan where the driver's window slid down silently.

'So?' the driver of the sedan asked the other man.

'He said we wait.'

'Then what?'

'He'll call when it's time. When he's about to move.'

The sedan driver nodded, looking past the other man and down the street to the diner.

'After that we go in shooting?'

The pick-up driver nodded. 'Everyone is a target.'

'Just the way it should be.'

'Okay, we can't wait here. It's too close to the diner. The Feds will be scoping the place out and probably holing up somewhere nearby.'

The sedan driver nodded.

'Let's park up somewhere else. Not too far. We need to be close when it goes off.'

The pick-up driver went back to his vehicle and got inside. He grabbed a baseball cap from the floor and pulled it on.

'Let's go find somewhere to hang. Get some sleep,' he said.

His passenger looked at him solemnly.

'What?' the driver asked.

'We're really doing this? I mean, we could get out of this now. Before, you know . . . '

'Chain of command. And we never leave a man behind.'

'We're not at war.'

'Yeah, we are.'

15

Irvine's thigh muscles started to shake from the effort of holding her position at the door. She eased back up and shook her legs to loosen the muscles.

'You're doing fine,' Armstrong told her from the floor.

She looked down at him. He looked alert. Kind of.

'You okay?' she asked.

He held his injured hand up, dripping blood on to the carpet.

'Right,' Irvine said. 'Sorry.'

Armstrong smiled. Or, at least, that's what it looked like he was trying to achieve.

Irvine whipped her head around at the sound of more movement down the hall. Four shots sounded in quick succession, blasting through the door frame. Irvine threw a hand up to shield her eyes from the splinters.

Butler made his move.

Irvine heard the sound of his feet running. Coming at her.

She stepped into the doorway and swung the bat high. She knew from his army records that Butler was around six feet tall.

Her aim was good. The timing a little off.

Butler was almost past the door when Irvine completed her swing. The tip of the bat caught him on the ear and sent him thumping into the opposite wall. He stayed on his feet, dazed, and swung the gun round at Irvine.

She ducked and fell into the room as the wall where she had been standing evaporated, showering her and Armstrong in dust.

She threw the baseball bat full force out into the hallway.

Butler put a protective arm up in front of his face and fired again into the doorway.

Irvine closed her eyes and felt the snap of the bullets as they passed through the air beside her head, thinking: *Now he's got us.*

The sound of the gunfire stopped.

Irvine heard Butler's footsteps as he ran down the stairs and outside. A gunshot sounded and the woman's screaming stopped. Other people shouted and screamed.

Irvine grabbed her mobile from the floor and went to the window in time to see Butler get into a car and drive off, the tyres screeching as he floored the accelerator.

This time she was sure she heard sirens.

16

They got up at five-thirty with a wake-up call from the hotel. Cahill picked up the phone in a daze and said hello before he realised it was automated. He grunted, slammed the phone down and went for a shower.

Logan got up straight away and opened the curtains because he knew that if he stayed in bed he would doze off again. He'd slept fitfully, his stomach flip-flopping at the thought of what the morning to come might hold for them. He boiled the kettle and used a sachet of branded coffee. Drank it strong and black.

Cahill spent a brief five minutes in the bathroom getting dressed then came out. Logan went to the bathroom and sank to his knees at the toilet, jettisoning the coffee and what was left of the food he ate yesterday into the bowl. He hacked out a cough when his stomach settled.

'You shouldn't go,' Cahill told him, standing in the door of the bathroom and pulling his shirt over the holster fixed to his belt.

Logan stood and went to the sink to brush his teeth, knowing that the bitter taste in his mouth would persist no matter what he did.

'I'm fine,' he told Cahill, not sure if he meant it himself.

Cahill stayed at the door, flattening his hair with his hands.

'I'm scared too,' he told Logan.

Logan stopped brushing his teeth and looked at Cahill. He looked the same as always.

'I've learned how to deal with it, that's all.'

Logan finished brushing and rinsed his mouth.

'Did you used to get nervous before?' Cahill asked. 'I mean, going into court or whatever?'

'Different thing.'

'Then you did?'

'Of course I did. But there was no risk of me getting shot and killed, was there?'

'Did you throw up the first few times?'

Logan didn't answer.

'Look, I'm not trying to embarrass you, Logan.'

'I know what you're doing. It won't change how I feel right now.'

'I'm only going to let you go with me if I can be sure you're okay.'

Logan looked at his friend for a moment.

'I'm going with you.'

Cahill nodded and went back to the main part of the room.

★ ★ ★

Cahill insisted that they eat something and walk down to check out the area around the diner. All that they could find in the room were a couple of biscuits so they shared them, Logan glad that he was able to keep them down.

'Put on a jacket that you can pull down over your belt to hide your gun,' Cahill told Logan. 'Don't want to be too obvious.'

Logan fitted the holster to his belt and when he had that in place around his waist he grabbed a light jacket and pulled it on. It hung long enough and loose at his waist. Cahill wore something similar.

'Follow my lead,' Cahill said. 'If it gets nasty, shoot to kill.'

Logan nodded, his jaw muscles bunching as he clenched his teeth.

'Try not to hit the Feds. Or the cops.'

Cahill smiled. Logan couldn't manage one in return.

It was six-thirty. Ninety minutes to go.

17

The armed response unit screeched to a stop outside the flat, followed by a traffic car which had been in the area and responded to the call.

'In the building,' Irvine shouted at the armed police as they got out of their car. 'Officer shot upstairs.'

She had time to see the body of the woman who had run from the flat lying on the grass. She had fallen face down after being shot, exposing the ugly exit wound in her back where the bullet had torn out of her after destroying her insides. Blood had soaked into the grass.

The driver of the traffic car, a powerful BMW, opened his door. Irvine shook her head and ran towards him waving him back into the car.

'No. I'm coming with you. Let's go.'

She got in the rear of the car and told them to go, pointing in the direction she had seen Butler drive off.

The cop in the front passenger seat got on the radio and asked for aerial support. He gave his position to the dispatcher, talking in short bursts.

Irvine tried to breathe, put her hand against her chest and felt her heart hammering inside.

She closed her eyes and listened to the radio chatter: more cars on their way to join the pursuit and then a voice from the helicopter. It was already in the air overhead. At the first report of an officer shooting, every spare resource had been deployed.

When she opened her eyes again they were racing down a ramp to join the eastbound carriageway of the M8 motorway. The passenger turned to look at her.

'You okay?'

She nodded, not trusting herself to talk in a steady voice.

The helicopter pilot's voice came on the radio telling them that Butler's car was about a half-mile ahead of them. Irvine saw the speedometer press on past a hundred.

She realised that she didn't even have her seatbelt on, grabbed at it and took three attempts to click it into place.

'There he is,' the driver said, pointing at a car weaving in and out of the traffic up ahead.

'Boy doesn't have the power to outrun us,' his partner added.

He got on the radio and alerted all other cars to their exact location. Activated the lights and siren. It was louder than Irvine remembered.

Cars in front of them started to slow and pull out of their way and they gained quickly on Butler. He was pulling the car recklessly across the road, almost colliding with a big four-by-four.

'He's going to get someone killed,' Irvine shouted.

'So long as it's only him,' the driver replied.

They passed another on-ramp and Irvine saw two more police cars with their lights flashing get in line behind the car she was in.

They pulled to within fifty yards of Butler.

We've got this guy now, she thought.

He swerved hard towards the outside lane to avoid a car slowing ahead of him. Didn't quite make it.

The rear panel of his car clipped the back of the other one. It sent Butler's car spinning through the central barrier and into the path of a truck on the opposite carriageway.

Irvine watched smoke billow from the truck's tyres as the driver slammed on his brakes. Thought she saw Butler's face looking back at her.

Then the car was obliterated.

18

Irvine was sitting with her legs out of the rear door of the traffic car when an unmarked car drew up on the stretch of motorway that had been closed to deal with the accident. The place was crawling with emergency service vehicles and personnel. Irvine looked over and saw Liam Moore and Paul Warren get out of the car. She raised a hand and they walked over to meet her.

'How's Kenny doing?' Warren asked. 'I was told he got shot but didn't get the details.'

'He lost two fingers,' Irvine said, holding up her hand and touching her own fingers. 'Otherwise he should be fine, I think. I didn't have time to wait around to find out.'

'Butler was waiting for you when you got to the flat?' Moore asked.

'He must have been hiding out there after what he did to the accountants.'

'What about the women at the flat?' Moore asked.

He looked around at the carnage on the road and shook his head.

'One dead for sure. Touch and go if the other one will make it. Both shot.'

'Jesus,' Warren said, shaking his head. 'What a psycho.'

'Yes, sir,' Irvine said.

'You don't look so good,' Moore told her.

'Thanks. I feel as good as I look.'

She tried to smile at her own joke. Didn't succeed. Couldn't seem to get her muscles to do anything that she wanted. The constant chatter from the car's radio sounded like white noise buzzing in her ears.

'Let me get someone to drive you home,' Moore said.

She nodded and rested her chin on her hands. Didn't have the energy to know how she felt about it all now that it was over. Tears welled in her eyes and she wiped at them, unashamed to do so in front of Moore and Warren.

'You did good,' Moore told her. 'You and Kenny. Busted this thing open.'

Warren nodded.

'Thanks,' Irvine managed to say, hearing the tremor in her own voice.

She didn't trust herself to hold it together and speak at the same time so she said nothing else.

A member of Warren's team came over to speak to him. He walked away with the man for a moment then turned back to Irvine and Moore.

'Word from the hospital is Kenny will be fine,' he said.

One of these days, Irvine thought, no one around me will get shot or killed.

19

Logan looked right along the block of Market Street as they crossed the intersection with Sixteenth Street heading north. He saw the lights on in the diner at the far corner of the block. The buildings across the street were dark. A homeless man lay in a doorway two buildings along from the diner. Everything looked normal.

'They must be in the diner now,' he said to Cahill. 'The FBI, I mean.'

'Yeah. Which means they'll be across the street also. Probably put blackout coverings up at the windows so that they can have lights on inside without anyone outside being able to notice.'

They reached the sidewalk on the other side of the intersection and kept on walking.

'How will they know what's going on outside?'

'Radio communications will be open all the time. Plus they'll probably have cameras set up to give them a view of the street and the interior of the diner. Technology's good for that stuff. It'll be small and unobtrusive.'

'Can't see it unless you know what you're looking for.'

Cahill nodded.

They passed the bus station, crossed the road at the intersection with Blake and turned right on to Wazee Street. The street was parallel to Market, two blocks north. There was another diner there open for the breakfast trade.

Cahill stopped outside the diner and checked his watch. Saw that it was seven in the morning.

'Let's grab something here. Those biscuits didn't do it for me. I need a muffin.'

Logan followed him inside. The place was basic, but they didn't need anything beyond a hot drink and a muffin. They ordered and ate in silence, Logan wondering how he was going to keep the muffin in his stomach.

★　★　★

'Did you see the two guys pass by at the end of the street?' Cooper Grange asked Randall Webb.

Grange pointed at one of the four monitor screens set up in the second-floor apartment across from the target diner. Webb nodded.

'They kept on walking?' he asked.

'Yes. But you want them checked out?'

Grange turned to look at the two agents standing behind him — men in their mid-thirties with ballistic vests on under FBI windcheaters. Webb had decided that he wanted more personnel after all. There were four of them in the apartment, Ruiz and Martinez in their car and three more agents in the diner. Plus the city cops, Hunter and Collins.

Eleven should be enough.

'No. Leave it for now. But if you see them again, get someone on it.'

Grange leaned forward and tapped the screen of a different monitor.

'What about him?'

Webb looked at the same screen. Saw the

homeless man lying bundled in a doorway.

'How long has he been there?'

Grange looked again at the agents behind them and raised his eyebrows. They looked at each other.

'Since before we got here,' the shorter of the two men said.

The other man nodded to confirm.

'Go roust him,' Webb said. 'Move him on, but don't create a fuss. If he gets too rowdy leave him be.'

The shorter man left the room. The three remaining men watched as he appeared on the screen in front of them. He went to the homeless man and crouched beside him, shaking his shoulder.

Webb glanced at a monitor to his left and saw Matt Horn enter the frame of the picture.

'Horn's here,' he said.

Grange looked at the same screen and then at his watch.

'He's early.'

They watched as Horn went inside the diner.

When they looked back at the other screen they saw the agent back away from the homeless man, turn and begin to walk back to their building. He looked up at the camera and shook his head.

They waited in silence until he was back in the room.

'Well?' Grange asked the agent.

'He's out of it. Stinks of booze and piss. He's not going anywhere any time soon.'

Webb looked at the still form of the man on

the screen. Decided he could live with his presence.

'How long now?' he asked, not looking up from the monitors.

'A half-hour,' Grange said.

The two men they had seen earlier appeared again on one of the monitors — the one that was showing the front of the diner.

20

A woman FBI agent moved to the door of the diner as Cahill pushed it open and stepped inside.

'I'm sorry, sir,' she said, holding up a hand. 'We're having a problem with the electrics today so — '

Cahill ignored her and walked into the main part of the diner. It was compact, with a dividing wall at the front between the welcome area and the actual diner. The wall extended halfway across the width of the building.

Logan followed Cahill as he stepped around the wall. The woman looked at them and over at the male agent standing behind the cash register just inside the door.

The tables were arranged in four rows between side walls featuring exposed brickwork. The back wall was painted white and had a set of double doors leading to the kitchen.

Jake Hunter was at a table by the left-hand wall. His partner, Danny Collins, was seated in the middle of the third row along from the wall and Matt Horn was at the table nearest the front on the opposite wall. He was hidden from anyone coming in the door behind the dividing wall. All three men looked up when they heard the agent talking to Cahill. Or trying to talk to him.

Logan heard a quiet commotion behind him

397

as he came around the dividing wall. The double doors at the back opened and another woman agent looked out at them. Cahill nodded at her and went to a table two up from Hunter against the same wall. He nodded at Hunter as he passed by. Hunter returned the nod and went back to reading, or pretending to read, the newspaper in front of him.

Horn watched them, expressionless.

Collins shook his head and sipped from a cup of black coffee.

Cahill sat in the chair nearest the front, turned the chair sideways so that he could see the entrance. Logan sat with his back to the rear wall.

The male agent at the cash register walked to the gap in the dividing wall and stared at Cahill.

'Can we get some coffee?' Cahill asked loudly.

★ ★ ★

'What the hell are they doing here?' Grange shouted after watching them on the monitor. 'I told you he was trouble.'

He turned to face Webb, his lip curling up into what was almost a snarl. Webb thought that it was the most angry he had ever seen Grange.

'He timed it well,' Webb said impassively.

'What?'

'There's nothing we can do. It's too late.'

Grange looked like he was ready to explode. Webb held up his hands.

'Tell them over there,' Webb said, pointing at

398

the diner on the screen. 'To be cool.'

Grange boiled. Then he got on the radio and told them to be cool.

*   *   *

Logan saw the agents at the front move back to the cash register. Heard them talking quietly and then the woman in the kitchen came out with coffee and filled their cups. She even smiled.

Logan noticed for the first time how rigid Horn's body language was. Everyone else was doing a passable job at looking relaxed.

*   *   *

Outside on Seventeenth Street Agent Ruiz watched from the driver's seat of his car as a pick-up truck pulled up and stopped on the block north of the intersection with Market. He and Martinez were on the block of Seventeenth Street immediately to the south of the intersection. The pickup was no more than fifty yards from them.

Ruiz nudged Martinez who was dozing beside him. He jutted his chin to point at the pick-up. They could make out four people in the cab, but not much else. No one made a move to get out of the truck.

'What do you think?' Martinez said.

'Get on the radio.'

Ruiz reached inside his jacket and unsnapped the catch on his shoulder holster.

'We got a vehicle on Seventeenth,' Martinez

said into his radio. 'Pickup truck. Four occupants. Copy?'

Hiss

'Copy that,' Webb's voice sounded. 'What are they doing?'

Martinez paused. Still no movement in the truck. 'Nothing, sir.'

'Keep watching. Let me know the second anything changes.'

'Copy that, sir.'

Martinez followed the lead of his partner and unsnapped the catch of his holster. They exchanged a glance. Neither of them had ever discharged their weapon on active duty.

A sedan passed by their car heading north with two occupants. It slowed as it passed the truck, then sped up and turned left on to Blake.

Martinez spoke into the radio again.

'Got another one. A sedan. Passed us and turned on to Blake behind you. Copy?'

Hiss

'Follow the sedan.'

Ruiz started the car, checked for traffic and pulled out. Martinez looked into the interior of the truck as they passed by.

'Four men,' he told Ruiz as they turned on to Blake. 'Didn't look at us.'

Ruiz nodded, his jaw clenched tight shut. He knew it wasn't good when four men in this situation didn't look at a car passing by. It would have been natural for at least one of them to glance their way.

The sedan was at the far end of Blake Street, at the intersection with Sixteenth Street. Its brake lights burned red. It turned left going south on to Sixteenth, towards the intersection at Market.

Doubling back.

Ruiz followed the car and stopped at the intersection where the sedan had been. He and Martinez looked left, saw the sedan stop short of the next intersection. The one at Market Street.

They had now covered both ends of the block where the diner was: the truck at the far end and the sedan at this end.

Not good.

Martinez looked anxiously at Ruiz.

'Tell them,' Ruiz said urgently.

21

'They have the street flanked.' Ruiz's voice sounded in the room.

Webb looked at the monitor with the diner displayed on the screen. There was no movement there. He didn't notice, on one of the other monitors, the homeless man roll over, stand up and walk down the short flight of stairs on to the sidewalk. His legs looked steady enough for a man reeking of booze.

Webb looked at Grange.

Grange turned to the two agents behind him.

'Let's go,' he told them, moving towards the door of the room.

'Get them out of that truck,' Webb told him. 'Ruiz and Martinez can cover the sedan.'

Grange nodded.

The three men left Webb alone in the room. He turned and saw the homeless man standing outside the diner. The man was looking at something in his hand, appeared to be prodding a finger at it. Webb leaned in to have a closer look, but the definition on the picture was too grainy close up to make much of it.

★ ★ ★

The driver of the pick-up looked at his vibrating phone. Saw that it was Raines calling. He didn't answer the phone, turned to the two men in the rear of the cab and nodded. The two men opened their doors and got out, walking round to the bed of the truck. One of them pulled at the canvas cover, exposing the weapons underneath.

The other man reached under the cover and grabbed two of the handguns, slipping them into the rear waistband of his jeans. After that, he picked up the rifles and moved to get back in the truck. The man holding the canvas cover reached in and took the other two handguns.

Back in the truck, each of the four men took a handgun, checked that the magazine was full and that the slide mechanisms were working. The two men in the rear of the cab sat with the rifles across their laps.

*　*　*

Grange came out of the building on to the street and saw the homeless man open the door of the diner across the road. He stopped briefly, watching the man. The two agents came out behind him and Grange forgot about the homeless man.

They walked briskly to the corner of the building at the end of the street and stopped. Grange took his gun from its holster and gripped it with both hands, bringing the gun up until it was just under his chin. The two men copied him. Grange turned to them.

'We go out together,' he said. 'You guys move to cover the sides of the truck and I'll cover the front. Any movement you don't like, anything you see you don't like, you shoot.'

403

The men nodded.

'On three.'

Grange held a hand up with three fingers extended. He started to count down silently from three.

★ ★ ★

Webb's voice sounded in Ruiz's car. They were stationary at the intersection, watching the men in the sedan.

'Get the men in that sedan out and secured. Grange is covering the truck.'

'Copy,' Ruiz said, opening his door and stepping out on to the street.

Martinez got out after him on the other side of the car. They drew their weapons and started towards the sedan.

★ ★ ★

The driver of the sedan was looking at his phone as it glowed in the car. The driver of the pick-up truck was calling. That meant it was time.

'Get the guns out of the trunk,' he told his passenger.

The passenger nodded and opened his door. The driver reached around to the floor behind his seat and picked up a handgun.

He looked in his rearview mirror and saw the two FBI agents approaching at a fast walk, their guns raised. He reached over to grab his passenger, but the man had stepped out of the car.

He heard them shouting.

'Freeze. FBI.'

22

Grange moved quickly to stand directly in front of the truck, maybe eight feet from the front grille. He raised his weapon and pointed at the driver's head through the windscreen.

The two agents with him ran to their positions on either side of the truck, level with the front doors. They trained their guns on the men in the rear seats.

No one in the truck moved.

'FBI,' Grange shouted. 'All of you in the truck slowly put your hands out of the windows where I can see them.'

Still no one moved.

'Do it now.'

* * *

Ruiz stopped after shouting his warning and aimed his gun at the back of the headrest of the driver's seat of the sedan. Martinez was focused on the passenger who had stepped away from the car by about three feet. The man stood still with his hands by his side. He held a gun in one hand.

'Driver,' Ruiz shouted. 'Hands out of the window slowly. Do it now.'

The passenger looked from Martinez to Ruiz and into the car.

The driver made no move to put his hands out of the window.

Ruiz felt like his head was about to explode. His finger tightened a fraction on the trigger of his gun. He started to walk slowly forward. Martinez copied him.

They were fifteen feet from the rear of the car.

★ ★ ★

The driver of the truck looked past his passenger at the FBI agent pointing his gun into the rear of the truck's cab. He turned his head to look at the agent on his side. Finally, he looked back at Grange.

The two agents at the side looked scared.

Grange didn't.

Looked like a gunfighter.

That was a problem.

'Hands. Out. Of. The. Car. Right. Now,' Grange shouted. 'Last warning.'

The men in the back turned the rifles on their laps until they were able to get their fingers inside the trigger guards. They eased them slowly forward until they were, as best they could tell, aimed through the doors of the truck at the two agents.

★ ★ ★

Grange was done. These guys were not moving. Which meant only one thing. He squeezed the trigger of his gun twice in quick succession.

The truck's windshield burst in a cloud of red as the bullets tore into the driver and killed him.

The two men in the back of the truck pulled

the triggers of their rifles, the roar of the powerful guns deafening within the confines of the truck's cab.

The rifle bullets crashed into and through the truck doors, most of them deflected from their true path as a result of the impact.

The two agents with Grange fired almost simultaneously, shattering the rear windows of the truck.

The truck's passenger lifted the handgun he held in his lap to aim at Grange. Fired.

Bullets cracked out of the ruined windscreen and fizzed by Grange's head.

Grange didn't flinch. Took aim at the passenger and fired twice.

One of the bullets took the top of the passenger's head off.

The agent to Grange's left fell silently to the ground, half his face missing.

Grange emptied his clip into the interior of the truck.

The air in the truck fogged with blood and dust from the shredded seats.

The gunfire stopped.

The exchange had lasted less than five seconds.

In the truck: three dead and one seriously wounded.

Outside: one agent dead.

If Grange had notches on his belt the count would have increased to six.

23

Ruiz heard the gunfire; cracks in the near distance, the sound dissipating quickly in the air.

It stopped.

'Man down.' Grange's voice sounded in his earpiece. 'He's dead. Truck is out of commission.'

Ruiz and Martinez kept walking. The passenger of the sedan came to a decision. He dropped his gun and slowly lifted his hands into the air.

Ruiz reached the door of the car, yanked it open and hauled the driver out on to the road with one hand. The man didn't resist, a handgun slipping from his grasp and skittering away across the road. Ruiz put him face down on the tarmac, crouched over him and pinned the man's neck with his knee.

Martinez told the passenger to turn around. When he did, Martinez stepped up and kicked the back of his knees hard. As the man fell forward with a shout, Martinez pushed him in the back. He moved quickly to put plastic ties around the prone man's wrists. Ruiz did the same with the driver.

'Sedan secured,' Ruiz said over the radio.

He turned his head to the side, felt like vomiting on to the road. Managed to hold it in.

24

Webb had been watching the diner on the monitor when the gunfire at the truck started. The radio traffic that followed was brief. Both vehicles were secure, but he had lost an agent.

When he looked back at the monitor, the two agents at the front of the diner were now out on the street sprinting towards the sound of the gunfire. Webb had not told them to leave their positions.

The homeless man was walking around the internal dividing wall of the diner.

Webb turned and ran for the door.

* * *

Logan smelled the man before he saw him, his nose wrinkling at the stench. Cahill saw him come in and the gunfire started outside.

Cahill stood, his chair clattering back against the wall.

Logan noticed the homeless man did not even flinch at the sound.

Hunter got up and walked to the front of the diner as the FBI agents there drew their weapons and ran out the door.

Collins stayed seated.

The homeless man walked to Matt Horn's table and stopped in front of Horn. He had on several layers of old clothes, including a hooded

409

sweatshirt with the hood up. He reached up, pulled the hood back off his head and raised his other hand to point a gun at Horn.

Logan reached for his gun. Knew he wouldn't make it in time. No one else was watching.

'I loved you like a son,' Seth Raines told Horn.

Then shot him in the face.

Horn toppled back off his chair, blood, bone and brain matter splattering the wall behind him.

Raines turned in a sweeping motion towards Hunter, pulling the trigger of his gun.

Hunter had flinched when Raines shot Horn, the movement saving his life.

Raines fired twice at Hunter as he turned, the motion taking his aim just a little off and Hunter's flinch bringing his head down under the trajectory of the bullets.

Raines kept on turning and firing.

Cahill shouted out in pain and went down.

Logan saw blood on Cahill's head.

Raines aimed at Logan.

Logan raised his gun and fired.

The bullet tore through the layers of cloth on Raines's gun arm, grazing a shallow track along the flesh of his forearm. Raines dropped the arm to his side.

Danny Collins shot Raines three times.

Part Ten:
Blood

1

Logan sat on the kerb as blue light strobed around him, the place awash with cops and paramedics.

It had been an hour since Collins shot Raines.

Randall Webb walked to Logan and stood over him on the sidewalk. Logan looked up at him.

'The next thing you're going to do,' Webb said, 'is go back to your hotel, pack and get on the first flight home.'

Logan frowned.

'What about the guns? Our guns.'

'What guns?'

Logan nodded and bowed his head.

Webb walked away from him.

Logan stood, his legs still unsteady. He wasn't sure if they would hold him. They did.

He walked to the far side of the street to an ambulance which was parked with its rear doors open. As he came around the doors Cahill looked up from the ambulance steps and smiled at him.

'How's your head?' Logan asked.

'Feels like someone hit me with a hammer,' Cahill said, touching the padded dressing a paramedic was securing on the side of his head.

'He'll be fine,' the paramedic told Logan. 'Bullet just grazed him. But he should get it looked at when you get home.'

Cahill thanked the man and stood.

413

'Webb told us to go home,' Logan told him.

Cahill shook his head. 'I can't. Not yet.'

Logan stared at him.

'I need to ask Webb a favour.'

'Don't you think that we've used up all our goodwill already?'

'Maybe. But I need a favour anyway.'

'You are a stubborn — '

Cahill waved him off and started walking across the street to find Webb. Logan didn't have the energy to follow him so he sat on the steps of the ambulance and watched.

Jake Hunter and Danny Collins walked over to the ambulance from the chaos of the diner.

'How is he?' Hunter asked, looking at Cahill.

'He's got a hard head.'

Hunter laughed.

'I noticed. And you?'

'I'm okay. But if you don't mind I won't stand.'

Hunter reached out a hand. Logan took it and they shared a firm handshake. Collins did the same.

'You probably saved someone's life in there,' Hunter told him. 'We owe you a thanks.'

Logan didn't know what to say, so said nothing.

'I heard that Raines is still hanging on,' Collins said. 'Tough son of a bitch. Took three slugs.'

'And the rest of his crew?' Logan asked.

Collins shook his head.

'That guy Grange,' Hunter said. 'He's some cowboy.'

'Still an asshole,' Collins added.

414

Logan wanted to laugh but found that he couldn't.

'Take care,' Hunter said.

They turned to leave Logan at the ambulance. Hunter stopped halfway across the street and turned back to Logan.

'They got the guy over in Scotland,' he shouted. 'Shot a cop before he went down.'

The words rattled around in Logan's head like a bullet, tearing through the delicate tissue of his brain.

Shot a cop.

Becky.

2

Cahill found Webb outside the door of the diner talking to an FBI press officer.

'Is he dead?' Cahill asked. 'Raines.'

Webb turned to look at Cahill and told the press woman to give him a few minutes. She headed off to a wooden barrier where the massed ranks of the press had already assembled, their flashbulbs popping as she approached.

'No,' Webb told Cahill. 'Not so far, anyway.'

'Will he make it to trial?'

'Initial indications are that he will.'

Cahill looked back over at the ambulance where he had been treated and saw Logan walking away from it frantically punching a number into his phone.

'Why did he do it?' Webb asked. 'The suicide mission. I mean, walking into a place full of men with guns and opening up.'

'Maybe he got tired of it all. It happens.'

Cahill scuffed his feet on the sidewalk. 'Sorry to hear about your agent,' he said.

Webb nodded.

'I appreciate that,' he said. 'But I want you and your friend out of here, like, yesterday. I don't need the headache.'

'Logan's leaving today.'

Webb's head tilted to one side. 'And you?'

'There's something I need to do.'

416

'What's that?'

'I need your help doing it.'

'You've got stones, I'll give you that.'

'It's been said before.'

★ ★ ★

'I'm fine,' Irvine told Logan as he walked away from the noise and the crowd outside the diner.

He put a finger in his ear as another ambulance whooped on its way to the hospital. Or maybe it was the morgue.

'It wasn't me who got shot,' she said.

'What happened?'

'It's a long story.'

'I've got the time.'

'We were following up a lead. Going to speak to some witnesses — a couple of prostitutes. Turns out this guy Butler had been hiding out with them and he came out shooting. He got Kenny Armstrong.'

'Is he okay?'

'Yes. Lost a couple of fingers, though.'

'What about Butler?'

'He's dead. I watched a truck crush his car while he was still inside.'

'How do you feel about that?'

'Probably for the best.'

Logan was surprised at the cold venom in her voice. Had never heard her sound that way before.

'He was a bad guy,' she said, as if feeling the need to explain her reaction.

'I've seen my fair share. You don't need to apologise for saying that.'

'I know. It's just . . . '

Neither of them knew what else to say.

3

Twenty-four hours later Logan embraced Ellie in the airport arrivals area until she started to squirm. He released her and hugged Sam Cahill briefly.

'Everything okay?' Sam asked, squinting at Logan. 'I mean, you look a little pale.'

'I'm fine. Jet lag.'

She didn't look convinced. 'And Alex?'

'Said he'd be back in a couple of days.'

'I know that, Logan. I meant, how is he?'

'He's, you know. He's just Alex.'

Sam did some more squinting before turning and leading them towards the escalator up to the car park. Logan put an arm around Ellie and squeezed.

'How was your holiday?' he asked.

'It was good.'

She sounded less than enthusiastic.

He stopped and turned her to face him.

'What's wrong?'

She blinked and he saw tears shining in her eyes. Sam Cahill watched from a distance.

'Ellie?' he said. 'Tell me.'

'It was fun, you know,' she told him.

'But?'

'I didn't know when you'd be back.'

'You knew I was coming back though, right?'

She looked uncertain.

'I'm not going anywhere any time soon,' he said.

419

She smiled and hugged him as tight as she ever had. Sam Cahill smiled and turned her head away, bringing a hand up to her face. Logan hugged Ellie back.

★ ★ ★

In the car Sam explained that they were having dinner at her house and she wouldn't entertain any debate on the subject. Logan was hungry after the long flight and didn't argue.

It only occurred to Logan that the Cahill girls had not been with Sam at the airport and that someone must have been looking after them when he followed Sam into the living room of her house. Irvine stood up from the couch and beamed at him. He went forward and hugged her without hesitation. He pulled away from the embrace and looked at the ugly bruising still on her face.

'Glad to be back?' she asked.

It was Logan's turn to beam. 'Like you wouldn't believe.'

She put her hands on his cheeks and kissed his mouth.

'Get a room,' Ellie said.

4

The house was a modest two-storey affair with a small front yard and a late model Toyota in the driveway. Cahill didn't know Kansas City, but it looked like a good neighbourhood. He stood at the foot of the path leading to the front door and patted the rear pocket of his jeans, feeling the slim presence of the gift he had brought here.

The doorbell chimed inside when he pressed the button by the side of the door. After a few seconds a woman not much younger than his own wife answered the door. She put a hand up to her face to shield her eyes from the glare of the low sun.

She looked better than he had expected, though her face still bore the tell-tale signs of grief. Her hair was blond and cut short, shaped to her face. Her eyes were the palest blue he had ever seen.

'Melanie,' he said. 'I'm Alex Cahill.'

Her hand dropped to her side. Cahill had no real expectation of how she would react to his presence. Her expression was neutral but she stepped back and told him to come in.

He waited on a couch in the living room while Melanie Stark made coffee in the nearby kitchen. She handed him a mug and sat in a chair by the window, watching him drink.

He felt self-conscious because she did not have a drink so he took two quick sips and set the mug down on the floor at his feet.

'You must have seen the news reports?' he said.

She nodded. 'They didn't mention Tim,' she replied.

'I know. But they will.'

This time her face was more animated.

'What do you mean?'

'I spoke with the FBI chief in Denver. He's going to make sure that Tim's part in all of this is put front and centre.'

'I'm not sure what you mean, Alex.'

'I mean that he was a hero. He set in motion a chain reaction that broke an international drugs ring. He saved who knows how many lives.'

She stood and looked out of the window.

'You mean his death set that in motion?'

'I suppose that's right, yes. I'm sorry.'

She sniffed with her back turned to him.

'But that's the job. We put ourselves in harm's way every day. That's what we signed up for. Tim knew it.'

'Doesn't make it any easier.'

Cahill reached into his pocket and took out the wallet. He ran his hand over the smooth surface.

Melanie Stark looked round at him, watching him turn the wallet over in his hands.

'What's that?' she asked.

'It's why I came here.'

Cahill got up and walked to her, placing the wallet in her hand. Her skin felt dry and rough. He saw up close that she had no make-up on and had probably given up on looking after herself since Tim's death. He hoped what he had

422

given her would speed the healing process. It was all he could do.

She looked at the wallet, the skin between her eyes creasing into a frown.

'Open it,' he said.

She put her fingers at the edge of the wallet and pulled it open.

A hand fluttered to her mouth. Cahill wondered if she might faint, but she held it together.

On one flap of the wallet, her husband's photograph was set in an official FBI identification card behind a clear, plastic sleeve.

On the other flap was the gold shield of a special agent.

A single tear splashed on the plastic sleeve holding the photograph.

'Tim . . . ' She crumpled. Fell into his arms and sobbed.

Cahill held her up, feeling her tears soak his chest.

Her sob turned into something more. All the raw emotion of the last week pouring out as the dam burst.

And all the time she held the wallet tight, her fingers splayed against the image of her husband's face.

When the tide subsided, he heard her say something, but it was muffled as her face was still pressed into his chest.

He asked her what it was.

'Thank you,' she said.

I did it for you, Tim, he thought. *You were one of the best.*

DAISYCHAIN

G. J. Moffat

Over the course of three days, the paths of three people's lives will intersect and change forever . . . Logan Finch is sitting pretty, with his penthouse apartment and a shot at making partner in Glasgow's largest law firm. Yet he still pines for the woman he thought was 'the one' and who left him with no word of explanation twelve years ago. Alex Cahill is a client and friend of Logan. The American owns a security business, but has a shadowy past. Detective Constable Rebecca Irvine, of Strathclyde Police's CID, is stuck in a failing marriage. On her first day in the new job she is called to a murder scene. The victim is Penny Grant, Logan's former girlfriend. And her eleven-year-old daughter, Ellie, is missing . . .

THE LAST MINUTE

Jeff Abbott

Sam Capra has one reason to live: to reclaim his baby son from the people who abducted him. And now the kidnappers have offered a deadly deal: they'll surrender Sam's child . . . if Sam agrees to commit a spectacular murder. Teaming up with a young mother whose daughter went missing, Sam tracks his child across the country in a dangerous desperate race against time.

THE SILENCED

Brett Battles

Professional 'cleaner' Jonathan Quinn has a new client and a strange job: find and remove the remains of a body hidden over twenty years ago inside the walls of a London building, before the building is demolished. But Quinn and his team are being watched. Suddenly caught in the crossfire between two dangerous rivals, Quinn must unravel the identity of the body and why it still poses so great a threat even in death. Because a plot stretching from the former Soviet Union to Hong Kong, from Paris to London, from Los Angeles to Maine is rapidly falling apart. And Quinn hasn't just been hired to tie up loose ends — he *Is* one.

CARTE BLANCHE

Jeffery Deaver

Fresh from Afghanistan, James Bond has been recruited to a new agency. Conceived in the post-9/11 world, it operates independent of Five, Six and the MoD, its very existence deniable. Its aim: to protect the Realm, by any means necessary. The Night Action alert calls Bond from dinner with a beautiful woman. GCHQ has decrypted an electronic whisper about an attack scheduled for later in the week: casualties estimated in the thousands, British interests adversely affected. And 007 has been given *Carte Blanche* to do whatever it takes to fulfil his mission.

I, ALEX CROSS

James Patterson

Detective Alex Cross is pulled out of a family celebration and given the devastating news that his niece, Caroline, has been found brutally murdered. Cross vows to hunt down the killer and soon learns that Caroline was mixed up in one of Washington's wildest scenes. And she was not this killer's only victim. The search leads Cross to a place where every fantasy is possible, if you have the credentials to get in. Alex is soon facing down some very important, very protected, very dangerous people in levels of society where only one thing is certain — they will do anything to keep their secrets safe. As Cross closes in on the killer, he discovers evidence that points to the unimaginable — a revelation that could rock the entire world.

FLASH AND BONES

Kathy Reichs

Right next to the Charlotte racetrack, a flash of lightning illuminates a hand reaching out of a barrel of asphalt . . . Dr Tempe Brennan, forensic anthropologist, must determine why before thousands of NASCAR fans arrive. But no examination is possible when the FBI, inexplicably, confiscates and destroys the body. A young NASCAR engineer's sister had disappeared with her boyfriend twelve years before. So, trying to find answers, Tempe comes up against the Patriot Posse, a shadowy right-wing group. Then the young man is found, crushed under the wheels of a racecar, his body covered in a mysterious substance. Tempe is involved in something extremely sinister. While the FBI and the Patriot Posse monitor her movements, where does the danger come from? Will it threaten her own life . . . ?